Here's what critics are saying about Catherine Bruns' books:

"Catherine Bruns has whipped up another delicious treat with this delightful cozy. If you like your mysteries to taste sweet this one is a good choice."
—*Night Owl Reviews*, Top Pick!

"I want to visit more with all of the quirky characters just to see what crazy and outrageous things they will do next!"
—*Fresh Fiction*

"Catherine Bruns has found a winning recipe for an exciting mystery mixed with a dash of humor and a heap of danger. Add in a little romance for spice, and you get one sweet reading treat."
—Mary Marks, bestselling author of the Quilting Mystery series.

"Ms. Bruns is an excellent writer—her style was definitely to get out of the way and let this reader enjoy the experience. I'd recommend Killer Transaction as one of those books to take to the beach or curl up with by the fire for an afternoon of easy reading."
—*The Kindle Book Review*

BOOKS BY CATHERINE BRUNS

Cookies & Chance Mysteries:
Tastes Like Murder
Baked to Death
Burned to a Crisp
A Spot of Murder (short story in the Killer Beach Reads collection)

Cindy York Mysteries:
Killer Transaction
Priced to Kill

Aloha Lagoon Mysteries:
Death of the Big Kahuna

BURNED
TO A CRISP

---

a Cookies & Chance mystery

Catherine Bruns

Acknowledgements:

First and foremost, I must thank Joseph Francis Collins, Paramedic/Firefighter, whose help with this book was immeasurable. Any errors or omissions are entirely my own. Retired Troy Police Captain Terrance Buchanan always has the answers I need, and special props go to attorney Lisa Proskin for assisting me with all the legal jargon. Constance Atwater, Krista Gardner, and Kathy Kennedy are the best beta readers in the world, and I'm so lucky to have you! Profound thanks for the mouth-watering recipes to Stephanie Nicole Schwenke, Amy Reger, Karen Clickner-Douttiel, and Paula Shappy. To my wonderfully patient husband, Frank, who has the difficult task of living with me. Last but not least, thank you to publisher Gemma Halliday and her amazing staff. It's truly an honor to be a part of your publishing company.

CHAPTER ONE

———

I sat down on the front steps of my cookie shop, Sally's Samples, and took a rare moment to enjoy the warm June sunshine on my face. The sky was a perfect blue, with nary a cloud to be seen. A gentle breeze flapped around my apron and my curly, shoulder-length, black hair. I kicked off my sneakers and wiggled my toes, enjoying the feel of the overgrown blades of grass between them. Content, I closed my eyes and leaned back, thinking about my life.

In a few weeks I would be Mrs. Michael Donovan. Heat flooded my cheeks, but not as a result of the shimmering sun above. I'd loved this man for so many years, even though we'd spent most of them apart—the result of misunderstandings and a lack of trust that stemmed from when we were teenage sweethearts.

"See before you jump," my wise Grandma Rosa had instructed me. That was her distinct way of saying, "Look before you leap." How I wished I'd listened to her back then.

It had taken ten years, but Mike and I had finally found our way back to each other. Now nothing and no one would stand in the way of our life together.

"Why you daydream?" A sharp elderly voice pierced my eardrum. "You gotta get me more fortune cookies."

As recognition set in, I winced and opened my eyes. I'd know that voice anywhere. Nicoletta Gavelli made her way up the steps of the porch and thrust a stubby finger in my face. She was dressed in her usual black housecoat and Birkenstock shoes, gray hair pulled back from her stern face in a severe bun.

"Hi, Mrs. G. Josie's inside. Go on in, and tell her what you'd like."

She frowned, the lines in her leathery-looking face

deepening further, and shook her head. "*You* wait on me. Josie—she no have respect for her elders. And you ain't so hot either, missy."

I managed to contain my smile as I followed her into the shop. Mrs. Gavelli had been my parent's next-door neighbor since I was a baby. She took immense pride and pleasure in insulting me whenever she could, but I had recently learned that it was her unique way of expressing affection. Since there was never any winning with Mrs. G, I'd learned to just shut up and take it.

Josie Sullivan, my best friend and partner, was an entirely different matter, though. She had no qualms about telling anyone what she thought of them. Sometimes she was a little too outspoken. I tried to keep her calm, but that was often a full-time job in itself.

She was in the back room, our kitchen and prep area, removing a tray of mocha cookies from the oven. My mouth watered from the smell. She peered out the doorway, having heard the bells jingle, and I watched as her expression changed from content to sour in a split second. She tossed the oven mitts aside and came toward us.

"Well, look who's here." Josie's blue eyes regarded Mrs. Gavelli with irritation. "My favorite customer."

Mrs. Gavelli pointed at me. "Sally wait on me. Not you. She lesser of two evils."

Josie's face turned as red as her hair. "Stop bothering Sal. She shouldn't even be here." She placed her hands on her hips and stared at me. "Speaking of which, why *are* you still here? The engagement party starts in an hour. And where's Mike?"

"He'll be here soon. He just started a new job today." My fiancé owned a one-man construction company, although at times he did hire people to assist him. "There really isn't anything for me to do, except show up. Mom's taken care of everything."

Mrs. Gavelli sniffed as she spread her hands all over the front of the bakery case like an eager child. "Engagement party. Big wedding. Is not right. You already married once, and that not end good. Shameful. I hope you not gonna wear white."

The old woman was the proverbial thorn amongst my roses. Defeated, I decided to change the subject. "Who are you bringing tonight? Is it Mr. Feathers?"

Mrs. Gavelli gave me a saucy grin. "Is big surprise. You find out soon."

Great. I hated surprises.

Josie pointed out the window. "The grass is loaded with dandelions. Who gets the honor of mowing the lawn tomorrow? I had Rob fill the gas can earlier, so it's out in the shed, waiting for its next victim."

"Mike did it last time. Think I can talk him into it again?"

Josie grinned. "I believe you have that power of persuasion. The lock on the shed is broken too."

"I know it is. I'll have Mike look at that as well." It wasn't the way I wanted to spend Sunday, our only day of the week off, but when you owned a business—or two, in our case—things frequently came up.

Our employee, Sarah, appeared from the back room with a tray of fortune cookies for the display case. She caught sight of Mrs. Gavelli, instantly paled, and closed her mouth. Mrs. G had that effect on many people.

"Aha!" Mrs. Gavelli's eyes resembled round jewels as she caught sight of the fortune cookies in Sarah's hands. Without even bothering to ask, she removed a cookie from the tray. Sarah made no effort to stop her, frozen in place with a deer-in-the-headlights look. "I choose my own. That way I no get bad fortune."

Josie pressed her lips together angrily. "You don't grab food off the trays in a bakery without gloves, old lady. Don't ever do that again."

"Who you call 'old lady'?" Mrs. Gavelli started toward Josie in a fury.

I was quick to jump between the two of them. "Okay, both of you knock it off. Mrs. G, was there anything else you wanted?"

She stared at me in annoyance. "Where you go for honeymoon?"

Man, she was nosy. "We haven't decided yet."

Mrs. Gavelli let out a long harrumph. "Every day a honeymoon for you two. I see the way you carry on. You will be pregnant on wedding night. I know these things."

I didn't say anything but hoped for once that her premonitions were right. More than anything, Mike and I both longed for a large family. My ex-husband, Colin, never wanted children and had been up-front about his feelings from the beginning. I had foolishly believed I could get him to change his mind over time.

Josie had four boys, all age ten and under. The baby was a year old and had just begun to walk. Even though she had started her family much sooner than she'd planned—right out of high school—and they'd gone through some tough times financially, I envied her lifestyle. Had it not been for my father and his old country morals, I might have tried to tempt fate before the wedding. Heck, Mike was all for it.

Mrs. Gavelli glanced at her message and gasped. "*Stay home and order take-out tonight.*" She flung the paper onto my blue and white checkered, vinyl floor. "I tell you get new fortunes. Why you no listen?"

Josie's mouth curved upward into a sly smile. "You're lucky I didn't poison the cookies. I was feeling extra nice today."

Mrs. Gavelli started to say something, but we were interrupted by the bells jingling on the front door. A man slightly older than me walked in, and the old woman gave me an arrogant smile as she pointed at him. "Here your surprise. Is early wedding present."

My mouth fell open in shock. "Holy cow. Johnny, when did you get into town? My grandmother never said a word."

Johnny Gavelli extended his arms and captured me in a tight hug, literally lifting me off the floor in the process. "Hey, Sal, how's my girl?"

Mrs. Gavelli's grandson had grown from a buck-toothed little boy with nerdy glasses into a dark-haired dreamboat of a man. He had classic, good Italian looks, complete with black, lazy eyes that had laughed at me for as long as I could remember. He was about Mike's height, six feet tall, with a lean, taut body and eyelashes so long I practically drooled with envy.

He grinned at me mischievously. "I got in last night. Had

to see my best girl." He put an arm around Mrs. Gavelli's shoulders, and her face glowed from the attention. "Then Gram invited me to your party. I can't believe my very first conquest is getting married."

My cheeks were on fire. "Johnny, we never did anything, and you know that."

He winked. "Oh, but those times in the garage with you were priceless. Too bad Gram caught us before we could proceed any further. That underwear you used to wear, printed with the days of the week, was quite a turn-on."

Josie shook her head. "Still the same old pig, Johnny."

Mrs. Gavelli smacked him lightly across the cheek. "Is enough. You stop nasty talk." Then she grabbed his face tightly between her hands and smiled. "He something, no?"

He certainly was. Still, I was happy to see him and delighted he'd be accompanying Mrs. Gavelli to my engagement party.

Once a perverted little boy who'd coerced me into playing doctor with him in his dark garage when I was six and he eight, Johnny had grown up into a respected college professor at Southern Vermont College. Who would have thought?

Johnny's mother, Sophia, Mrs. Gavelli's only daughter, had died of a drug overdose when he was five. He'd never known his father. I had been told by my grandmother that I resembled Sophia, a possible reason for the old lady's somewhat shabby treatment toward me. Mrs. Gavelli had raised her grandson without assistance from anyone, and I was the first to admit she'd done a wonderful job.

Johnny pointed toward the ceiling. "Is Gianna upstairs? I haven't seen her in ages."

My sister lived in the apartment over my bakery. "No, she's going to the party straight from work."

The bells chimed again, and my heart took a leap when my fiancé walked in. Mike stopped for a brief moment to wipe his work boots on the mat inside my door, nodding to the Gavellis and Josie before his eyes found mine.

"Is my bride-to-be ready to go yet?"

"Aw," Josie and Sarah said in unison.

Mrs. Gavelli snorted. "You is all dirty. Why you roll

around in mud?"

"He's been working on a roof, Mrs. G," I explained. Tar dotted the front of Mike's gray T-shirt, and there was a large gaping hole in the knee of his jeans. He smelled of the turpentine he'd used to wash his hands, but I caught the faint scent of the spicy cologne he wore mixed in. His dark hair curled over the nape of his neck, and as always, he sported a five o'clock shadow and needed a shave. His midnight blue eyes sparkled as they gazed at me. Ever since the first time I'd looked into those eyes at the tender age of sixteen, I'd been hooked.

He might have been a bit dirty but was still sexy as all get-out, and every ounce of him was mine.

Mrs. Gavelli reached again for the tray of fortune cookies, and Josie slapped her hand away. One fell onto the floor.

Josie glared at the woman. "I told you, no touching the merchandise."

Mike reached down to pick up the smashed cookie, which lay at his feet. He read the message, and a strange expression crossed his face. "Hmm. Interesting."

"What does it say?" I asked, not positive I really wanted to know. The fortune cookies in my shop seemed to carry a weird kind of aura. Patrons received a free one whenever they bought a cookie from the bakery. The predictions usually came true in some shape or form. To be honest, I wasn't sure I wanted to carry them any longer but knew my customers—Mrs. Gavelli in particular—would be outraged if we discontinued making them.

Mike smiled as he read aloud. "*All things are difficult before they are easy.*"

Mrs. Gavelli grunted. "You see. He get bad fortune too."

Mike laughed and put his arm around me. "I don't think it's bad. It just means that we've been through our rough patch, and now's the time to enjoy ourselves." He kissed the top of my head. "Don't you agree, princess?"

"Sure," I said with uncertainty.

Josie gave me her *I told you so* look. She knew how I felt about the cookies. From the beginning, she'd never been completely on board with the idea, but I had insisted the bakery had to have a theme. "A waste of time and money" is what she called them.

"Those silly messages don't mean anything," she said.

Johnny stepped forward. "Hey, Mike. Remember me? I was Sal's first."

"Oh, you." I gave him a shove to the shoulder. "He's still the same egotistical eight-year-old who promised me an ice cream cone if I followed him into the garage."

Mike suppressed a smile as he shook Johnny's hand. "I thought it was you. Long time no see. Bet you're teaching those kids a lot in sex ed class, huh?"

Mrs. Gavelli shot my fiancé a dirty look. "We go now. Make sure we have good table tonight. And you no put me next to bathroom."

With that, she pushed the glass door open with a vengeance, and the welcoming sound of the bells drifted through the warm air. We all seemed to sigh in relief at her departure.

Sarah started to place the fortune cookies in the display case as she watched Mrs. Gavelli and Johnny cross the street together. She was in her late thirties with dishwater blonde hair and thoughtful brown eyes that lingered on their retreating figures. "That woman scares me."

Josie grunted as she took the tray from Sarah's hands. "Ah, Mrs. G is all talk and no action. It does my heart good to piss her off every now and then."

"You are so bad," I laughed.

Josie pointed toward the front door. "You two need to get out of here. I'll see you at the restaurant. Sarah, you're okay to close, right?"

Sarah nodded. "Oh, sure. No problem." She smiled at Mike and me, but I glimpsed sadness in her eyes.

Mike's phone buzzed, and he checked the screen. "I've got to take this. One of my customers. I'll be out in the truck waiting for you, babe."

I went into the back room to grab my purse. When I returned to the storefront, Sarah startled me as she pulled me into a tight hug. "I just wanted to tell you how happy I am for you. Mike seems like a great guy. You're very lucky."

"Thank you. I know I am." Sarah was usually so quiet

and reserved. Half the time I didn't even know she was around. She'd started working for us this past January, and we'd been very happy with her performance. Sarah was also a single mother and had an eight-year-old daughter who was the center of her world.

A tear leaked out of her eye. "I hope you guys have a long and happy life together. And that he truly deserves you."

I exchanged glances with Josie. Where was this coming from? "Is something wrong, Sarah?"

"I'm sorry," she stammered. "I didn't mean to imply anything. I've never had much luck with the opposite sex, so I have a tendency to be a bit negative about love and marriage."

Josie folded her arms across her chest and raised one eyebrow at me. Sarah had never mentioned if she was dating anyone, so I assumed the topic was off-limits. Her daughter, Julie, had already captured a special place in my heart. Even though I assumed it must be tough for Sarah to make ends meet, I envied her for having that little girl.

"What about Julie's father? Does he help out at all?" I asked.

"Not as much as he should." Sarah wiped her eyes. "I don't mean to feel sorry for myself because I wouldn't trade Julie for the world. Some days I just need a break, you know?"

My heart went out to her, and I placed an arm around her shoulders. "I'm so sorry. I wish you'd said something before." Julie had been in my shop on numerous occasions and was another one who loved the fortune cookies.

Sarah shrugged. "I didn't want you to think I was a problem employee."

A thought occurred to me. "Maybe I could take her overnight next weekend and give you some free time? I'd love to have her. We could go out for pizza and then watch movies together. It would be so much fun."

Josie looked at me like I was nuts but said nothing.

Sarah smiled. "That's so sweet of you, Sally. I'm sure she'd love it."

Josie pointed toward the door and gave me a look that said *Go—I've got this.* She put an arm around Sarah's thin shoulders. I felt terrible. My life was overflowing with happiness while this poor woman had almost none. Maybe if I gave her another raise that would help.

"Come on, Sarah," Josie said. "I'll help you clean and lock up. Sal really needs to leave." She shooed me toward the door. "I brought a change of clothes with me, so I'll head over afterwards. Rob's going to meet me at the restaurant."

A sudden thought crossed my mind. "Sarah, you're invited to the party too, you know. After you close up, please come meet us at the restaurant."

She wiped her eyes with her apron. "I—oh, Sally, I didn't expect an invitation. Honest."

"I'd really like you to be there. Please bring Julie too."

She reached out and grabbed me in such a tight hug I couldn't breathe. "I'd be honored to come, but I need to see how Julie's feeling first since she's had a bad cold the last couple of days. Thanks for thinking of us."

"Give her a hug from me." I waved at them both and hurried out the door. I climbed into the passenger side of Mike's truck. As I reached for the seat belt, he grabbed me and crushed me to him, placing his mouth over mine.

When we finally broke apart, I was breathless. "Hmm. Maybe we should skip the party."

He laughed. "I've been thinking about kissing you all day. I was tempted to do it in front of Mrs. Gavelli but figured I'd give the old lady a heart attack." He controlled the truck with his left hand, his right one stroking mine. "Any chance we've got a few extra minutes for alone time before the party?"

"Maybe a couple. We're running on a tight schedule, as usual," I said glumly. For the last few days, I hadn't seen much of my fiancé. Mike was busy trying to finish up a long list of jobs customers wanted completed before he took time off for the wedding and our honeymoon. Josie and I had been swamped at the bakery and were putting in overtime with special orders for graduation parties, baby showers, and weddings. "Maybe I should tell my mother we can't make it. I think I just caught the flu."

Mike stopped for a red light and turned to look at me, his beautiful eyes startled in his tanned, rugged face. "Babe, you have to go. I mean—your mother has put so much work into this."

I sighed. "I didn't even want a big wedding. I had that once before, and it ended in disaster. And now we're having an engagement party just weeks before we get married—who even does that? Only my kooky mother."

He watched me closely. "Sal, what's bugging you?"

"Let's pack a bag and fly to Vegas like we planned months ago. Or go see the nearest justice of the peace tomorrow. We've got the license. I want to be married to you now. No more waiting. We can still go through with the original wedding—we just won't tell anyone we're already married."

Mike laughed as he pulled into the driveway of the small yellow ranch house he owned, a ten-minute drive from my bakery. The house had belonged to his mother until she had succumbed to cirrhosis a couple of years ago.

He turned and placed his arms around my waist. "Please tell me you're not letting that stupid message get to you?"

"Of course not," I lied. Mike, like Josie, knew of my anxiety over the cookies. "I just don't want to wait anymore. We've waited long enough. Ten years is a long time."

He was silent as he pushed the hair back from my face, his expression thoughtful. "It's not a bad idea, but it does seem kind of unfair to your mother when she's devoted so much time to this. Besides..." He smiled as if teasing me. "I'm looking forward to showing you off to the world. I want to let everyone know you're mine. Forever."

The love in his eyes reflected my own. My eyes started to fill as I cradled his face in my hands. "I'll always be yours. Nothing will ever change that."

He kissed the tip of my nose. "Your mother would be crushed if she found out we got married before the actual wedding. And your grandmother would know. Don't ask me how, but she would know."

I sighed. He was right, of course. "Okay, forget that idea." I reached for the door handle and let myself out of the truck. "It was crazy anyway."

Mike unlocked the front door and stepped back, allowing me entrance first. "Nothing is going to happen, baby. We've had our share of bad luck and then some. What could possibly go wrong now?"

CHAPTER TWO

———

Forty minutes later, after a quick shower and a few stolen moments of intimate time, we were on our way to Mama Lena's, the location my mother had chosen for our engagement party. Since no one could even attempt to match my grandmother in Italian-style cuisine, we'd decided on a buffet with a variety of different dishes from this popular family restaurant.

Technically, Mike and I had been engaged since last January when I, as he liked to teasingly remind me, had proposed to him. We'd celebrated that night with champagne and romance and planned to fly off to Vegas a few days later. The next morning, my father, Domenic Muccio, had suffered a minor stroke. My mother, beside herself with worry, had made me promise that day at the hospital that I'd let her throw me the big wedding I so rightly deserved. Feeling guilty about my father's condition, I had relented. Those kind of preparations took time, especially with my mother planning them. Why she was throwing me an engagement party now, five months after the fact, was a complete mystery.

"I'm surprised Mrs. Gavelli didn't make a snide comment about holding the party so close to the wedding," I said and stepped out of the truck. I noticed my parents' car and Gianna's Ford Fiesta parked nearby.

"Hmm," Mike said as he opened the door of the restaurant for me.

I had turned twenty-nine years old yesterday, and it was the happiest birthday I could remember. The last year had been a tumultuous whirlwind with my divorce, a murder investigation when a high school nemesis had dropped dead on the front porch of my bakery, and the death of my cheating ex-husband. But I had survived and was a stronger and more confident person because of it. I could handle anything life threw at me with my true love by my side.

I glanced sideways at him suspiciously as we walked down the red-carpeted hall to the private dining room where the party was being held. "What's up? You're awfully quiet."

Mike grinned but said nothing. He opened the double doors to the room and gave me a gentle push forward. I was met with a chorus of "Surprise!"

I stood in the doorway for a moment, thoroughly confused and unable to say anything. My parents, Grandma Rosa, Gianna, Mrs. Gavelli, Josie and her husband, plus a few other friends were gathered. Pink balloons and streamers decorated the room. In one corner, there was a table piled high with envelopes, gift-wrapped presents, and a two-tier birthday cake decorated in pink and white icing that read *Happy 29th Birthday, Sally*.

Dumbfounded, I stared at my fiancé. "You tricked me."

He leaned over and kissed my cheek. "Happy Birthday, princess. It's a day late, but we knew you'd never fall for an engagement party on your actual birthday."

"Happy birthday, sweetie!" My mother, Maria Muccio, threw her arms around me. As usual, she was dressed conspicuously in a bright red sundress, cut low in the front and back and barely covering her rear. She had paired the dress with four-inch, matching stiletto heels that accented her sensational-looking legs.

"Don't bend over, Mom," I whispered in her ear.

She giggled and bussed my cheek. "Wasn't it smart of me to have a twenty-ninth birthday for you? I'll bet you don't know why I picked this year to do it."

"I give up. Why?"

She straightened the collar on my white silk blouse. "Because now when people ask your age, you can always tell them, 'I had a 29th birthday party recently.' You can keep that charade up for at least another ten years!"

I sighed. "Mom, your philosophy never ceases to amaze me."

She gave Mike a hug. "I tell everyone I'm only thirty-nine. And you know what? They believe it."

I was certain they did. Mom had a perfect size four figure and rich, dark hair the same shade as mine but not quite as curly. Paired with soft brown eyes, a small nose, and teeth she whitened religiously, my mother looked better than me most days.

My father, sixty-six years old, stout, and balding, came over and put an arm around her. He kissed me on the cheek and grunted a greeting at Mike. My father didn't have anything against Mike personally. He was just old-school and convinced there wasn't a man alive good enough for either of his daughters.

"Come on, *bella donna*," he said. "Everyone's waiting for you to grab a plate so we can start eating. I can't wait to dig in to those baby back ribs myself. Your grandmother never makes good stuff like that."

Grandma Rosa gave him the evil eye and put her forefinger to the side of her white head in a circular motion. "Crazy fool. The doctor said they are not good for you. More salad and vegetables is what you need."

"Hogwash," my father growled. "I stopped going to Denny's. What more does he want."

Grandma Rosa sniffed. "Lies. You were at Denny's yesterday." She looked at Mike and me. "That man is full of salami."

My father cut his eyes toward her and frowned, a confused expression on his round face. I placed a hand on Grandma Rosa's shoulder. "You mean bologna."

She nodded in approval. "That works too."

I looked up to see Josie standing on a chair, clinking a spoon against the side of a wine glass. "Attention, everyone!"

The thirty or so people in the room stopped talking and turned to stare at her.

Josie's gaze met mine, and she smiled. "I'd like to make a toast to Sal. I just want to say how lucky I am to have had a friend like you for over twenty years. Thank you so much for giving me a job that I enjoy waking up for every day."

She wiped away a tear while her husband Rob helped her down from the chair and placed an arm around her shoulders. He was a good-looking guy, over six feet tall with brown hair in a buzz cut and a matching well-trimmed beard.

"I'm so happy for you and Mike," Josie continued. "I've always known that you were meant to be together. Jeez, I don't know of two people more in love."

"Ahem." Rob cleared his throat.

She gave him a playful nudge in the side with her elbow. "Oh, get over yourself. Romance died after the first kid, babe."

Everyone laughed as Josie raised her glass again to us. "I have a feeling you two will find out about that very soon."

Oh, good grief. I stole a sideways glance at my father who was smiling broadly, his arm around my mother's tiny waist. I was afraid he'd misunderstand Josie's words and think I was already pregnant. I didn't want to be the reason for another stroke.

"Love you, Sal." Josie grinned as she made her way over to us. I reached out and enveloped her in a tight hug, unable to speak for a moment, while everyone clapped.

When the noise had subsided, my mother spoke up. "All right everyone, I have some news to announce. In fact, the Muccio family has quite a lot to celebrate these days. First off, my beautiful Gianna won her first court case today."

Everyone clapped again while Gianna stared at my mother, openmouthed, her jaw close to hitting the floor. My baby sister was my pride and joy, both beautiful and brilliant. As a public defender, she'd just landed her first case, and it had been huge. Gianna had defended a local man, who was rumored to have ties to the mob, on racketeering charges. A mistrial had been deemed earlier today.

Gianna's cheeks flushed pink with agitation and embarrassment. "Um, Mom, I didn't win. They—"

Mom ignored Gianna's comment and prattled on, announcing to everyone that Gianna got both her looks and her brains from her mother's side of the family, which made everyone laugh. I locked eyes with my sister, and she scowled at me. I understood her annoyance. Technically, Gianna had not won the case. She was waiting to hear if and when her client would be retried. We both loved our mother dearly, but she tended to present the facts in a way that suited her, whether they were true or not.

My mother beamed with pride. "And last but not least, I won the local Hotties Over Fifty pageant last week. What that means is now I'll be competing for a modeling contract and a trip to Hawaii in the statewide Foxes over Fifty contest, which starts in a couple of days!"

Everyone whistled and cheered appreciatively again.

My father grinned and lowered his hand from my mother's waist to her behind. He nodded at Mrs. Gavelli, who stood to his left side with Johnny. "This caboose won first prize."

Mrs. Gavelli grabbed Johnny's arm and moved away from my father in disgust.

Even over the laughter, I could hear Gianna gasp out loud. She hated my parents' public—and frequent—displays of affection. As much as I adored them, I had to admit they were tough to take sometimes.

Grandma Rosa sighed and shook her head. "May the good Lord help us all."

Everyone clapped again politely while my mother giggled and held up an 8 x 10-inch, framed photograph of her in a yellow bikini that brought to mind the old song "Itsy Bitsy Teenie Weenie Yellow Polkadot Bikini." I averted my gaze in embarrassment, as did Gianna, her face scarlet and probably mirroring my own.

Mike bowed his head and traced a pattern on the floor with his foot, attempting to hide his smile. My family had always been a source of amusement to him. Maybe he figured a whacky family was better than no family at all since he'd grown up with a drunken mother and abusive stepfather. I guessed we looked pretty tame when compared to what he'd endured.

"Okay, everyone, time to chow down," my mother giggled. "Please help yourselves."

Everyone formed a line behind me for the buffet. Still in shock and not especially hungry, I looked around at the covered hot trays, trying to decide what to get. Sitting down with an empty plate was a sign of disrespect in our family. I would have preferred my grandmother's homemade braciole but didn't say so for fear of hurting my mother's feelings. I settled on a slice of prime rib, mashed potatoes, and salad. My mother directed me to the center seat at an oblong table that had a balloon tied to it which read *Birthday Girl. Jeez, was I five years old again*?

Mike sat down to my right and reached for my hand, pressing it to his lips. "In a few weeks we'll be seated like this at our wedding, babe." He started to eat. "By the way, you'll get my present when we get home later."

I waved my wrist at him. Fastened around it was a gorgeous heart-shaped Tiffany bracelet he'd given me last night. "This was more than enough. Please tell me you didn't spend any extra money on me."

His smile was wicked as he leaned closer, his lips pressed against my ear. "I wasn't talking about *that* type of gift."

Heat flashed through my body as I understood his intended meaning. "You're naughty, Mr. Donovan."

"We haven't had any time alone all week," Mike complained as he cut into his meat. "We've got a lot of making up to do. I say let's blow this party early."

"Eat up," I teased. "You'll need to save your strength for later."

He roared with laughter as Gianna sat down to my left. I hadn't seen her in a few days, and she appeared to have lost weight. People always commented on the fact that we looked like twins, but I was never convinced. Gianna's rich chestnut hair was lighter than mine and enveloped her shoulders in perfect waves. Her face, although beautiful, was drawn and tired.

I leaned closer to her. "You're not still mad at Mom, are you?"

She pressed her lips together tightly. "Is it too much to ask that we could have a normal mother—or, shall I dare say, normal parents? Grandma is the only one who is completely sane."

"Not including me, I hope," I teased.

Gianna grimaced as she dug into her potatoes. The past few weeks had been rough for my sister. Her boyfriend of two years, Frank Taylor, had decided he'd had enough of playing second fiddle to what he called Gianna's "unnatural fascination with the law." They'd gone their separate ways, and now there was this whole incident with the mistrial that she had to deal with.

What my mother had failed to tell everyone was that an

enamored juror had asked Gianna out on a date. She'd had no choice but to report the incident. The juror was dismissed, a mistrial called, and now my poor sister was left feeling humiliated after details had leaked out to the press.

"Hey." I touched her arm. "There's something else going on with you. Let's have it."

Gianna glanced around the room, but everyone else was busy eating, talking, or milling about. No one paid us much attention. She leaned closer. "I don't want to defend this guy again, Sal, and it's a pretty safe bet he's going to be retried. Bernardo's a total sleaze. I don't mean to sound unprofessional about this, but for now the trial is over, and I know I can trust you not to say anything. Frankly, I'm not convinced of his innocence."

"How did you wind up with him anyway?" I asked. "You're a public defender, and his family has oodles of money."

Bernardo Napoli, the man Gianna had represented in court, came from a prominent Italian family in Colwestern. His stepfather, Luigi, owned and operated Napoli Furnishings. It was a large, red-brick building where you could buy anything from a porcelain soap dish to a gold-plated dining room set. Most people in Colwestern knew the place was just a cover-up for mob operations, but no one dared to blow the whistle for fear of reprisal.

"His stepfather has all the money," Gianna explained. "Bernardo doesn't have any assets in his name. Even if he did, he probably still would have gotten a public defender since that's pretty much the way it works in this state. He was very pleased when they told him I'd be representing him. I've no idea why since this is my first case, and I'm more than a little green."

Mike, who'd been eating and listening without comment, wiped his mouth with a napkin. "He probably thought you were cute."

My sister narrowed her eyes. "*Cute?* I am an attorney. I am not *cute.*"

Mike smiled but wisely said nothing. Like the rest of the family, he knew when Gianna was in one of her moods.

"You look exhausted," I said. "You've been working way too hard."

She sipped at her wine and then squeezed my hand. "I'm sorry. I didn't mean to be such a snot. This is your party, and I'm doing a great job of trying to ruin it."

"Forget about that. All I want to know is that you're okay."

Josie came up behind us and put a hand on each of our shoulders. "Hey, Gi, there's a guy out in the hallway looking for you. He said his name is Bernardo. Isn't that your client?"

Gianna's face paled, and she hurriedly rose to her feet. "Crap. I told him I was coming here tonight. Did he say what he wanted?"

Josie shook her head. "He asked if you were in here and said he didn't want to come barging in. He seemed polite enough and is very good looking—for an older man."

I laughed. "Bernardo's only about forty, Jos. Not exactly ancient."

She made a face. "Oh, whatever." She turned back to Gianna. "Anyhow, he said it was urgent that he talk to you."

Gianna muttered under her breath. "Great. I wonder what's going on now." Her hands shook as she grabbed her purse off the back of the chair.

I placed a hand on her arm. "Are you sure you're okay? Let me go with you to meet him."

She shook her head. "I'm sorry, Sal, but I know he'll want to go somewhere and talk. I may not make it back in time. Will you forgive me?"

I kissed her cheek. "As long as you don't do this at the wedding, I'm good."

"I'll call you later." She glanced toward the other side of the room where my mother and father were deep in discussion with Grandma Rosa and a friend. "Tell Mom and Dad I had to leave. If I go over there to say good-bye, they'll never let me out of their grasp."

"I'll save you a piece of cake and bring it to the bakery tomorrow."

"You'd better." She grinned then made her way over to the double doors.

When I'd moved in with Mike this past January, I'd rented Gianna my old apartment over the bakery. She was thrilled to be out on her own. My parents' house resembled a zoo in many ways, and Gianna desperately needed her private space.

I watched her graceful figure disappear behind the doors and caught a glimpse of Bernardo waiting on the other side for her. Bernardo had sultry Italian good looks—black, wavy hair, piercing brown eyes, and an olive complexion, slightly darker than my own. Something about him screamed wolf and left me concerned for Gianna's welfare. I saw his smile widen as she approached, and then the doors closed, cutting off my line of vision.

Loud giggles distracted me. I turned my head in time to see my mother and father kissing and winced. Mom was obsessed with my upcoming wedding, and I was afraid it had as much to do with Gianna as myself. She'd confided to me last week, after my sister's recent breakup, that she was afraid beautiful and brilliant Gianna, who would turn a ripe old twenty-six next month, was destined to become a spinster. I'd had a difficult time not rolling my eyes.

I noticed Johnny holding the door open for his grandmother. His eyes met mine, and he smiled and waved at both Mike and me, then followed her out. It seemed odd that they were leaving so early, but Mrs. G. did look exhausted. Harassing people for a living had to be tiring work.

Mike ran a finger down the side of my face. "Everything okay?"

"I'm worried about Gianna," I said. "She hasn't been the same since this case started."

"Do you want me to go check on them?" Mike asked. "I can't say that I trusted the looks of Mr. Mafia there."

"She'd be furious if you did. I'm sure she can handle him. He probably just wants to talk about the case." At least I hoped so.

I wondered if Gianna was allowed to tell Bernardo she didn't want to represent him again. I had a feeling he was enamored with her—as most men were. All Gianna had ever wanted was for people to take her seriously. Unfortunately, they seemed to be more focused on her beauty than brains, and it drove her crazy.

Someone touched my arm from behind. Grandma Rosa

sat in Gianna's discarded chair and placed a small white box on my lap. "Happy birthday, *cara mia*."

Next to Mike, Grandma Rosa was the other love of my life. She had come to live with her daughter and son-in-law when my grandfather passed away, shortly after Gianna's birth. She was an excellent cook, made the world's best ricotta cheesecake, and her sound advice never failed. Growing up, she was the one person Gianna and I would run to with our problems. My grandmother had never been too busy to listen or lend a shoulder for us to cry on, which had been quite often.

"You didn't have to do anything." I removed the top of the box and revealed an ancient silver cameo brooch set with a glittering blue topaz stone in the center. My breath caught. As a little girl I had loved playing dress up with Josie and Gianna. Grandma Rosa sometimes allowed us to play with her costume jewelry, but this prized piece had always been off-limits no matter how much I'd begged and pleaded.

A lump formed in my throat as I stared into her brown eyes and the wrinkles that formed around them when she smiled. Grandma always said that they were lines that came from wisdom, not age.

"I can't take this. Grandpa gave it to you when you got married."

She shook her head. "No. He did not like to buy me jewelry. He did once give me a ring from a Cracker Joe box, though."

I laughed. "It's Cracker Jack." I fingered the brooch, intrigued. "Who gave it to you, then?"

She waved a hand dismissively. "That is a talk for another time. I insist you take the brooch. Why do you think I did not want you to play with it when you were a little girl? Because I knew someday it would belong to you. It is not only a birthday present. You will wear it at your wedding as well. You know the saying 'something old, something new, something borrowed, something blue'? Well, right here you have the old and the blue. You can borrow the pearl necklace I gave your mother at her wedding. That will look beautiful with the new gown."

I blinked rapidly, but the tears came anyway. I reached

out and wrapped my arms around her while she laughed and patted my back. "You are a good girl, my Sally. I did not give the brooch to you for your first marriage because I knew it would not last." She released me and nodded toward Mike, who watched us with affection. "This one—it will be different."

Mike's hand tightened around mine.

"Thank you," I whispered, too choked up to say anything else.

"Guess what, honey?" My mother squealed from behind me. "Look what we have for dessert? I had the restaurant order them special!" She held out a tray of homemade chocolate fortune cookies.

Ugh. I caught Josie watching us from across the room, amused. Okay, I was probably being silly. Just because the fortune cookies we used in the shop sometimes had an uncanny way of predicting the future didn't mean that these would have the same effect, right?

"Come on, Sal. They won't bite." Mike handed me a cookie and then whispered in my ear. "Leave that part to me later."

It suddenly grew warm in the room. "We are so leaving after this." I broke the cookie apart and stared down at the strip of paper.

Things will heat up for you tonight.

Mike studied the message with interest, and a broad smile broke out across his face. "Damn. How did it know what I was thinking?"

CHAPTER THREE

———

About an hour later we were in Mike's Ram truck, headed back to his house—or our home, as Mike had always referred to it since I'd moved in. He lifted my hand to his lips. "Happy, baby?"

I gazed into those deep-set blue eyes that I adored so much. "More than I ever thought I could be."

It hadn't always been clear sailing for Mike and me. I'd first met him at the age of fifteen, when his family moved into town. Mike's stepfather had been a construction worker who taught Mike the trade—when he wasn't smacking him around, that is. The first time I'd spotted him during my sophomore year, I had been a goner. The feeling was apparently mutual, and within two weeks he'd asked me to a school dance.

We'd quickly become everything to each other, but Mike had been insecure and insanely jealous of every male I'd talked to back then. When I'd spotted him in the backseat of Brenda Snyder's car—aka Backseat Brenda—on the night of our senior prom, that had been more than enough for me to call it quits. On the rebound, I'd hooked up with Colin Brown and later married him. I had only discovered last year that nothing had even happened between Mike and Brenda that night. He'd tried in vain back then to tell me the truth, but I had refused to listen.

It had taken me several months to stop dwelling on the fact that we'd lost ten precious years together. Instead, I now looked ahead—to an entire lifetime of love with this man.

Mike came around to my side of the truck to help me out and took the box full of gifts and envelopes I'd received from my guests. I made a mental note to write thank-you notes tomorrow. He placed the box on the porch while he opened the front door, silenced the alarm system, and then stepped back for me to enter first.

Spike, our black and white Shih Tzu, greeted us at the door. He looked at both of us and wagged his tail hopefully. He wanted to go for a walk.

Mike addressed the dog as he placed the box down on the coffee table and scooped me up in his arms. "Sorry, buddy. You're gonna have to wait a little while. I've got to heat things up like the fortune cookie said."

I giggled and kissed Mike's neck while he carried me down the hallway. After he laid me on the bed, I removed my phone from the pocket of my slacks. "Maybe I should call Gianna first and see how she is."

Mike reached for the phone and placed it on the nightstand. "Later. We need to follow the protocol of that cookie first."

I unbuttoned his dress shirt, a light blue that brought out his eyes so well. "You're taking that message very seriously, Mr. Donovan."

He grinned. "Well, my wife-to-be seems to regard those words very highly, so it's my job to make them come true."

He wrapped his strong arms around me and kissed me. His mouth was hot and tender, and desire spread through my body.

"We are so lucky," I whispered.

The musical notes on my phone sounded.

Mike removed his mouth from the path he was making down my neck and looked at the offending phone with disdain. "Someone has lousy timing."

I tried to reach my phone but couldn't with Mike on top of me. "Please, honey, see who it is. What if it's about Dad? He had three pieces of cake tonight."

Mike sighed and rolled off me to grab the phone. He studied the screen, and a look of utter irritation spread over his face. "What the hell."

I sat up, worried. "Is it Mom?"

He held the phone out so I could see the name on the screen. "It's Jenkins. Your not-so-secret admirer. Why is *he* calling *you*?"

Brian Jenkins was a cop in Colwestern with dirty blond

hair and a handsome Greek godlike profile. We'd first met last September, when a former nemesis of mine had dropped dead on the front porch of my bakery. We'd become fast friends and almost something else.

"Press *Ignore*," I said.

"Gladly," he muttered. He tossed the phone back on the nightstand then blew out a long breath. "Sorry. That guy still gets under my skin. He just won't go away."

In fact, Brian had recently been in my bakery. Last week he'd mentioned something about a fellow police officer who wanted to place an order for their son's upcoming graduation party. Well, if that was why he was calling, it could wait until tomorrow.

I ran a finger over Mike's lips. Brian and Mike had both asked me out on a date for the same evening when I'd first returned to Colwestern, and I'd been forced into a decision I wasn't sure I was ready to make, or even wanted to, so soon after my divorce. It hadn't taken me long to realize I'd never stopped loving Mike. "I hope you know that I haven't been encouraging him in any way. And he's well aware that we're getting married."

Mike made a face. "I know, baby. But I hate the way that cop looks at you—like you're a dozen doughnuts."

I burst out laughing and ran my hands down his smooth, muscular chest. "Don't get your feathers all ruffled, Mr. Tough Guy. You know who my heart belongs to."

He lay down next to me and kissed me, tracing his fingers lightly down my stomach. "No offense, Sal, but I've got other parts of your body on my mind right now."

I giggled as his tongue probed my mouth open. In a second I had forgotten all about Brian, my crazy parents, and even Gianna. I closed my eyes and thought of nothing but my fiancé and sharing this intimate moment with him.

"I wish we could stay like this forever," I whispered.

His eyes were dark and passionate as they gazed into mine. "We will, if I have anything to say about it."

Spike barked, and a loud banging on our front door commenced.

Mike swore softly. "I don't believe this. It's a little late for visitors. Whoever's at that door is going to be sorry that they stopped by."

"Jeez, don't say things like that." I shivered, superstition getting the best of me again.

He shrugged on his shirt. "Don't go anywhere." He stared at me hungrily, and my entire body tingled from the look. "I want to keep this picture of you in my head. Give me one minute to get rid of whoever the hell's out there."

I took the opportunity to roll over and check my phone to see if Gianna had texted. There were no messages from her. She'd probably gone to bed right after her meeting with Bernardo. My heart ached for what she was going through. How lousy was it to have your first case end in a mistrial because a juror was hitting on you?

At that moment I heard Mike's voice, loud and angry about something. I put the phone down and listened.

"Jenkins, when are you going to take a hint?"

"Sally!" I heard Brian's voice yell. "You need to get out here! The bakery is on fire!"

He didn't mean *my* bakery, did he? There had to be some type of mistake. Panic ensued, and I jumped off the bed and threw my blouse on, adrenaline flowing through my body. I buttoned my shirt as I ran down the hall. I met Mike halfway, coming to get me. He had his truck keys in hand and pulled me toward the front door. Brian followed us, dressed in his dark blue uniform. He closed the front door behind us.

I clutched Brian's arm when I got to the side of Mike's truck. "What happened? Where's Gianna?"

He stared back at me with concerned green eyes. "I don't know anything else. A passerby noticed flames shooting out of the back room of the bakery and called 9-1-1. The fire department was there within minutes. I heard the dispatch over my radio and recognized the address. Which was why I tried to phone you." Brian stared accusingly at Mike, as if suspecting he was the reason I hadn't answered the call.

Mike shouted from behind the wheel. "Sal, let's go!"

"Come on!" Brian practically pushed me into the truck and slammed the door when I was inside. "I'll follow you guys over."

The ten-minute ride to the bakery was perhaps the

longest of my life. Somehow I had managed to call Josie, who'd been sound asleep, and told her what had transpired. She'd started crying and said she'd be there as soon as she could find a babysitter. I'd also dialed Gianna's cell over and over but got no answer.

Mike was quiet during the ride but held my hand tightly. I chided myself in silence. Why hadn't I let him answer the phone? Who would have thought that was the reason Brian had been trying to call me? Never mind. It wouldn't have changed anything. I had more important things to worry about now, such as where my sister was. Fear gripped me tighter than a lover's arms and wouldn't let go.

I was afraid I was going to be sick to my stomach. I prayed over and over that Gianna wasn't inside the building. Maybe she and Bernardo had gone for drinks somewhere. She still wasn't answering her phone. Perhaps she'd stopped to see my parents. *Oh my God. My parents!* I needed to call them.

Mike was forced to stop for a red light and faced me. "She's fine, Sal. Don't do this to yourself."

My response, of course, was to burst into tears.

Even from the next street over, we could see the strobe lights from the fire truck and hear the activity. Mike was forced to park the vehicle about halfway down the street. Before he could even put the truck in park, I had the door open and started to run toward the shop.

"Sal!" He yelled after me.

I stopped suddenly, mesmerized. The sight that met my eyes both terrified and froze me in place. I'd never seen a fire up close before. Several firefighters surrounded the building with hoses that twitched in the air like snakes in the night sky. Water gushed forward from them in all directions. A couple of men moved quickly back and forth, carrying tools and shouting commands. The smell of smoke filled my nostrils. I hesitated, not sure what to do next. Then I spotted an EMS ambulance, and my heart filled with sickening dread as it dropped into my stomach.

My sister could be inside the building.

I ran across the lawn toward the bakery at full speed. A policeman was near the entrance, shouting something into his radio, and caught me by the arm.

"Ma'am, you need to get back across the street."

"It's my bakery!" I screamed. "My sister lives upstairs. I've got to see that she's okay."

Someone from behind me touched my shoulder. I assumed it was Mike and, without thinking, turned and threw my arms around his waist, sobbing into his chest. "I need to know she's all right. I have to get in there. Please tell them, babe."

After an awkward silence, a hand patted my back softly. I looked up and found myself staring into Brian's shining green eyes flecked with gold. Mike stood beside him. He said nothing, but his face hardened as if it was carved out of stone.

This definitely was going down as one of the most embarrassing moments of my life. I struggled for composure and inched away from Brian. "I'm sorry. I—I thought you were Mike."

Neither man said anything as Mike reached out and pulled me into his arms. To his credit, he didn't fly off the handle. Ten years ago, he would have punched Brian in the face first and asked questions later. Now he cradled my face between his hands. "I just called your parents' house. Your grandmother answered the phone. They'll be here soon."

"Gianna," I whispered hopefully. "Is she there?"

His expression was sorrowful. "No, baby. They haven't seen her since the party."

I looked at the two-story, white-painted building with the large front porch that held my wicker table and chairs for customers to sit outside during the warm weather. Several people had been doing that earlier today. I already knew that the damage was going to be significant. Maybe the place would even have to be torn down. My eyes filled, and the tears gushed down my cheeks.

I grabbed the arm of the other policeman. "My sister Gianna lives upstairs."

The man shook his head at me. "The firefighters were able to get upstairs immediately after they first arrived on the scene. No one was inside the apartment, ma'am."

I collapsed against Mike in sheer relief. "Thank God." But something continued to gnaw away at my brain. If Gianna wasn't in the building, then where was she? Had she gone to Bernardo's house to spend the night? No, that wasn't her speed. Gianna hadn't even liked the man. She hated this entire case and the embarrassment it had caused her.

"Sal!" I heard Josie scream.

I turned to see my friend running toward me. Her gorgeous, long, red hair was a tangled mess, and she wore cropped, pink, cotton pajamas with flip-flops. Mike released me so that I could hug her.

Her face was streaked with tears as she clung to me. "What the hell happened?"

"I don't know. A passerby reported it."

Josie's face went pale. "Gianna—"

I shook my head. "She wasn't in the building."

"Thank God." Josie looked at the bakery in angst, and her lower lip trembled. She continued to cling to me. "What are we going to do?"

"It's insured." Mike leaned over and kissed the top of my head.

I sniffled as smoke continued to spew from the building. "The important thing is that no one got hurt."

At that moment two firemen came out of the building carrying something between them. It only took a split second for me to figure out that it was a body—and a lifeless one at that. Mike placed his arms around me in a tight grip to prevent me from running toward it. The EMTs pushed a gurney toward the firefighters as we all continued to stare, frozen in place. Blood roared in my ears as Brian strode over to them. As they spoke, one of the firemen shook his head. I watched, not daring to breathe, as the victim was placed on the gurney and secured in the ambulance, which immediately rushed off, sirens blaring. Mike's firm grip still held me in place.

A small, strangled cry escaped from my lips. *No! No, it can't be her.*

Brian turned in my direction, and our eyes met. His expression was sober as he started toward me. "Sally—"

I never heard what he said. I was vaguely aware of Mike catching me in his arms as I struggled for air and my legs collapsed out from underneath me.

In one brief second the entire world—like my bakery—turned black.

CHAPTER FOUR

―――

"Sweetheart, open your eyes, and look at me."

My head resembled a jigsaw puzzle. The pieces were all there but not in any logical order. I opened my eyes in confusion to see Mike bending over me. His midnight blue eyes were anxious as they met mine. Why did he look so upset? Then I saw my building behind him, the clouds of smoke billowing in the night sky, and remembered what had happened. I shrieked and tried to push myself up from the gurney that I was lying on.

Mike held me down firmly. "Stay here, Sal."

"Please let me up," I sobbed. "I have to go to her. I need to—"

"It's not her, baby," he said. "Gianna wasn't in the building."

Overcome with relief and joy, I reached up and wrapped my arms around his neck. Over his shoulder I noticed that while there was still plenty of smoke, I could no longer see flames shooting out from the building.

Mike held me close, whispering reassurances in my ear. Then he pushed back my hair and kissed me. "You fainted before Jenkins could tell you that the body they found in the back room belonged to Bernardo Napoli."

Josie was standing to my right. She reached down and gave my hand a tight squeeze and then wiped at her eyes with a tissue. She asked the question that was rapidly taking shape in my mind. "What was he doing in there all by himself?"

"Where's my sister?" I sat up and looked around. My parents were across the road, huddled together and leaning against their car, talking to a police officer. Mom was smoking a cigarette. Grandma Rosa was standing with them, her sharp eyes focused on me.

"I need to go to them." I jumped off the gurney and felt a bit shaky, but Mike's arm steadied me.

"They're okay. A bit shocked, but your grandmother's been great at keeping them calm."

"This doesn't make any sense. Where is my sister?" I repeated. Gianna would never leave my bakery with someone inside, especially a man she'd defended in court.

Brian approached us. "Fire's out. The firefighters will be here for a while doing overhaul. We'll leave an officer overnight to prevent looters from coming in."

Mike eyed a tall man dressed in black, holding a clipboard. He was talking to one of the firemen. "Who's that?"

"The arson investigator." Brian studied me. "He'll want to speak to you in the morning."

My mouth went dry. Never in my wildest dreams would I think this might have been done on purpose.

Josie swore. "They think the fire was deliberately set?"

Brian's mouth set in a hard, firm line. "It's a possibility. We'll know more in the morning. But for now, you might as well go home. There's nothing else you can do here." He gazed at me with sympathy. "You need some rest. Please let me know if you hear from your sister. We'd like to speak to her and find out why Bernardo was in the back room."

"We'd like to know why too," Mike said grimly.

My entire body was numb as I tried to make sense of this. "Why? Why would someone deliberately set my bakery on fire?"

Brian shrugged. "Personal vendetta? I don't know, Sally. There are some shady characters out there. And you've had the bad luck of being involved with several as of late."

He had a point. I removed Mike's arm from my shoulders and walked toward my once beautiful little bakery. I thought of the day, almost a year ago, when I had first laid eyes on the building. I remembered how the real estate agent told me it had been a former Chinese restaurant, which led to my idea of handing out free fortune cookies to patrons whenever they made a purchase.

Evil fortune cookies. I thought of the message from earlier, and my stomach grew queasy.

Things will heat up for you tonight.

What the heck were the odds I'd receive a message like that and then have my building burn down hours later? Did someone really hate me enough to do this, and why? Even worse, had they been hoping that I was inside the bakery at the time of the fire? Or maybe Gianna?

The air was still thick with smoke, but I walked closer anyway. I'd almost reached the porch when Brian caught me by the arm.

"You can't go in there, Sally. Not while an investigation is pending. Plus, it isn't safe right now."

Josie ran up to me and started to sob again. "What are we going to do, Sal?"

Mike reached for my hand and tried to lead me away. "Come on, sweetheart. Jenkins is right—there's nothing we can do. Let's go home. You need to sleep."

As I looked at the building again, my own fire raged from within. "*No.*"

Mike opened his mouth in surprise. "You're upset, Sal. Come on. We'll go home and talk this through."

Yes, of course I was upset, but more than that, I was pissed. Royally pissed. Why me? What had I ever done to deserve this? I tried to lead a good life. I always gave people the benefit of the doubt, yet murder and destruction followed me at a merry rate these days. Josie and I had worked so hard to build a successful business, and neither of us deserved this. Heck, I wouldn't wish it on my worst enemy.

Then again, perhaps it had been *my* worst enemy that had done this. I didn't know what to think anymore. My rage reached a boiling point, and I exploded.

"I don't want to go home. How can I? My sister is missing. Someone might have torched my bakery. This is my livelihood. A man is dead because of all this. How the hell can I rest?"

Mike's eyes widened. "Baby, you need to stay calm. It's not going to do any good to freak out."

"Don't tell me what to do!" I shook his hands off and saw the look of amazement that crossed his face. I knew I was being unreasonable but couldn't help myself. I was so angry at the latest curveball life had thrown at me. Whenever I was in a good place in my life, it seemed that something terrible happened. How was this even fair? All I wanted was to have a family and run my little cookie shop. Was that too much to ask?

Mike tried to reason with me once again, wrapping his arms around me. "I've got something back at the house that will help you sleep."

A feeling of suffocation was settling over me as I pushed him away. "I don't need to sleep. What I need is to find my sister."

"Sal." My father's gruff voice sounded behind me. "She's going to be fine. Just keep checking your phone. If she calls anyone, it will be you."

Grandma Rosa stood there quietly, watching me, while my mother sniffled and reached out to hug me. "Sweetie, do you want to come back to the house with us? It would be nice to have you there."

I didn't want to be around anyone, but these were my parents, and they were hurting too. "Sure." My voice sounded hollow to my own ears. "I'll be there soon."

My parents started in the direction of their car with Grandma Rosa following. I was overwhelmed with sadness as I watched their hunched figures depart. They stopped at the driver's side door, and my father stared back at the bakery while Mom rummaged for something in her purse. I guessed she needed another cigarette.

My mother didn't smoke often, usually only when she was stressed, and that was a rarity, since Maria Muccio didn't let many things in life bother her. When my father was sick a few months ago, she'd been outside the hospital lighting up so often I was afraid she'd burst into flames. I'd come to rely on her sunny outlook, so this upset me even further.

"I'm going home too." Josie reached out to hug me. "Rob's working the overnight shift, so I asked my neighbor to come over and stay with the kids. She wasn't thrilled about me waking her up, so I need to get back. Brian's right—there's nothing more we can do tonight." She turned to him. "What time can we talk to the investigator tomorrow?"

Brian cleared his throat. "I'll let you know. I'll call Sally in the morning." He glanced at me. "You might want to call your insurance company too. I'm sure they'll send a representative out tomorrow to assess the damages."

I said nothing as I stared from him to Josie and then back to Mike.

Josie walked across the street and then stopped to hug Grandma Rosa before getting into her van. My grandmother nodded and said something to her. My grandmother was the person everyone turned to in a time of crisis. Only I didn't want to turn to anyone now. The anger was fighting a war against me, and I was determined to let it win.

Mike put an arm around me and once again tried to lead me away from the building. "Come on, baby. Let's go home."

Furious, I turned to face him. "I can't go home. Don't you understand? I need to be with my family. They're hurting over my sister. My shop is destroyed." I stopped to catch my breath. "Why do rotten things always happen to me?"

Mike stared at me like I was a complete stranger. "I know it looks bad, but we'll get through this together. You'll see."

"Go home. I want to be alone."

"Sal—"

"Leave me alone!" I ran toward the bakery and fell to my knees, sobbing as I surveyed my building and the mass disarray still going on around me. The firefighters were packing up their truck and putting away hoses. Two of them stood just inside the front door while the arson investigator nodded and wrote something on his chart. The urge to scream and start throwing things was great. Complete hopelessness had overwhelmed me.

In the past year, I had come in contact with several murder incidents. The first had been my great-aunt Luisa, Grandma Rosa's younger sister. Then a former nemesis from high school had dropped dead on the front porch of my bakery after eating our cookies. Colin, my ex, had returned to town in early January with plans to manipulate me and take away my bakery. He'd gotten into a fight with Mike, who had later been arrested after Colin was found shot to death. Now there was the fire and death of Gianna's client—in my bakery. *Again.*

This building was cursed. No, wait a second. It wasn't

the building. *I* was the one jinxed. A fortune cookie's happy victim. Why had I ever started making those stupid pieces of dough in the first place?

Not knowing what else to do, I buried my face in my hands and continued to sob.

Someone placed a hand on my shoulder, but I didn't look up. "Mike, I said to leave me."

"*Cara mia*, do not do this to yourself."

Grandma Rosa stood beside me. She placed a soothing hand on my head and smoothed back my hair. I rose to my feet, still crying. She reached out and placed her arms around me, as if willing me all her strength.

I wiped at my eyes. "Go home with my parents. I need to be alone."

"You must stop this, dear heart. Do not let the grief win. It solves nothing."

"It's already won. I'm done. I give up."

She shook me slightly. "No. You are upset and not thinking straight. Stop feeling sorry for yourself. Be grateful that your sister is still alive. These are all material things. They do not mean anything."

"But it's not fair," I whined like a six-year-old. "I put my heart and soul into this place. Now it's ruined, and a man is dead."

I heard the rumble of a truck engine and saw Mike's pickup take off down the street. Grandma Rosa shook her head at me. "Why did you lash out at your young man? He loves you very much."

"He doesn't understand how I feel."

"You are doing it again," she said. "After all the suffering he has been through in his life, you have the nerve to say that *he* doesn't understand? Think about that for a minute, my dear."

Crap. She was right. Mike had a horrible childhood in an abusive household. And here I was, pushing him away when he'd tried to comfort me. What they said was true. You always hurt the one you love.

"He wanted to stay and wait for you, but I told him to leave," Grandma Rosa continued. "I said I would take care of you. He is very worried about you, my dear. All he wants is to help."

"I didn't mean it," I choked out. "He knows I love him. Everything will be fine when I see him."

Grandma Rosa raised her eyebrows at me. "Everything is *not* fine. You are about to be husband and wife. It is not wise to start your marriage out like this. You go to him."

"No. I need to be with my family."

She grunted. "Do not tell me no. I will take care of your mama and papa. Mike is your family too. Perhaps not in name yet, but that does not matter. You go. That is an order."

I knew better than to argue with her. Reluctantly I rose to my feet and took one last look at the building. As we turned to make our way across the street, we saw my parents' Chevy take off. Grandma Rosa threw up her arms in pantomime.

"You see? They forget all about me until it is time for dinner." She tapped the side of her white head. "Your parents are—what do they say?—nutsy cookies."

Despite the despair I was feeling, I managed a smile. "Cuckoos."

"Bah. Same thing."

I placed an arm around her shoulders. "Well, I guess you and I are walking."

Brian's voice startled me from behind. "I'd be glad to give you ladies a lift. Go make yourselves comfortable in my squad car. I want to speak with one of the firemen for a second."

Grandma Rosa snickered as I opened the door to Brian's vehicle and settled her into the backseat. "He is very charming and handsome, the police officer. But I do not trust him around you, my Sally."

"Grandma, you sound just like Mike now."

She wagged a finger at me. "It is the truth. He looks at you the same way you look at my cheesecake when I take it out of the oven."

Ouch. That was bad.

Grandma Rosa shook her head. "Mike is not going to be happy when he sees the young officer bringing you home. That is more trouble that you do not need."

I knew she was probably right, but I was tired and had

no energy left. This had been a long draining day that had started out wonderfully and then ended in tragedy for both Bernardo and my bakery.

"Grandma, I would hope that Mike and I have learned to develop some type of trust between us." I could have bitten my tongue off as soon as I said the words. How trusting had I been of him minutes ago when I'd had a meltdown for everyone to witness?

She chuckled. "You still have a lot to learn, granddaughter."

I leaned my head against her. "I do everything wrong."

She kissed me. "No. You are being tested. You are a survivor, *cara mia*. You will get through this and become an even stronger person because of it."

"I don't feel very strong right now," I admitted.

"We are all tested every day in many ways." A shadow crossed over her face as she stared out the window. "I have had my tests too. You, my dear, are a lot like me."

I lifted my head and examined her face. Grandma Rosa never cried, but I could have sworn I saw her wise brown eyes mist over for a second. "What happened?"

She looked at me and smiled. "Someday I will tell you. But not now. You go to your young man and work things out. Everything will look better after you get some sleep. Trust your grandmother."

As I'd suspected, Brian decided to drop Grandma Rosa off first, even though Mike's house was closer. I think she was aware of this too, although she chose not to say anything as she thanked him for the ride.

Brian went around to open the door for her, and I gave her a kiss on the cheek. "Tell Mom and Dad I'll stop by tomorrow."

She nodded. "Get some rest, dear heart. Let the sun rise on a new day and happy thoughts. Life is what you make of it."

We waited until she got inside, and then I slid into the front passenger seat across from Brian, thinking about what she'd said. Neither one of us spoke for the first few minutes.

Finally, he cleared his throat. "I hope there's no trouble between you and Mike."

"We'll be fine."

There was another awkward pause. "When's the wedding?"

Oh, jeez. I really didn't want to discuss this with him, on top of everything else currently going on in my life. "In a couple of weeks."

Brian grew silent again. "Sally, I wanted you to know that I still—"

I cut him off, having a premonition of what was coming next. "Brian, please don't say it. I can't deal with this right now."

His response was to pull the car over to the side of the road and place it in park. I wanted to run and hide as he turned to face me, but we were in a desolate part of town after midnight. Still, I thought being in the car with Brian might be even more dangerous.

"I'm still in love with you."

I sucked in some air. Another awkward moment of the day for me. "Brian, nothing ever happened between us. A couple of kisses. How could you possibly be in love with me?"

"I have been since the first day I laid eyes on you in the bakery. Does that make any sense?"

Actually it did, for that was the way I'd always felt about Mike, although I chose not to mention it at the moment.

I rubbed my eyes wearily. "I love Mike and always have. No one else ever stood a chance, not even Colin, to tell you the truth."

"Do you think Mike's worried you might still have feelings for me?"

Okay, he clearly wasn't getting it. After everything that had happened tonight, I couldn't believe that Brian—a police officer who was supposed to uphold the law nonetheless—was putting me through this crap.

I reached deep down inside for some patience, currently in short supply. "Brian, I'd like it if we could be friends. That's all."

Brian's voice was low and emotional. "But I don't want to be just friends, Sally." He reached across the seat and pulled me into his arms. Furious and stunned, I pushed at his massive chest. The back of his head hit the driver's side window, and I was shocked. From the expression on his face, so was he. I hadn't realized that I possessed so much strength. Maybe it was a result of my newfound anger.

I edged as far away from him as possible and spoke to my side window. "You need to move on."

From the corner of my eye, I could see him staring at me, motionless. Finally he turned and meekly put the vehicle in drive, saying nothing. A few minutes later, we pulled up in front of my house. The porch light was on, a welcoming sight. I sat there staring into the night, wondering what I was going to say to the man I loved.

Brian's voice interrupted my thoughts. "I'm sorry. I can't believe I just did that."

"I can't believe you did either." I refused to look at him. "What time is the investigator coming by the shop in the morning?"

"I'll call you first thing and let you know," Brian said. "I'll be glad to help in any way that I can."

I opened the door. "You've helped enough. Have him call me directly. Thanks for the ride."

"Sally—"

My answer was to slam the car door as hard as I could. As I ran across the driveway, I spotted Mike standing on the porch, one hand on the door jamb, the light enhancing his handsome face. He watched me in silence, and then his eyes narrowed on Brian's squad car. *Wonderful.*

I approached him cautiously, wondering if it might be his turn to slam the door in *my* face. "Hi."

He held the screen door open, allowing me to enter, but said nothing. I reached down to pet Spike, who had come out to greet me. Mike closed and locked the door behind me and set the security alarm. I followed him into the kitchen, where he grabbed a beer out of the fridge.

"Want one?"

"No thanks." I waited, but Mike said nothing else. He turned and stared out the window over the kitchen sink, sipping his beer. I glanced at the wall clock. Almost one in the morning. I was bone tired and ached all over. The ache wasn't just physical—it was emotional as well. What on earth had possessed me to do such a thing? I'd never lost control like that before. It was both terrifying and surreal. The only thing I'd accomplished was hurting the man I loved more than life itself.

I reached out and wrapped my arms around his waist. "I'm sorry. I acted like an idiot."

Mike didn't move or respond.

"Please don't be angry with me." I leaned my head against his back.

He turned around and gathered me into him, brushing a soft kiss across my lips. I could see the unmistakable shadow of pain reflected in his eyes and longed to take it all away.

"It's okay, Sal. You were upset."

I buried my face in his chest, relief washing over me as he stroked my hair. "That was wrong of me. I didn't mean to push you away. I need you so much."

He tipped my chin up so I was forced to look at him. "This is a lot for someone to deal with. I know how much you love your sister—and the shop. But don't shut me out next time, okay? You're going to be my wife very soon, and it's my duty to be here for you, now and hopefully in fifty years too."

Tears fell from my eyes and blurred his image. "I was so worried you'd be upset with me."

He swiped his thumb underneath my lashes and spoke quietly. "I'm not going anywhere, Sal. I lost you once. Remember? It took me ten years to get you back. I'm never going to let that happen again."

A sob escaped my lips as Mike leaned down and kissed me. He crushed me against him as the kiss deepened and became more urgent. Without saying another word, he scooped me up into his arms as if I weighed nothing and carried me down the hallway toward our bedroom.

"Fifty years isn't enough," I whispered. "I'll love you for eternity."

CHAPTER FIVE

———

My cell phone rang at eight o'clock sharp the next morning, startling me out of a deep dream I couldn't remember. I glanced over at Mike's side of the bed, which was empty, then reached onto the nightstand for my cell, rubbing sleep out of my eyes. I prayed for my sister's name to pop up on the screen, but instead it was Brian's.

Great. "Yeah?"

There was a brief pause. "Sorry. Did I wake you?"

"It's all right." My voice sounded shrill. I was still peeved at him after the stunt he had pulled last night. I hadn't told Mike and didn't plan on it. Mike had more self-control these days than I did, but there was no reason to tempt fate.

"I spoke to the arson investigator," Brian said. "He'll be at the building around nine and would like to speak with you then. Will that work?"

I jumped out of bed and searched for clean clothes while making a mental note to text Josie. "That's fine. Josie and I will both be there."

"Have you been in touch with your insurance company yet?"

"I left a message for them before I went to sleep last night. They have a 24-hour hotline. I'll follow up on my way over to the shop this morning."

He cleared his throat. "Okay. I don't work until this evening, so I'll be there as well."

"That's nice of you, but there's really no reason to bother."

An uncomfortable silence ensued. "Sally, I know you're probably still pissed at me about last night—"

"Gee, why would I be pissed at you?" I snapped. "A man

is dead, my bakery caught fire, and Gianna's missing, but all you cared about was getting cozy in your cop car with me."

"I'm sorry," Brian said quietly. "I didn't mean for that to happen. Honest." He hesitated. "Did you tell Mike?"

The shower was running, so I knew Mike couldn't hear our conversation. "No. I didn't tell him—for *your* sake."

He laughed out loud. "Well, that's nice of you, but I'm not afraid of Mike."

Oh, you should be. "Look, I think it's best if we stay away from each other."

"Your sister is wanted for questioning. A neighbor saw her and Bernardo entering the bakery after closing last night."

An overwhelming chill of fear ran down my spine. That would have been after she'd left the party. What the heck had happened? "She didn't do anything, Brian."

"I wasn't implying she did," he said quietly. "But we do need to speak to Gianna, so please let me know if you hear from her."

Don't think so. "Sure. No problem."

"I'll see you in a little while." He disconnected.

Annoyed, I clicked off and noticed I had a text message. My heart almost leaped out of my chest when I saw who it was from.

Got your texts and calls. Sorry. Didn't mean to scare you. Just needed to get out of town. Tell Mom and Dad I'm okay. Love you.

Gianna.

I sent up an infinite prayer of thanks to the heavens above and hugged the phone tightly to my chest. Then I checked the time on the text. She'd sent it after three in the morning. Even though I was relieved, I still worried about her and the tone of her message. She'd clearly been upset at the party, and I wondered if something had happened afterward to push her over the edge—maybe related to Bernardo.

I typed a message back. *Where are you? Need to see you. Things to tell.* I didn't want to come right out and tell her about Bernardo in a text, or that she no longer had a place to live. Some things were best relayed in person.

I waited a few minutes, but there was no response. I tried

phoning, but my call went directly to voicemail. Something was definitely wrong.

The door of the bathroom opened, and Mike appeared with a towel wrapped around his waist. He grabbed a pair of jeans out of the closet as I ran toward him and leaped into his arms.

"Let me get rid of this towel first," he joked.

"Smart aleck. Gianna's all right. She just texted me."

He held me close against his bare chest. "You see? I told you she'd be okay."

I released him and dashed off a quick text to Josie. "But I'm still worried. There's something wrong. I know my sister."

Mike reached for a T-shirt in the dresser drawer then walked back into the bathroom to shave. "Where is she?"

I grabbed a towel out of the linen closet for my shower. "Gianna didn't say. I texted her, but she hasn't answered yet."

He turned his attention back to the bathroom mirror. "At least you know she's all right. She'll come back home soon, and everything will be fine, sweetheart."

"I hope so." I studied the screen of my phone, as if somehow I could will Gianna to send another message. "Brian called me while you were in the shower. The arson investigator is willing to talk to me in an hour. Can you come too?"

"Dammit, I can't," Mike said. "I'm meeting a client about a new job."

"On a Sunday? You never schedule work then."

He hesitated for a moment. "It was the only time the guy had available, but I can cancel if you really need me. I don't want you going there alone or—excuse me—with doughnut cop. I wouldn't put it past him to try something with you, even though he knows we're engaged."

Oh, boy. I definitely wasn't telling him about last night now. My phone pinged, and I glanced down at the screen again. "No, that's all right. Josie just texted and said she'll be here to pick me up in forty minutes. We'll probably head over to my parents afterwards if you're able to meet me there."

He wiped his face with a hand towel and then gazed at me, concern in his eyes. "Sal, maybe you shouldn't do this to yourself. Ask the inspector to call you or wait a couple of days.

You haven't even had time to process everything yet. I've seen the damage a fire can do. It was dark last night, and you have no idea how bad the building is going to look today. It's going to break your heart."

I bit into my lower lip. I knew he was right, but I had to face it sometime. "Can we rebuild the shop? You could do it, right?"

Mike sighed and reached out to stroke my cheek tenderly. "I don't want to lie to you. It all depends on the extent of the damages. My guess is it would take several weeks at least, maybe longer. Plus, if it is arson, like they suspect, your insurance company might not pay out."

That stopped me cold. "But—but they have to! There's a mortgage on the building I need to pay. They won't think I did it—will they?"

"I'm not sure of all the details," Mike said. "Why don't you wait and see what this fellow has to say? Somehow, somewhere, you will have your bakery again, I promise. But for the time being, maybe you and Josie can rent a space. Plus, you're going to need all new equipment too. I've got about twenty grand in the bank. It's yours."

"No. That's your money," I objected.

"Wrong. It's *our* money."

My throat went tight with tears as I threw my arms around his neck. "Thank you. I hate feeling so helpless right now. But I do have to find another place soon. This isn't just about me. Josie needs the job, and so does Sarah."

"We'll find something." He motioned toward the shower. "You'd better get moving if you want to get there on time. I'll bring you some coffee."

I smiled up at him gratefully. The rest of my life might be in shambles, but at least I'd hit the jackpot with this man. "How can I thank you?"

He grinned wickedly. "I'm sure I can think of something later."

* * *

Mike was right. I shouldn't have gone.

Since we weren't allowed inside the building yet, Josie and I stood helplessly on the lawn, inhaling the remnants of smoke that still lingered in the air. Peering inside, I'd noticed that the firemen had torn down the wall between the front room and the prep area. This had been done last night, Brian explained, to ensure that the fire didn't spread. I couldn't see the entire portion of the back room and wasn't sure I wanted to. I already knew it was probably a total loss, not to mention the thousands of dollars to replace my appliances. The front part of the building wasn't as bad as I'd feared, but the overall picture left me nauseated. I turned away for fear I might be sick.

Josie and I moved near the shed. She wiped at her eyes and blew her nose into a tissue. "Sal, what are we going to do? I've got to have a job."

"We'll rent space until I can afford to buy a new building," I said. The question was where, though. For the life of me, I didn't know of any vacant buildings in Colwestern right now. So many questions were jumbled inside my head. What had Bernardo been doing in the bakery alone? What had happened between him and Gianna? Where was my sister now? And last but not least, who had done this?

Brian and the arson investigator I'd seen last night walked toward us. "Sally, this is Clint Rogers. Clint, Sally Muccio. She's the owner." He gestured toward Josie. "And this is Josie Sullivan, her head baker."

We all shook hands. Clint tapped his pencil against his clipboard, wrote something down, and then stared up at both of us.

"Well?" Josie asked impatiently.

I nudged her slightly in the side with my elbow.

Clint spoke with a slow Southern drawl. "In my opinion, there's no question about it. There are things that are consistent with the fire being deliberately set."

Dread as heavy as a mountain settled in the pit of my stomach. "But how? Did they turn on the ovens? I don't understand."

"Matches or a lighter?" Josie asked.

He shook his head. "We've seen this before. Pretty common. A fire doesn't usually start in the middle of a bare concrete floor unless someone has used an accelerant. My guess is gasoline. I can tell from the unusual burn patterns. It has to be confirmed in a lab analysis, of course."

"But why?" I sputtered. "I don't have any enemies. Who would do this to me?"

Clint ignored my question. "I'll have the report to your insurance company as soon as possible." He turned to Brian. "Sorry to rush off, but I've got another place to investigate. You'll see that I get the details on the autopsy?"

Brian nodded. "Thanks for coming out."

Clint cut his eyes to Josie and then back to me. "Sorry about your bakery, ladies." With that, he turned and walked toward his car while still making notes on his clipboard.

"Gee, thanks for the concern," Josie muttered under her breath.

Dazed, I watched as Clint got into his vehicle. "Wow. That was quick."

Brian sighed. "Sally, you have to understand. There's only so much he's going to tell you. For all he knows, you could have been the one to set the place on fire."

"What?" Josie exploded. "Why the hell would we do something twisted like that?"

Brian held up a hand. "I know you two didn't have anything to do with the fire. But, sad to say, there are plenty of times when the owner has played a part. Maybe someone's in debt and trying to get out from under. The business might not be doing well, so they think they'll collect on the building. I could give you half a dozen different scenarios."

This was all too much for me to absorb right now. "I don't believe this. It's bad enough that my place was torched, and now they think I might have committed the deed?"

Brian put a hand on my shoulder, and I flinched. His face reddened, and he removed it quickly. "There are other possibilities. Bernardo might have been the intended victim, not your bakery. Maybe someone followed him here. That would really stink for you guys—a rotten twist of fate, so to speak."

I glanced at Josie. For some reason I was thinking about those blasted fortune cookies again. "So you're saying someone might have deliberately set the fire to kill Bernardo?"

"We're going to have to wait until we hear from the coroner's office," Brian replied, "and discover exactly how he died. There's a chance I might have the results tonight. Would you like me to stop over at your house after I get the report?"

I was tempted to say no, but the urge to find out what had really happened surpassed everything else. "I'd appreciate that. Thank you."

He watched me closely. "Have you heard anything from Gianna?"

I debated about how much to tell him. "Yes, earlier this morning. She texted me and said she needed to get away for a while. Brian, she doesn't have anything to do with this mess."

He leaned against the shed and watched me, the sun reflecting off his fine, blond hair. "Where is she?"

"She didn't say."

Brian held out his hand. "Can I see the text?"

I stepped back from him, furious. "No, you *can't* see the text. Maybe you should get a court order, and then I'll let you see it."

Josie's mouth fell open, and she looked at me in amusement. "Wow. Way to go, girlfriend."

Brian's mouth twitched. If he started laughing, I wasn't going to be held responsible for my actions. "Sally, I don't believe Gianna killed him. But she may have been the last person to see him alive. A lot of things don't add up here. So if you know where Gianna is, you'd be doing her a huge favor by sharing the information with us. She's not under arrest for anything. We only want to talk to her."

Shoot. Here I was flying off the handle again. As much as I wanted to, I couldn't afford to alienate Brian since he might prove to be a valuable source of information, especially where Bernardo's autopsy was concerned. "Sure. Sorry I overreacted, but I'm still upset. In answer to your question, I really don't know where she is."

He nodded, but the look in his eyes was untrusting. "It's okay, Sally. I believe you."

A female voice came over his radio at that moment, addressing him by name. He reached for it, and then his gaze met mine again. He studied me in such a way that brought to mind

Grandma Rosa's reference to her cheesecake last night.

Brian was sweet and handsome, and while sparks had flown between us for a brief period in the past, that was all over now—well, for me anyway. I was in the midst of planning a wedding, dealing with a destroyed business, and trying to locate my sister. I didn't have time for his lovesick antics.

"Maybe I'll see you tonight." Brian started to say something else then he cut his eyes to Josie, and his face reddened immediately. He turned and walked toward his squad car.

Josie grinned. "Gotta give him credit. Officer Hottie is one persistent little bugger." She stared at the building again and sighed, her face mournful. "Let's go. I can't bear to look at this place anymore."

"I know. It seems unreal, kind of like a bad dream."

Josie's lower lip trembled. "Sal, I can't believe I'm asking this, but what's Gianna's connection to this mess?"

"I don't know," I said. "Hopefully nothing. There's no proof that she was involved in Bernardo's death."

"She didn't give you any clue as to where she was?"

I shook my head. "She hasn't answered any of my calls or texts since the first one. What if somebody's holding her against her will? Maybe they made her type that message to me."

Josie pinched a blade of grass between her fingers. "Ah, you watch too much television."

Perhaps she'd forgotten how a lunatic had once done the same thing—made her call me and say everything was fine as she'd been held at gunpoint? I decided not to remind her. If Josie had somehow managed to block that horrible episode out of her life, then all the better for her.

She dug her keys out of her purse. "Maybe someone wanted Bernardo dead, and they hoped Gianna would take the blame for it."

"I don't understand this at all," I said. "Was someone angry that he wasn't going to prison? Maybe they blamed Gianna for that too?"

"It's possible. They may have been sure he'd be convicted, but then that juror came on to Gianna and screwed up their entire scheme." She opened the driver's door of her van.

"Come on. Let's go grab some coffee and hopefully cheesecake—courtesy of your grandmother."

I pulled the seat belt around me. "Sounds like a plan. Besides, I want to see how my parents are doing."

Josie observed me suspiciously. "Speaking of plans, you're up to something. I can tell. Let's have it."

I stared out the window at my smoke-stained and battered bakery one last time. "We're going back in later to search Gianna's apartment. Maybe then we can find out where she's gone."

She gazed at me in astonishment. "You can't, Sal. That would be tampering with an investigation."

"Then we'll get Brian to let us in somehow. Gianna could be in trouble. I need to find her before the police do." I averted my eyes from the building and told myself that I wouldn't cry again. After all, what would it solve?

Josie started the engine. "Why does this stuff always happen to us?"

I thought of the fortune cookie message from last night and shivered. "I don't know. But I can tell you I'm getting a little tired of so much drama in my life."

"Yeah, I hear you on that one."

CHAPTER SIX

———

We found my parents and grandmother in the large, sunny, yellow kitchen, drinking coffee and arguing in their typical Italian fashion. I'd already phoned Grandma Rosa earlier to tell her about Gianna's text. My parents were back to their old selves, acting as if nothing had ever happened. This was the usual manner in which they dealt with disaster. They put their rose-colored glasses on and saw only what they wanted to see. It was a mechanism that worked well for them, so perhaps I was jealous.

"Come here, baby girl." My father put a protective arm around me. "There's no need to worry. We've got your new bakery all ready."

Josie and I sat down while Grandma Rosa set a large piece of her ricotta cheesecake in front of each of us. My mouth immediately started to water. I hadn't eaten since the party last night and until this moment hadn't realized how famished I was.

Grandma Rosa brought us each a cup of coffee and snorted at my father. "*Sei pazzo.*"

With the exception of my grandmother, was there anyone in my family who wasn't acting a bit crazy these days? Lord knows I'd come close to teetering on the edge last night too.

Grandma Rosa shook her fist at my father. "I tell you, this idea is no good. It will never work. You have had some winners before, *si,* but this one really takes the pie."

"You mean cake, Grandma," I said.

She shrugged. "Same thing."

"Can someone please tell me what's going on?" Josie asked. "Did you find a new location for the bakery?"

"Yes." My mother giggled and spread her arms out wide. "Here you are, honey."

Josie and I exchanged confused glances.

She had to be joking. "Mom, I have no idea what you're talking about."

"It's the perfect solution. You'll run your bakery right here until you find a new place." My mother gave a proud toss of her head. "I can tell you firsthand from my professional connections that there is very limited rental space available in Colwestern at the moment."

My mother was a licensed real estate agent. She'd been working at the job for over a year but hadn't made any actual sales yet. It was a good thing that my father had a generous pension from the railroad and didn't have to depend on her to bring home the bacon because they would have starved long ago.

Josie's face was pale underneath her freckles. Somehow I'd managed to keep myself from choking on the coffee I'd been swallowing. How crazy was this idea?

"Mom, what about permits and everything? It will never work."

She waved a hand impatiently. "Of course it will. Don't you remember my friend, Claire Houston? Well, she's a health inspector now. She gave me an application for you to fill out. She's coming here tomorrow to check out the place, and she said if everything looks good, she'll pull some strings and issue you a permit right away. In the meantime, you two should go out and buy some new equipment today so you'll be all set to go."

The panic in Josie's eyes undoubtedly mirrored my own. I found myself grasping for more excuses as to why this would not—could not—work. "Wh-what about zoning? I don't think we'll be allowed to run a business here."

"Sure can." My father looked up from the obituary section of the paper that he was reading. "This street is zoned both commercial and residential. You're forgetting about Mona at the end of the block."

I desperately wanted to forget about Mona. When I was ten, my mother had thought it would be nice to send Mona some business after she'd opened a hair salon inside her house. Somehow she'd managed to mix color with shampoo, and my hair had wound up a mysterious shade of purple that I hadn't been able to wash out for weeks. I had never returned to the salon. Thanks to the rumor mill in town, it appeared not much had changed with Mona and her dye problems.

"Besides…" My father looked at my mother. "After Sal finds a more permanent location, we'll be getting ready to move another business in here."

Uh-oh. I pushed my empty plate forward. "Okay, I'll bite. What are you thinking about doing now?"

My father reached for another piece of cake. "I'm taking an online course. Of course, I'll have to complete my traineeship at a lab afterward, but these 60 credit hours will have me on my way."

"How is this possible?" I asked. "You don't even know how to turn on a computer."

My father shoved half of the cake from his plate into his mouth and talked around it. "Your mother has been showing me things."

"What course of study are the credits for?" I asked nervously, but deep down I already knew the answer.

He beamed. "I'm studying to become a mortician."

Josie's fork clattered noisily to the floor.

My grandmother shook her head in disgust as she removed both of our plates from the table. "You want more, *cara mia*?"

"No, thank you." I had officially lost my appetite. I stared at my father, who was grinning from ear to ear. "You can't be serious."

"Of course I am." He exchanged glances with my mother, who wore a proud smile on her face. "Someday we'll be running our own funeral home here. Your mother will greet the guests while your grandmother bakes cheesecake for the mourners."

Grandma Rosa turned around from the sink, a knife in hand. "That will *never* happen. You can go to the store and buy the Sara Lee kind for all I care."

He prattled on as if he hadn't heard her. "I have to pass a test too. Anyhow, you girls can bake in here all day. Plenty of counter space for your goodies, and there's the two freezers out in the garage, so you can store dough there. I've already cleaned them out for you. You even have room for a small display case too. This will work out great."

Oblivious to our dazed state, my father stood and calmly removed the napkin tucked into his shirt. He reached out and patted my mother on the behind. "Come on, hot stuff. Let's go take a walk on the wild side."

Mom giggled as she put her arms around him. "I thought you'd never ask."

After they'd left the room, Josie shook her head in disgust. "Your parents are—guess the word I'm thinking?"

"Unique?" I prompted.

"Nice try. More like whackadoodle," Josie said.

My grandmother slammed a kitchen cabinet shut. "Crazy loons."

"Just when I thought I'd seen it all," Josie muttered. Her cell phone rang, and she glanced at the screen. "It's Rob. I'll take it in the other room."

I leaned forward in my chair, covering my face with my hands. Grandma Rosa patted my shoulder. "Did you and your young man straighten everything out, my dear?"

I smiled. "Yes. We're fine. You were right, as usual."

"I always am." She sat down in the chair next to me. "You two were always meant to be together. Such love like yours is rare. Never take it for granted. I do not want to see you make another mistake."

She was referring to my marriage to Colin, a mistake that had been big enough to shock the Richter scale.

I stirred my coffee absently. "Lord knows I've made several. Plus, I acted like such a baby last night. I'm sorry."

She patted my hand. "It is all part of growing up. We are always learning. You were upset, but remember that Mike is there to provide strength. You will be life partners soon. That is his job, and you will do the same thing for him."

That was pretty much the same thing Mike had said to me last night. I reached out, and she took my hand in her tiny, warm one. "Grandma, I know Mom and Dad mean well, but I'm not sure I can do this."

She nodded in understanding. "It is a bad idea. I love you and Josie but do not want you both in my kitchen all day. But it is your only option for now."

"Well, hopefully it won't be for too long. That's not fair to you."

"Do not worry about me." She smiled. "We must think of others besides ourselves. Josie needs the job, and so does Sarah. And you do not want people to forget about your bakery, so it must stay open until the other one is fixed."

I knew this spelled disaster, but she was right. "Josie and I will have to buy new equipment. There won't be room for much, but we'll manage somehow."

"It will be fine." She pursed her lips together. "Now on to other things. I am worried about your sister."

"So am I. Why would she take off like that and leave Bernardo in the shop? Who started the fire? None of this makes any sense."

Grandma Rosa shook her head. "I knew she should have refused to defend that man. That family has a very bad reputation."

"She didn't have a choice, Grandma," I said.

"Furniture shop, my foot. His stepfather thinks he is the next Marlon Brando." She sipped at her coffee. "Someone did not want to see Bernardo go free. That is why he died, I am sure of it."

An uneasy feeling washed over me. "Do you think Gianna might be in danger?"

She nodded soberly. "Yes, I do think so. You must find her, *cara mia*."

"I was told there wasn't much damage to her apartment. Maybe she left something behind that will tell us where she went."

She patted my hand. "It is good. You will find her. And Josie will help. You are like those famous women television detectives."

Josie walked back into the room and sat down at the table. "Charlie's Angels? I love those old reruns."

"No, the other ladies. Cagney and Stacey."

"It's Lacey, Grandma."

Grandma Rosa shrugged. "Close enough."

I spread my arms out wide as I addressed my best friend. "Well? Do you think you can bake in here, partner?"

"Shoot, I can bake anywhere," Josie replied. "But your father and mother need to promise to stay out of the way."

I rolled my eyes. "You know that isn't going to happen."

"Hey, I can dream, right?"

I placed my coffee cup in the sink. "Grandma and I were talking about Gianna. We're both worried about her."

"It is not like her to not answer your messages," Grandma Rosa said. "If it was your parents, yes, she might try to ignore them for a while. Who could blame her? But Sally, my love, Gianna looks up to you. And she has been so stressed from this trial. She thinks it is all her fault."

"It wasn't Gianna's fault," Josie protested. "It was that stupid juror's doing. But of course, everyone will blame her instead."

"I do not like this," Grandma Rosa muttered under her breath. "Think. Where could she have gone?"

"She has friends in Canada. Maybe there?" Josie asked.

"Your handsome officer friend," Grandma said. "He will know more when the autopsy comes back. Maybe that will show how Bernardo died. You should call him."

I frowned. "I don't want to call him."

She raised her eyebrows at me. "Did something happen last night after I left the car?"

I wasn't going there again. "Let's not talk about him anymore. Plus, Mike won't be pleased if I go near him again."

Josie leaned forward on her elbows. "But *I* want to talk about it. I want to hear every sordid detail."

I made a face. "You're sick."

She grinned. "Hey, I'm living vicariously through your life. I'm an old married lady with four kids. Of course I want to hear how the hot cop tried to seduce you in his car last night."

"Mamma mia." Grandma Rosa shook her head in disbelief.

My cheeks warmed. "It wasn't anything drastic like that, okay? And for God's sake, don't breathe a word to Mike. He's about ready to shoot Brian as it is."

Grandma Rosa snorted. "The young officer is still in love with you. This nonsense must stop. You will be a married woman soon."

"I won't see him anymore," I promised.

"But you *have* to see him."

Thunderstruck, Josie and I both looked at her. "What are you talking about?"

"He will tell you things that the other officers will not because he is smitten with you," Grandma Rosa said. "You must play the game for a little while. Be nice to him. I realize that your young man may get upset, so you should be honest with Mike about what you are doing, and then everything will be fine."

What she said made sense. Brian had already offered to share the autopsy details with me, and I was tempted to take him up on it, but I didn't want to give him the idea I was interested in him romantically. Last night's episode had been extremely uncomfortable. I intended to be honest with Mike about the scheme, but that didn't mean he in turn would be happy about it. I didn't want to risk hurting our relationship—heck, I'd almost done a bang up job of that last night. But this was my sister we were talking about. She was in some kind of trouble, and I needed to find her.

Josie snapped her fingers. "I've got it. We'll have Brian let us into Gianna's apartment tomorrow. I'll go through her things while you distract him."

I didn't like the sound of this. "Distract him how?"

"Wear a tight, short skirt and bend over right in front of him," Josie said. "I'm sure your mother has something that will work. Officer Hottie won't know what hit him."

"Dear God in heaven," my grandmother muttered. "You must stop reading those romance novels. They are giving you too many naughty ideas."

Josie grinned. "But I *like* ideas, Rosa."

Grandma Rosa said something in Italian that I could have sworn meant "nutsy cookie." She heaved herself out of her chair and began to wash the dishes in the sink.

Josie winked at me with a pleased expression. "You'll have him eating out of your hand."

A visual I didn't even want to let myself think about.

CHAPTER SEVEN

———

Josie and I went on a shopping spree at the bakery supply store and bought mixers, cookie sheets, spatulas, utensils, and several other necessities. There would be limitations on the cookie variations we could make because we lacked the extra space that had been available in the bakery.

We'd placed a sign out in front of my torched shop, informing people of the new, temporary location. I ran an ad in the local paper to announce that the bakery would be open for business on Tuesday morning. We planned to spend a good portion of Monday getting things in order. Claire Houston had already dropped off our permit, and I'd been forced to admit that my mother had really come through for us this time.

In addition to all of the preparations for Tuesday's opening, I wanted to get Gianna's personal items out of the apartment and figure out where she might have gone. I was anxious to hear a determination from my insurance company, but when I'd called again, they'd only told me that the claim was still pending. There were several things related to my upcoming wedding that I needed to finish as well. Life, in a word, was nuts.

Josie and I had returned to my parents' house and moved the kitchen table and chairs into the basement. We'd found a small folding table to hold the cash register we'd just bought. Luckily, there had also been enough room for the mini display case we'd purchased as well.

I phoned Sarah and brought her up to speed on the new developments and location. Josie had texted her last night to tell her about the fire. Sarah was happy but surprised by the news that we'd be reopening so soon.

"Is this really going to work?" The doubt in her voice was apparent.

I chuckled. "Let's hope so."

She was quiet for a moment on the other end of the line. "Um, Sally, I—"

"What's up?"

Sarah paused for a moment. "I don't know how to tell you this. It's just that I figured the bakery wouldn't be reopening for quite a while, so I applied for a job at Wrigley's Grocery Store today. I'm supposed to start work in a week. They have someone going out on maternity leave who's not coming back and need the help immediately."

"Oh." I was stunned by her news and didn't know what else to say.

"I'm sorry. I was planning to call you tomorrow and tell you."

"Are they paying you more money?" I asked.

She was silent, and I immediately regretted my question. "Forget I said that. It's none of my business."

"Oh, I don't mind that you asked," Sarah said, "and yes, they are. I'm also going to be trained for a management position. You've been terrific, but I really think this will work out better for me in the long run."

For some strange reason, I was hurt by her decision. It almost felt as if she was rejecting me. I tried to see things from her perspective. She had a child to think of. "Could—could you still work this week at least? I've got a lot going on and need the help while we settle in at my parents'." I also didn't know how involved the search for my sister might get, and if Josie came along with me, someone would have to hold down the fort. I didn't want to burden Grandma Rosa with it.

"Oh sure. I should give you notice anyway—it wouldn't be right if I didn't." Her voice suddenly became shaky. "You've been wonderful to me, Sally, and I appreciate everything. You gave me a job when no one else would."

"Hey, I'm just glad I could help," I said. "Do you think you can come over to my parents' house tomorrow and help us do setup for Tuesday? You might be on your own for a while too. Josie and I will need to go over to the bakery and take care of a few things."

"Of course," she said. "Do you think you'll be able to

rebuild the shop?"

"No idea." I sighed. "Maybe it would be better for me to just make a fresh start."

"I know what you mean." Sarah hesitated. "I've been thinking a lot about that myself lately. I'll be there tomorrow morning to help. I just have to ask again..."

"Yes?"

"Well, do you think this is actually going to work? Running a bakery from your parents' house? No offense, but they are a little different, Sally."

That was putting it mildly. "I guess we'll find out." I disconnected and rubbed my eyes wearily. Yes, Sarah had a valid point. What the heck was I getting myself into?

"You're nuts." Mike grinned as he helped me clear the dinner dishes. We'd cooked steaks on the grill with steamed vegetables. As I stacked the dishes in the sink, he wrapped his arms around my waist and kissed my neck.

I handed him a sponge. "You can wash, and I'll dry."

He turned on the faucet. "You drive a hard bargain, princess."

I glanced at him with uncertainty as I placed a glass in the cupboard. "Josie and I—we spent three thousand dollars today. And I still need to get some more supplies."

Mike turned to gaze at me with thoughtful blue eyes. "I didn't ask how much you spent."

Feeling anxious, I babbled on. "I know, but I feel like this is all my fault. I should have had more money in the bank. I didn't realize that my business would slow down in the spring. Plus, we had all the expenses with the new roof you had to install and the plumbing. If I'd been more careful it—"

He calmly dried his hands on a dish towel then gathered me in his arms. "I told you that was *our* money. You did the same thing for me once too. Remember?"

He was referring to the time he'd been arrested for the murder of my ex-husband, and I'd put up the bail money. That money hadn't actually belonged to me either—most of it had been borrowed from my grandmother. "That's not the same thing. Besides, you were totally ticked off about it at the time."

Mike stroked my cheek tenderly. "Yeah, but I know you

did it because you love me. And that's why I'm doing this now. Frankly, I don't care if you spend all of it, Sal. I know how important this business is to you. But I've got to say my piece first."

"Okay." I had no idea what he was getting at.

"Running the bakery out of your parents' house is just asking for disaster."

"You're not the first one to say that. Believe me." I finished drying the dishes and walked over to the kitchen table. I picked up the newspaper, idly glanced at the real estate section, and squealed. "Hey. There's a building available on Carson Way for rent. That's only about five minutes away from my shop. I think I know the place—it's even got the same setup as my bakery." It was hard not to contain my excitement as I grabbed my cell phone and punched in the number.

Mike watched me intently. "What are you doing?"

"I want to see if I can make an appointment to see the building. You'll come with me, right?"

Before he could respond, a man's voice came on the line. "Hello?"

"Yes, I was wondering if I could make an appointment to see the building located at 13 Carson Way sometime tomorrow. Whenever the owners are available."

His deep voice permeated through the phone. "I'm sorry—you're too late. I rented it earlier today."

My heart sank to the pit of my stomach. "Okay, thank you." I disconnected then tossed the paper into the garbage. "Well, I guess I'm out of options for now."

Mike wrapped his arms around my waist and kissed me below my ear. "I can think of some *fun* options."

Despite my disappointment, I managed a smile for him. "I'm being serious here."

"So am I." He spoke in that bedroom voice that warmed me from head to toe.

Desire flooded my body as I pressed my lips against his, and he uttered a guttural sound low in his throat.

"You looked mighty sexy while washing those dishes, Mr. Donovan."

His breath was hot in my ear. "Oh, tell me more."

Spike started to bark, and Mike turned and glanced out the living room's front window. A patrol car had just pulled into our driveway.

He shook his head in disbelief. "What the hell? It's Jenkins again. That guy has got the worst possible timing. I'm starting to think he's doing this on purpose."

I grabbed his arm before he could start toward the door. "Uh, I need to talk to you about him."

His expression was grim. "Did he try something with you last night?"

I purposely avoided the question. "He's my only source of information right now to find out what happened to Bernardo. I'm afraid they think Gianna might be involved. I asked Brian to keep me informed about the autopsy, so maybe that's why he's here. I'm hoping it will clear my sister from any suspicion."

Mike pursed his lips together and frowned. "I don't like the sound of this, but for Gianna's sake, I'll go along with it."

"Please don't start anything with him. I know you're going to hate hearing this, but I have to be nice to him."

He lifted one eyebrow. "How nice?"

I waggled my hand back and forth. "A couple of steps above civil."

"Do I have to be nice too?"

I ran a finger across his lips and grinned. "Can you?"

Mike leaned down to kiss me. "Not likely." There was a tap on the door, but he didn't move. "So what does this mean, Sal? Are you going to pretend to be interested in him so that he'll share more information?"

"No," I said quietly. "You trust me, don't you?"

"Of course I trust you. It's Jenkins that I don't trust." He ran a frustrated hand through his dark hair and gave me a resigned look. "Oh, fine. But I'll be watching him."

I opened the door to Brian, who was standing there in his uniform. A wide grin spread across his face as his eyes focused on me. At that particular moment, a low growl sounded from behind me, and I prayed that it came from Spike.

"Hi, Sally. Do you have a minute to talk?" Brian asked.

"Of course." I opened the screen door. "Come on in."

He nodded at Mike, whose only response was to fold his

arms across his chest and glare back at him. When I shot Mike a disapproving look, he sighed in resignation. "Want a beer, Jenkins?"

Brian looked surprised at the suggestion. "Not while I'm on duty."

"Oh, right."

Brian bent down to pet Spike and then focused his attention back on me. "Bernardo's autopsy came back. There were some interesting findings."

I didn't dare breathe. "Such as?"

"He didn't die from the fire, Sally." Brian cleared his throat. "Bernardo was already dead."

The blood pounded in my ears as I exchanged glances with Mike.

Mike leaned against the partition that led to the kitchen. "How do you know that?"

"Because the coroner said he didn't die from smoke inhalation," Brian said, "and there was blunt trauma to the right side of his face. He was hit with something several times."

Panic surged through my body. I tried to maintain a calm exterior, but on the inside cold, dark fear was engulfing me. Had Bernardo tried to make a move on my sister? Now that she was back on the market, Gianna was attracting men like a magnet, and Bernardo seemed like the type that took anything he wanted. Could Gianna have been forced to protect herself?

Mike moved next to me. "Do you know what he might have been hit with?"

"We're not sure yet," Brian said. "They did find a rolling pin on the floor in the back room. It was burned from the fire, so we can't be positive it was the weapon, but there's a good chance."

My heart stuttered inside my chest. "Someone killed Bernardo with my bakery equipment?" The whole scenario sickened me.

"We're not positive." Brian hesitated. "But I can tell you one thing. The person who did this to him was left-handed."

I shivered but said nothing. Only one person in my entire family was left-handed. Gianna.

On several occasions Grandma Rosa had proudly

declared that Gianna had inherited the trait from her late husband. When we were growing up, she had always told my sister, "Left-handed people are very smart."

Brian must have caught the look that passed between Mike and me. "Your sister is left-handed, isn't she?"

I put a hand over my chest to steady myself. "So what? Lots of other people are too."

"Maybe he tried something with her," Brian said. It was almost as if he could read my thoughts. "Bernardo had quite the reputation. Rumor has it he was cheating on his wife with several other women. His wife said he has at least one child from a past relationship but didn't know any other details. She said he never sees the kids."

What a role model of a father Bernardo must have been. "You've been to see his wife? How's she taking his death?"

Brian waggled his hand. "She's not exactly grief stricken, but then again, she wasn't jumping up and down for joy either."

"Did anyone actually like the guy?" Mike wondered aloud.

"His stepbrother and stepfather are pieces of work too," Brian added. "And it appears Bernardo had no shortage of enemies." He looked at me. "As his attorney, Gianna could tell us things about him that might help with the investigation. So if you know where she is—"

Mike took a step toward Brian. "Sal doesn't know where Gianna is, Jenkins. She already told you that."

I tried to change the subject. "Brian, what about my building? Anyone can get in there through the back door and take things from Gianna's apartment. How bad is it upstairs?"

Mike interrupted. "I'll stop over tomorrow and secure it. If it needs a new door, that won't take long to install."

"You'll have to wait until the investigation is finished first." Brian turned to me. "One of my fellow officers is patrolling the place tonight. If you want to go in tomorrow and get Gianna's things, like clothing, I'll escort you."

Mike snorted but said nothing.

"Can't I just run over there tonight?" I pleaded.

"Like I already mentioned, the investigation is still

pending," Brian said, "but I expect it to wrap up tomorrow, and then you'll be allowed inside. I'll call you as soon as I know for sure. I also need to go through your sister's things. I want to see if we can find any evidence of what happened or where she might have gone."

Aargh. That had been my plan. Maybe I would have to borrow that skirt from my mother after all. I glanced at Mike, whose expression was stern. I hoped he didn't know what I was thinking.

Mike put his arm around my shoulders. "Is the place structurally sound?"

"Yes," Brian nodded. "That's what I've been told by the firemen."

"Well, that's not good enough for me," Mike said. "Even I can't tell for sure. I've got a friend who's a structural engineer, Dave Perkins. He's hard to catch, but I'm hoping he can get in there during the next couple of days to look around." His arm tightened around me. "It's probably okay for you to get Gianna's things, but I don't think you and Josie should plan on spending any significant amount of time in there until we know exactly what's going on. Sometimes buildings have to be demolished after a fire."

Brian frowned at him. "Not always."

"I think I know a little more about this than you do, Jenkins," Mike retorted. "I'm not taking any chances with Sal and Josie's safety."

A muscle ticked in Brian's jaw. "I'd never let anything happen to either one of them under my watch."

Both of them were starting to drive me crazy. They were like two little boys fighting over a piece of birthday cake, and I was getting tired of it.

I squeezed Mike's hand in reassurance. "I'm sure we'll be fine. Please don't worry. Hey—maybe you could come with us?"

Mike's face fell. "I wish I could, babe, but I'm starting another new job tomorrow. I tell you what. Text me before you go over, and I'll try to break away for a little while."

"There's no need," Brian said quietly. "I'll take care of her."

Mike's eyes flashed angry, blue sparks. "Oh, I know

you'd like to."

Brian ignored the comment. "You can only take her clothing and toiletries, Sally. Nothing else leaves Gianna's apartment until I go through it first."

"My sister is not a criminal." I pressed my lips together tightly.

Brian looked pained. "I know that, but what if she didn't leave of her own free will? We have to take that into consideration. Maybe something could even give us a clue as to what happened to Bernardo. Would Gianna have locked him inside the building?"

Startled, I stared at him. "No, of course not. Why would she do that?"

He answered my question with another. "Then why was he in there alone?"

I didn't have a response for that and merely shrugged.

"You don't have to answer those questions, Sal." Mike gave Brian a surly look. "My fiancée is not on trial, Jenkins, so don't treat her like she is."

Brian clenched his fists at his sides. "I'm only trying to find out how Gianna's client wound up dead in Sally's bakery. You must admit it seems a bit odd."

"I don't want Sal involved in your investigation," Mike said. "She's had enough brushes with danger lately. You and your department need to handle this by yourselves. You're the detectives, not her."

"Excuse me?" My tone was so shrill that both men stopped arguing to look at me. "I'm already involved in this. I own the building, which someone deliberately torched. The most important thing right now is finding my sister, so I'd appreciate it if you two could stop your bickering for a few minutes."

Mike's face reddened. "You're right, Sal. I'm sorry."

Brian edged toward the door. "I'll call you tomorrow and let you know when it's a good time to come over."

"Thanks for stopping by to fill us in."

Brian nodded. "Did you know that Bernardo was also being investigated for tax evasion? Plus, he managed to hide all his assets so he could seek out a public defender and not pay for an attorney. This whole scenario stinks like rotten eggs. If there's anything I can't stand, it's someone who lets other taxpayers foot the bill for him."

"I've got to side with you on that one, Jenkins." Mike opened the door for Brian's departure.

Great. How wonderful to hear that my poor sister had gotten mixed up with such a sleaze. Then another scenario occurred to me. Could Gianna have witnessed the killing and left town because she was terrified?

No, that wasn't my sister's way. She was an attorney, a lover of the law, and did everything by the book. But what if Bernardo had tried to attack her, or one of his buddies had shown up and hurt her? Would she have fled then?

I waited until Brian was in his squad car and out of earshot. "I have to find Gianna, and soon, Mike. I'm scared for her."

CHAPTER EIGHT

———

"Yes." My father pumped his fist in the air. "I've missed those fortune cookies."

I looked up in surprise from the oatmeal cookie dough I was mixing. "Dad, it's only been two days since you had one."

"Sure." My father leaned forward over the Formica kitchen counter next to Josie as she removed a tray of fortune cookies from the oven and set them on top of a trivet on the kitchen counter. She immediately laid the fortunes in the centers and started to roll them since they hardened quickly. "But it seems longer."

Josie kept her head down, but I could still glimpse the gnashing of her teeth. She didn't like people crowding around her while she was baking, especially my parents.

"Um, Dad," I said. "Shouldn't you be working on your course?"

He waved a hand impatiently. "As soon as I get a cookie." He reached his hand out toward the tray, and for a moment I was afraid Josie might slap it away like she had with Mrs. Gavelli. Instead, she moved the tray with her bare hands, forgetting it was still hot.

Josie yelped. "Damn it!" When she jumped, the entire tray of cookies went crashing to the floor.

Sarah was standing to my left, working on the cream filling for the cookies I was making. Her hands flew to her face as I set down my mixer and rushed over to pick up the broken cookies off the floor.

My father whined. "Aw. Now they're all ruined."

I glanced at Josie, who was holding her hand under the faucet. "You okay?"

Josie said nothing, but the look she gave caused me to

shiver. *Stupid question, Sal.* Who could be okay having to work here?

I picked up a still intact fortune cookie and handed it to my father. "Dad, do you think you could take this into the front room?"

"Let me read it first." He broke the cookie in two. "Hmm. This is a new one. Not sure what it means."

"What does it say?" I asked, only because I knew he wanted me to.

He read aloud in a theatrical voice. "*Don't go where you're not wanted.*" He laughed. "Hey, everyone wants me. I don't get this."

Josie muttered something inaudible under her breath.

"Uh, Dad, I think Mom was looking for you. She's upstairs."

He grinned. "Of course she is. Your mother's a playful thing, that one." He put the cookie in his pocket and whistled as he walked out of the kitchen.

Josie threw up her hands. "I can't do it. There's no way. I love your parents, Sal, and God knows they were wonderful to me when I was growing up. Sometimes they were better to me than my own. But. I. Can't. Do. This."

I dropped to my knees to clean up the rest of the mess. "It won't be for too long. And I'll talk to him about staying out of the kitchen."

"It won't do any good." Josie blew on her finger.

I picked up the last cookie. The paper had come loose from the inside, and the message was staring me right in the face. Something inside me screamed *Don't look. Don't look.* Too late. Like at a bad car wreck, I couldn't turn away.

Your lover is keeping a secret.

Okay, that was it. I'd had enough of these cookies. Enraged, I ripped the small strip into even tinier pieces and threw them into the garbage pail. Then I kicked it for good measure. Josie and Sarah both stared at me in amazement.

Grandma Rosa entered the kitchen in time to catch my dramatic act. "Whatever is the matter?"

"Nothing," I lied. "Everything is just dandy."

Josie folded her arms across her chest. "It's those

freaking messages again, isn't it? What did it say? Wait. Let me guess. Something cynical like 'Your business is going up in flames.'"

I swallowed hard, trying to force the bile back down my throat. I hadn't told Josie about the previous fortune cookie message I'd received, so her teasing remark only succeeded in making me more upset. Chills ran down my spine, and my hands shook as I picked up the rest of the mess.

I kept telling myself that these messages didn't mean anything, but suddenly they had me doubting everything in my life. Things between Mike and me were wonderful, so why should a stupid piece of paper bother me?

Because they always seemed to speak the truth.

"*Cara mia.*" My grandmother patted my arm. "You are upset."

I exhaled a deep, noisy breath. "No, I'm fine. But I was thinking that maybe we should stop making the fortune cookies for a while."

Josie grunted. "Fine by me. I never wanted them in the first place. People are always looking for freebies."

Sarah gasped. "But everyone loves the fortune cookies! I think you'd lose business that way, Sally."

My grandmother studied my expression. "You are afraid of something. What did the message say?"

Agitated, I shook my head. "Nothing. We don't have the counter space for them now anyway. Maybe when we get a permanent location, we'll start making them again." *Yeah, fat chance.*

"What you say?" A voice bellowed from the other side of the kitchen screen door.

Sarah froze when she saw Mrs. Gavelli's face pressed up against the mesh, gesturing for her to unlock the door. "Sally, are we using this as the official entrance?"

"Might as well," I conceded. We couldn't have customers come in through the front door, which led to my parents' living room. My father had a coffin set up in there. Despite my pleading, he refused to remove it. He said it was part of his studying process.

I unlocked the door. Mrs. Gavelli was standing there,

accompanied by Johnny. He gave me a wide grin and smacked his lips together. "How's it going, hot stuff?"

Mrs. Gavelli turned and smacked him lightly across the cheek. "You stop. She engaged. She already try to ruin you for other women."

Good grief. As if my patience wasn't being tested enough today. "I was six years old, Mrs. G."

She ignored the comment and waggled a finger in my face. "What you say? You no make no more fortune cookies? You give me one now."

"We don't have any right now," I said. "There was a little accident."

She moved closer toward me. "Let me tell you something, missy. You better keep those cookies, or I not gonna be happy. I need them. They important."

I glanced at her, puzzled. "Why?"

Her face reddened. "You ask too many questions. You keep making cookies, or I tell everyone they no come here."

"Nicoletta," my grandmother growled. "You had better not make trouble for my granddaughter. I know things, remember."

Mrs. Gavelli's face clouded over. She said something in Italian that sounded way too similar to a swear word, turned on her Birkenstock heel, and flounced out the screen door.

Grandma Rosa exchanged glances with Johnny. He nodded at something unspoken between the two of them and then held the door open for her.

"I will go talk to her," Grandma Rosa said. "She is a bit of a fluke sometimes."

I had to think about that one for a minute. "Do you mean flake?"

"That is good too." I watched while she made her way across the lawn over to Mrs. Gavelli's house next door.

"You can't get rid of those cookies, Sal," Johnny said. His voice was almost wistful. "Grandma needs them in her life."

"Johnny," Josie asked. "What the heck is going on?"

He stared out the window in the direction of his grandmother's house for a moment before answering. "It's nothing, really." His eyes darted around the kitchen. "So, Gram told me that Gianna and her boyfriend broke up."

I reached for the kitchen faucet and helped myself to a glass of water. "That's right. He told her he was tired of taking a backseat to her career."

"Sounds like she's better off without him." Johnny leaned his head on my shoulder and grinned up at me in a teasing manner. He was impossible. I pushed him away, and he laughed.

"How long are you home for?" I asked.

A shadow passed over his face, and the mischievous expression in his eyes turned serious. "I've transferred to the high school. I'll be teaching in Colwestern this fall."

Josie and I exchanged glances. "But your grandmother always said how much you loved Vermont."

Johnny gave me a rueful smile. "Yeah, well, things change. So, where is your sister?"

That was the $64,000 question of the day. "She—ah— she took off for a few days."

"Sal." He nudged me playfully in the ribs. "Don't lie to me. Not your first love."

"Johnny, I swear. Some days I want to hit you over the head with something."

He grinned at me saucily. "Hey, I'm used to it. Now, back to the subject at hand. I heard about what happened. Is Gianna okay? Can I help somehow?"

I looked at Josie, and she wiggled her eyebrows at me in return. I placed my hands on my hips and turned to face Johnny. "You have a crush on my sister, don't you?" It was almost like I was eleven and he thirteen again, with me teasing him about riding his bike by the new girl's house for the millionth time in one day.

He winked. "Maybe."

"I always suspected you had a crush on her." When Johnny used to walk home with us from the bus, he'd carry Gianna's books but toss mine across the street. Gianna was nearly five years younger than him, making any type of relationship inappropriate back then. It looked like dear old Johnny might have been biding his time all these years.

"Well, I didn't like the way that client of Gianna's was looking at her the other night during your party," Johnny said. "I was afraid she might be in danger—hey, I just want to make sure she's all right after everything that's happened. Will you let her know I was asking about her?"

The look in his eyes touched me. For once, he wasn't kidding around. He was actually concerned about her. I had no idea what Gianna thought of him—if anything. Despite his constant pranks over the years and how he always managed to get me into trouble, Johnny was a great catch. Handsome, intelligent, and a nice guy. Heck, how many people could put up with Mrs. G all these years and live to tell about it?

I gave his hand a little squeeze. "Of course I will."

He gave me a peck on the cheek, nodded to Sarah, and blew Josie a kiss. She stepped forward and shoved him toward the door. "Get out, and go home to your crazy grandmother."

He laughed and then turned back to me. "If you could keep the fortune cookies around for a while, I think Gram would appreciate it. Trust me on that one, okay?"

We watched him run across the yard, back to his house. My mind was flooded with happy memories of Josie, Gianna, Johnny, and me playing statues in the backyard and Mrs. Gavelli screaming at him for the tenth time to come home. Life was so much simpler then.

"Something's going on," Josie murmured.

Before I could reply, my phone pinged from my jeans pocket. I glanced down to see that I had a new text message from Brian.

I'm at the bakery if you want to come by to get Gianna's things. Want me to give you a lift?

My fingers flew across the screen. *No thanks. Josie will be with me. We'll be there in about ten minutes.*

He shot back a quick *Okay. Looking forward to seeing you.*

Cripes. Josie was right—he was a persistent bug. The mental vision of a mosquito came to mind. Well, might as well get it over with. I grabbed my keys and my purse from one of the kitchen cabinets. "Would you mind making more fortune cookies while we're gone, Sarah?"

Her face brightened. "Of course not. You two take your time. And I'll help get things organized while you're gone."

Josie glanced at me, surprised. "I thought you said no more cookies."

"Well, let's appease our neighbor for a while." As long as I stayed clear of the cookies, there would be no problems, right? "We shouldn't be too long."

Sarah watched us with a sad smile. "Good luck. I hope the place can be salvaged."

In my heart I was thinking the very same thing but knew that the odds were not in my favor.

CHAPTER NINE

———

Josie and I didn't say much to each other during the drive to the bakery. Sometimes conversation isn't necessary between best friends. Neither one of us was looking forward to surveying the damage firsthand.

Brian met us at the front door and ushered us inside. From the front lawn yesterday, things hadn't looked so bad. Upon entering the building, it was an entirely different story. The smell of smoke still hung heavy in the air, and my eyes immediately began to water. The bakery case had been shattered—most likely by one of the firefighter's hoses or the actual heat of the fire. I spotted some remaining fortune cookies through the remnants of glass, mocking me. *Stop it, Sal. They don't mean anything.*

We entered the back room for only a brief minute, but what I saw left me heartbroken. The walls were blackened, and the appliances were waterlogged and ruined. The utilities had since been turned off. There was still a good deal of soot remaining on the floor. In short, the place was a disaster. I glanced around, trying to somehow make sense of the entire situation.

Brian helped us remove items that were salvageable from the front room, but there wasn't much. My Keurig and espresso machine both still appeared to be in working order, although I'd have to test them later. There wasn't room for them on the counters in my parents' kitchen, so I'd store them at my house for now. The artwork on the walls was ruined, and the shelf Rob had made for us with the two porcelain figures having tea and cookies had been smashed. I assumed it might have been in the way of the firefighters.

Josie wiped her eyes with the back of her hand as she

picked it up off the floor where it lay broken in several pieces. "Rob will make us another one, Sal."

"No, that would make the third one. He doesn't have to go through all that trouble again." A previous shelf had been shattered last year when someone had trashed my bakery.

She placed a hand on my shoulder. "He won't mind. You'll see."

With our arms around each other, we trudged up the stairs to Gianna's apartment, Brian following. There appeared to be some smoke damage in the main room, which was a dining and living room combo. The bedroom door was shut, which Brian said had probably saved the room from having further damage.

"The investigation is finished," Brian said. "Now we're just waiting on the lab results, which could take quite some time. If you want to do any cleaning, I don't suggest staying in here for prolonged periods until someone like Mike's friend can check on the safety of the building. I saw your insurance guy here earlier. He was leaving when I pulled in."

I whirled around at the door of the apartment. "Why didn't you call me? What did he say?"

"He was leaving," Brian said. "He didn't share any details with me. I'm sure he'll want to confer with the arson investigator before a final determination." Brian started to place a hand on my shoulder then must have thought better of it. He took a step back. "I wouldn't get my hopes up if I were you, Sally."

My lower lip started to tremble, and Josie wiped at her eyes. No, I wasn't going to cry and carry on again. I'd already had my moment of weakness. Now was the time to deal with the hand fate had dealt me. The problem was I seemed destined to lose this poker game of life.

A voice came over Brian's radio, and he excused himself to go outside and take the call. "Don't spend any longer up here than you have to."

Once he had disappeared, Josie turned to me. "Okay, what's the plan?"

"We'll pack up her clothes and anything else she might need for now. Then I'm going to do a little snooping to see if we can find out where she's gone."

I noticed only a few pieces of clothing missing from her bedroom closet, which gave me hope that she wasn't planning to be gone for long. Her laptop, much to my disappointment, was nowhere to be found. I went through her dresser drawers but came up with nothing.

Josie set some personal toiletries inside the suitcase I had brought along. "Any ideas yet?"

I shook my head. "None." I opened the main drawer to her desk and sifted through papers, doodles, and notes she had made. My sister was not a neat freak when it came to paperwork. I found a postcard from a casino near the Canadian border for a free night's stay.

"Look at this." I waved it excitedly at Josie.

She grabbed it between her hands. "Casino Regal. Do you think she could have gone there?"

I raised an eyebrow at her, and she grinned. We both knew there was a good chance. My beautiful and brilliant sister had a secret. She loved to play the slot machines. I wouldn't call her an addict, but she did tell me once she found them "relaxing." Her former boyfriend had enjoyed the tables, so they'd made a few trips last year, usually when Gianna required a much needed break from studying for the bar. She'd even dragged me along with her on a trip a couple of months back. Personally, I hated that type of environment, and Mike had no use for the places either. They were too smoky and loud for my taste. Plus, why did I want to give away the money I worked so hard for? However, Gianna had just passed the bar and wanted to celebrate, so I hadn't had the heart to refuse her.

"She needed to relax. Plus no one knows her there, making it all the better. She hates driving long distances by herself, so I'm guessing that's the farthest she'd attempt to go."

"If she went willingly," Josie chimed in. My face must have looked stricken because she quickly added, "I'm sure that's not the case, Sal. She's fine."

I took a deep breath, pulled out my cell phone, and dialed the number on the postcard.

"Thank you for calling Casino Regal," a pleasant female voice on the other end of the line said. "How may I assist you?"

I clutched the phone tightly to my ear. "Can you connect me with Gianna Muccio's room, please?"

"Spell the last name, please?"

I gave her the rundown, letter by letter. There was a brief silence, and I could hear the woman typing something. "One moment."

Yes. I gave Josie a thumbs-up. The phone rang several times, but there was no answer, so eventually I disconnected. "Well, at least we know she's there."

"Yes, but for how long?" Josie asked. "Maybe she's planning to take off soon."

"Are you up for a road trip this evening?" I asked.

She made a face. "Sal, if Brian finds out you know where she is and didn't say anything, you could be stirring up trouble again."

"I don't care. I need to find out what's going on with Gianna first. I'd rather go tonight, before we open for business tomorrow. The sooner the better. What about the kids?"

"Rob's off today, so that's not a problem. What about Mike?"

"He's on a new job today, and he said he'd be home late." I thought about the fortune cookie earlier that implied he was keeping a secret. Was Mike really working, or was it just my brain putting in overtime again? There was no reason for me not to trust him. At times like this, my past history with Colin crept into my mind and proceeded to haunt me.

Josie narrowed her eyes. "That's not what I meant. Are you going to tell him?"

I stared at her pointedly. "Are *you* going to tell Rob?"

"Hell no! He'd tell me to stay out of it."

I carried the suitcase to the front door of the apartment. "There's no reason for me not to tell Mike. I won't keep any secrets from him." Although he may be keeping one from me— *Okay, enough, Sal.*

Josie folded her arms. "Sal, you don't really think she had anything to do with Bernardo's death, do you?"

"Gianna would never intentionally hurt anyone." A flicker of panic crossed my mind. "But what if he tried something with her? Maybe things got out of hand. I have to protect her, Jos."

We heard footsteps on the stairs, and Brian appeared. "All set to go? Is everything of value out?"

"Yes, thank you," I smiled. "No laptop or electronics. She must have taken them with her."

He watched me thoughtfully. "Thanks for being honest with me. We'll probably be doing another check later on today, though."

"Knock yourself out," I said boldly. "And Mike's going to stop by and fix the back door at some point today so no one will be able to get in."

He cleared his throat. "You might want to ask Mike when his friend the engineer is supposed to come by and check on the building."

"I think he said the day after tomorrow, but I'll find out when he gets home tonight."

A sly smile spread across Josie's face. "He may be pretty late, right?"

I stared at her in confusion. "Yes, he's working on two different jobs right now—a roof, and he just started a new project."

Josie's eyes moved from Brian then back to me, and she winked. "Guess you'll have to ask him when he comes to bed, then."

Brian's face turned crimson while I gave Josie my best murderous glare. As much as I adored her, she was the world's biggest troublemaker.

I locked the front door of the bakery. It felt like a futile effort since people could still get in through the back door, but I couldn't worry about that right now. If people wanted anything that bad, let them have at it. Perhaps I needed to separate my personal feelings from the place because deep down I was wondering if it would ever be the same again.

"Thanks for letting us in," I said to Brian.

He took the suitcase from my hands and placed it in the back of Josie's van. Then he leaned against the side of it, making it impossible for me to open the door and get inside the vehicle. "Would you like to join me for a cup of coffee?"

I glanced over at Josie, who was wearing that smug

smile again. She gestured with her hand. "You should go, Sal."

God, I was going to get her for this. She got behind the wheel without another word and waited patiently.

"I don't think that's a good idea," I said honestly.

Reluctantly, Brian moved away from the door, but his eyes continued to search mine, and I was growing uncomfortable. "Sally, did you find anything upstairs to give you an idea of where Gianna might have gone?"

Man, I was the world's worst liar. I glanced over at the building then at the trees—anything except his gorgeous face and those green eyes with flecks of gold that shone brilliantly in the sunlight. "No, I didn't. How about you?"

A smile formed at the corners of his mouth. "No. But we'll be able to search her phone records. We can get a judge to grant us access to them."

I gave a sudden start. "Why would you do that?"

He gave me a sympathetic smile. "Because there's enough of a reason to label her as a suspect."

Josie's mouth opened wide in amazement.

I was furious. "You can't, Brian. You know she had nothing to do with the murder."

He reached for my hand, which I yanked away. "Sally, this wasn't my doing. Honest. I know Gianna's not guilty. I'm only doing my job."

I tried desperately to control the anger rising in my voice. "I've got to get back to my parents' house."

"Sally, wait—"

I flung open the door to the van. "Thanks again for all of your help."

As soon as I was seated, Josie drove away from the curb. I glanced into the side mirror and saw Brian still standing there, watching us.

"Do you think he bought it?" Josie asked.

I leaned my head back against the seat. "I don't care if he did. Once the police get a hold of Gianna's phone records, they'll be able to track her location. She sent me a text from wherever she is, remember? We have to get to her first."

CHAPTER TEN

Josie and I spent the rest of the day making and freezing doughs and attempting to get things into some sort of semblance of order for the bakery's grand reopening tomorrow. Since we were limited for space, there were some types of cookies we would not be able to make, unless people special ordered them. The smaller display case held less than half of what the other one in my shop had housed. I kept telling myself that working here was only a temporary situation, like having the flu or some other type of illness.

Grandma Rosa was trying to make dinner in the midst of all the confusion. My mother kept walking into the kitchen, asking my opinion on the different bikinis she was modeling and which one I thought she should wear for the pageant's bathing suit competition. When he wasn't cheering or shouting catcalls at my mother, Dad kept yelling from the living room that he was hungry, which only added to my grandmother's fury.

"If he keeps this up," Grandma Rosa growled, "he will be wearing his dinner."

It was six thirty before we had order established. I worried about leaving cookies in the mini display case overnight. "What if Dad tries to eat them?" I asked my grandmother.

She let out a harrumph. "Tell your young man to come by later and install a padlock on the case."

"That seems a little drastic, doesn't it?"

She shrugged. "If you want to have cookies for people to buy tomorrow, then drastic is the way for you to go."

After Sarah had left for the evening, Josie joined me outside and helped me position a new sign next to the mailbox. It announced that Sally's Samples was once again open for business.

Grandma Rosa wagged her finger at both of us. "You should eat. It has been a long day for both of you."

I shook my head. "There's no time. Josie and I have an errand to run. Maybe we can grab something on the way back."

"Nonsense," she said. "Both of you sit down. It is all ready."

When Grandma Rosa opened the oven door and I saw that she had made braciole, I reconsidered. Next to her cheesecake, braciole was my favorite. In my opinion, nothing quite compared to the thin slices of beef, pan fried with a filling of herbs and cheese then dipped into her rich tomato sauce. A definite comfort food ever since I had been a child. "Well, okay. But we have to hurry."

She eyed me suspiciously. "You have found your sister." It was not a question but a direct statement.

"Yes," I confessed. "I haven't told Mike yet, so please don't say anything until I have a chance to tell him. And Josie doesn't want Rob to know. He thinks she's here working late tonight."

Grandma Rosa clucked her tongue against the roof of her mouth in disapproval as she dished out braciole and spaghetti for the both of us. I took the plates into the dining room, and Grandma Rosa followed with glasses and a pitcher of her homemade raspberry iced tea. "It is not good to keep secrets in a marriage."

Josie sat down next to me. "Rob hates it when I play detective, so it's better if he doesn't find out the truth. I don't want him to get his panties in a bunch. We need to warn Gianna about what's going on before the police are all over her. That's all."

"She's my baby sister," I said with my mouth full. "I have to protect her."

Grandma Rosa frowned. "You are a good girl, *cara mia*. But you do not actually think Gianna was involved in that *stupido's* murder, do you?"

"Of course not. But she's been through so much lately." I put my fork down and stared at my grandmother in earnest. "I'm afraid for her well-being. She's been under constant stress ever since she started studying for that exam a year ago. I know she wants everyone to see her as this rough and tough lawyer, but with everything that's happened—especially Frank—I know how vulnerable she is." Heck, I had been down that road myself. At least Gianna hadn't caught Frank cheating on her like I had with Colin, but there had been rumors circulating around town about him and a possible indiscretion.

Grandma Rosa nodded in approval. "I am not sorry the man is dead. I never wanted Gianna to defend him. He threatened people. His family, and especially that stepfather of his, gives Italians a bad name. Furniture shop my foot. Bah."

"Rosa!" We heard Mrs. Gavelli bellow from the kitchen screen door.

Grandma Rosa sighed and rose to her feet. "I must go help Nicoletta with something. I will be back soon. You two enjoy your dinner."

We were finishing up and stacking the dishes in the sink when the doorbell rang.

Josie gestured at me. "I'll hurry and wash these while you grab the door. Probably someone who thinks we're still open. We'll have to put up another sign tomorrow, directing them to come through the kitchen door. I don't want customers coming in contact with your father and his—*ahem*—new business venture. No offense."

"None taken." I was in full agreement with my friend. As I crossed through the living room, the mahogany coffin displayed in the center of the floor was impossible to ignore. There was even a pillow and blanket inside. I'd actually seen my father napping in it earlier. *Good grief. How weird could my family get?*

The house, which had always seemed enormous to me as a child, was shrinking fast. Next to the coffin and the couch was a small computer work desk with a laptop that my father had recently bought. His "office" is what he now called the living room. I wasn't sure how long Josie could survive working here before she tried to strangle my father. I knew she loved him but had no patience for his "weirdo antics" as she called them. I couldn't say I blamed her. My patience was wearing thin lately too.

A tall, distinguished-looking man in his late fifties was

standing on the front porch. His black hair was slicked back behind his ears. I stared at the snappish, dark eyes underneath a wide forehead. His complexion was a shade lighter than my olive one, and he wore dress slacks with a white shirt opened at the neck, revealing an impressive-sized cross that hung from a thick gold chain. He seemed familiar, but I couldn't quite place him.

He greeted me with a cordial nod. "Sally, right?"

"That's right." I smiled. "Sorry. We're not open until tomorrow."

That drew a small chuckle out of him. "I'm not here about the bakery. I'd like to talk to you about your sister."

As I stared into the dark, calculating eyes, my palms began to sweat. I had a premonition of who this might be, and the thought unnerved me. "I'm sorry, but I didn't catch your name."

He extended his hand. "Luigi Napoli. An honor to meet you. Just as beautiful as your sister."

I knew it. Bernardo's stepfather. This couldn't be good. Reluctantly, I brushed a couple of fingers against his outstretched hand. He reached forward and grabbed mine in a tight grip. "Where's your sister, doll? I'd like to have a little chat with her."

"She's not here." I tried to stay calm. "Please let go of my hand."

He released it and laughed, opening his mouth so wide I could count the gleaming white teeth with prominent gold fillings. This was the master of the so-called Napoli Operation, as my grandmother often referred to it.

"I'm sorry about your stepson, but Gianna had nothing to do with his death."

He cocked his head to one side as he observed me. "Now that's where you're wrong, sweets. Your sister had *everything* to do with it."

Uneasiness stirred from within as the dark eyes continued to hold mine. I took a step backwards. "I don't know what you think she did, but I can assure you you're dead wrong."

"Ah." A deep voice behind Luigi piped in. "Nice play on words there, huh, Pop?"

I nearly jumped at the sound. Luigi stepped through the doorway and motioned to the younger man who had been standing behind him. "This is my son, Sergio."

The man, who appeared to be in his early thirties, nodded at me. Dark hair and eyes like his father's raked over me, and I suddenly longed for a cleansing shower. I had never met Sergio before, but Gianna had made reference to him once. Good looking, single, and another troublemaker. He was slim and about Mike's height but without Mike's muscular build.

Sergio's mouth turned up at the corners into a sly smile. "My. Beauty does run in the Muccio family."

I glanced uneasily in the direction of the kitchen. Josie could be heard chatting with someone on her cell phone. Grandma Rosa hadn't returned from next door yet. Mom and Dad were upstairs, probably doing things I didn't want to think about. It was silly to feel threatened here—in my parents' home—but right about now I was praying for a panic button to push.

I swallowed nervously. "Like I already said, my sister isn't here."

Luigi and Sergio walked past me and regarded the coffin in the middle of the floor with interest. "Hmm. Maybe we should have come here for Bernardo's casket, my boy."

My feet were frozen to the floor as I watched them. Having no choice, I shut the front door. They settled themselves comfortably on the couch and looked up at me expectantly. Sergio patted the cushion next to him. "Sit down. Let's talk for a while."

Nausea stirred in my stomach at a furious pace. "I-I, um, there's nothing to talk about."

He winked at me. "Sure there is."

"What's going on?" Josie's voice snapped suddenly from the hallway.

I breathed a sigh of relief. My face must have appeared terrified because she was watching me anxiously. She pointed at the Napoli clan. "Who are these two clowns?"

Luigi's smile left his face. "Who's the bombshell with the big mouth?"

Josie placed her hands on her hips and thrust her chest

forward. "What did you just call me?"

"Okay." I moved forward, stepping between Josie and Luigi. "Josie, this is Luigi and Sergio Napoli. They want to talk to Gianna."

Luigi's gaze rested on my friend. "Another sister? She don't look Italian."

Josie wrinkled her nose at him. "I'm Sal's partner and friend. What do you want to talk to Gianna for? She was Bernardo's lawyer. She can't reveal any information to you."

Sergio's eyes roamed over Josie, and he grinned. "I do like a girl with attitude."

She stared back at him in amazement. "You haven't seen anything yet, buddy."

"No," he agreed. "And *I want* to see more."

Josie seemed momentarily flustered, and it was one of the few times I could remember when she didn't have a clever response ready.

Luigi clapped his hands. "Okay. Let's get down to business. You tell me where your sister is, and nobody's gonna get hurt."

Josie's eyes bugged out of her head. "Are you threatening us?"

Luigi raised a hand. "No one said anything about threats, doll face. We just want to talk to her."

"Why?" I asked. "Like Josie said, she can't tell you anything about his case."

"Bernardo's dead," Luigi said in a matter-of-fact tone. "So she can talk. More specifically, she can tell us where the cash is."

Josie and I glanced at each other in confusion. "What cash?" I asked.

"Sweetie," Sergio said to me. "You might be cute, but you'd make one hell of a lousy actress. It's written all over your face."

Josie folded her arms across her chest. "Please explain what you're referring to."

Luigi stuck his index finger in his mouth and then smoothed it over his mustache. I tried to keep from gagging.

"Ladies, there's no need to get hostile." He studied me

for a moment. "We know your sister was the last one to see him alive. He told her where he stashed the dough. For all we know, he even gave it to her for safekeeping."

"This isn't making any sense," I said. "What cash? Gianna was his lawyer. She would never take money from him."

Luigi sighed. "You're not very wise to the ways of the world, my dear. Bernardo was in love with your sister. He was planning to leave his wife, Victoria, for her."

Josie gasped. "That's ridiculous. Gianna thought he was scum."

I elbowed her in the side, and she grunted in pain.

"Sorry," I whispered.

Luigi moved closer to us. I clutched Josie's arm, and we kept moving backward until we hit the living room wall.

"She didn't mean that," I whispered. "Gianna would never talk bad about her clients. Honest."

He smiled, putting his face next to mine so that the smell of sweat and Aqua Velva mixed together and infiltrated my nostrils, making it difficult to breathe normally.

"But your sister's right," he said. "Bernardo *was* scum. I'm not sorry he's dead. All I want to know is what he did with the freaking money. *My* freaking money, to be exact."

Sergio stood next to his father and winked at Josie. "How about you and I go for a drink, hot stuff?"

Josie clenched her teeth together, sucked in a deep breath, and then reached out and slapped him across the face.

Oh man. We were goners for sure now.

Sergio brought his hand to his cheek, momentarily surprised by her response. Then he laughed and elbowed his father in the side. "She's turning me on."

"Don't worry," Luigi growled. "I'll smack you around too if we don't find that money."

My internal alarm went off, and I prayed my fear did not show on the outside. "This money. How much are we talking about? Did it belong to you?"

Luigi ran a hand through his greasy-looking hair and sighed. "Yeah, it belonged to me, honey. My business funds. Bernardo stole it from me. He was planning to leave town and take your sister with him. For all we know, your sister's the one who killed him so she could have the loot all to herself."

Like an electric shock, anger surged through me. "That's ridiculous. My sister would never involve herself in something illegal like that. She is a lawyer, for God's sake, not a criminal."

"Ah." Luigi shook his head at me. "That don't mean anything. Bernardo said they were having an affair."

I shook my head vigorously. "I will never believe that."

Sergio held up a hand. "We ain't gonna hurt her. Not a sweet-looking dish like that. If she gives us the money, we'll let her go."

"And if she doesn't," Luigi gestured toward the coffin, "she's gonna be lying in one of those soon."

There was an angry grunt from the hallway, and we all turned in that direction. Grandma Rosa stood there, poised for action with a broom between her hands. She scowled at Luigi. "Why are you bothering my granddaughter and her friend?"

Luigi gave a mock bow to my grandmother. "*Ciao, signora.* How are you today? Allow me to introduce myself…"

Grandma Rosa cut him off. "Do not waste your time and mine. I know who you are." She stood in front of me and Josie, broom still between her hands. "You need to leave this house, sir. *Now.*"

Luigi stared at her in surprise. "I don't believe I've had the pleasure of making your acquaintance."

"No, you have not," Grandma Rosa snapped. "And you *will* not. You should be ashamed of yourself. Making innocent people pay you money. Plus, you do not even have decent furniture in that shop of yours. My daughter bought a lamp from you, and it never worked right."

Luigi's lips curled back from his teeth in a snide grin. "Well then, you should have had her return it for a refund."

"You are a disgrace," my grandmother muttered. "I will not ask you again. Leave this house now, or I will call the police."

Luigi took a step toward my grandmother, and I jumped between them. "If I hear from Gianna, I'll let you know, Mr. Napoli."

He glanced from me to Grandma Rosa then cocked his head at Sergio. "We have to go. Other things to take care of. But we'll be back."

Sergio winked at Josie. "Can I get your number, hot stuff?"

Josie closed her eyes in disgust. "Don't ever darken this doorstep again, you sick, disgusting pig."

He chortled and slapped his father on the back as they exited the house. "I think she likes me."

Luigi turned around, his hand on the doorknob. He smiled, but the piercing dark eyes that regarded us were as cold as ice. I was stunned at the venom contained in them as they locked onto mine.

"When you see your sister, give her a little piece of advice," he said. "You might tell her that she'd be wise to bring me the cash. Then again, maybe you should volunteer to bring the money back for her. That might be the smartest thing to do because if I find her first, she's going to be walking funny tomorrow."

Grandma Rosa stepped forward angrily. "Do not ever threaten my granddaughters again. If I were not a lady, I would spit on you, sir."

Luigi looked over Grandma's head at me. "Wow, that's harsh."

"Out!" she yelled.

Josie and I exchanged glances. Grandma Rosa never raised her voice, probably because most people knew better than to argue with her.

Luigi bowed to Grandma and smiled at me. "Tell your sister Bernardo's funeral is scheduled for Wednesday morning, if she'd like to drop by. She'll be pretty popular. I personally guarantee it."

CHAPTER ELEVEN

———

Grandma Rosa shook her fist at the front door. "Shameful. That is what they are." She looked from Josie standing there with her hands on her hips, face pale, to me chewing away on my fingernails. "Are you all right, my dears? Did they hurt you?"

I breathed a sigh of relief. "No, we're fine. What the heck is going on? They seem to think Bernardo was carrying on with Gianna and that she took the money he stole from his stepfather."

She snorted. "Ridiculous." Then her expression changed from irritated to somber. "Maybe that is why Gianna left town, because she knew they were trying to harm her."

I frowned. "But Gianna's a lawyer. She would have reported it to the authorities first."

Josie drew her eyebrows together. "Even if Bernardo had told her he stole the money, she couldn't reveal it, right? Because of client confidentiality?"

Grandma Rosa leaned the broom against the wall and put an arm around each one of us. "Make sure she is safe. That is all that matters right now."

"I wish she'd answer my messages," I sighed. "Why hasn't she returned my calls?"

At that moment, Josie's cell phone buzzed from her jeans pocket, and she glanced at the screen. "It's Rob. I'll meet you in the van, Sal."

I nodded and went into the kitchen to retrieve my purse, Grandma Rosa following me. My phone pinged, and I saw I had a message from Mike.

Working late. Don't wait up. Love you.

As I stared down at the text, that little voice of doubt

crept into my head again. I should have been relieved he wouldn't be looking for me for a while, but my thoughts kept returning to the fortune cookie message from earlier. Mike rarely worked nights anymore, his reason being that he was always anxious to get home to me. Of course I was overreacting. He had several jobs to finish before our wedding and not enough hours in the day.

I typed out a quick *Love you too* and placed the phone in my purse. When I looked up, I found Grandma Rosa watching me with eyes that stared straight into my soul. "What is wrong?"

It was always impossible to fool her, but I lied anyway. "Nothing. I'm fine."

She gave me a doubtful look. "No. There is something else bothering you besides your sister. Do not lie to me."

"It's silly."

"Silly Sally." Grandma Rosa smiled at the nickname she gave me as a child. When I'd come home after a rough day at school with an earth-shattering problem—like why the new boy was teasing me—Grandma Rosa would say I was being silly and subsequently set my mind at ease. Everything would be fine the next day, she'd assure me. Of course, she was always right.

"Is there a problem between you and your young man?"

As usual, I was amazed by her perception. "I got another weird message today. It was in a fortune cookie."

She nodded. "I suspected it was something like that. Sally, my love, you need to stop letting those cookies bother you. In time, they will consume you if you are not careful." She realized what she had said and then gave a low chuckle. "No fun intended."

I smiled. "That's pun, Grandma. See, I told you it was silly. The fortune said that Mike was keeping a secret from me."

She eyed me sharply. "Please do not tell me you think your young man is fooling around. He loves you more than anything. I will never believe that, and neither should you, my dear."

"I don't." I felt foolish but still couldn't help myself.

"You have been down this road before. Do not travel it again. Listen to your grandmother."

I blew out a long sigh. "It's probably just my imagination

running away with me."

She nodded in approval. "Then make sure you go catch it."

I laughed and leaned over to hug her. "Consider it done."

Her eyes were somber. "Go find your sister, *cara mia*. Bring her home, where she belongs."

*   *   *

It was close to eight thirty when Josie pulled up in front of the Regal Casino. A light summer rain had fallen during our trip, and the sun was sinking fast in a sky that resembled a giant orange fireball. As we exited the vehicle and I stared upward at the marvelous sight similar to an inferno, my thoughts returned to Mike. I couldn't wait for us to have some alone time together later. In a little over three weeks, I would be on my honeymoon with the man I loved more than anything in this world. It didn't get much better than that.

Grandma Rosa was right. Mike and I had a wonderful relationship. I was getting obsessed with the fortune cookie messages as I had done in the past, and it was time to end this nonsense.

"Everything okay?" Josie asked as we entered through the glass, revolving door.

"Yeah. Come on. Check-in is this way." To our right was a long reception counter with six employees standing behind it. Several people were impatiently waiting to be called from a single line. I guessed they were eager to hit the slots and start feeding their money into the machines. I had phoned the casino on the way over, and they had rung Gianna's room again for me. Still no answer. I wondered if she was choosing not to answer the phone. To my alarm, I found myself wondering if she wasn't alone. What if...

"Sal?"

Josie stared at me with eyes full of concern. I forced my thoughts away and tried to focus. "Sorry. I'm just worried."

She placed a hand reassuringly on my arm. "We'll find her. You'll see."

We took our place in line and waited our turn. The

woman in front of us kept turning around and staring with a longing look in the direction of the casino. She had short, blonde hair in a pixie cut and was wearing skintight jeans that didn't do much for her robust figure. They looked so snug that I wondered how she managed to move without pain.

She tugged at the shirt sleeve of the man she was with. "My machine will be gone if they don't hurry up. Can't you do the check-in?"

"No way," he growled in return. "It was your idea to come here, babe. I hate this place. And if I catch you asking for credit in the casino again, you're done for."

Josie and I exchanged a glance, and she whispered in my ear. "Classic gambling couple. Woman wants to spend money she doesn't have. Probably has three kids at home. Bet she feeds them ramen noodles. They'll be divorced within a year if she doesn't kick the habit."

I narrowed my eyes. "Are you an expert now?"

Josie shrugged. "Hey, all the classic signs are there."

It was finally our turn, and we approached a young woman behind the desk, who smiled at both of us. "Checking in, ladies?"

"I'm wondering if you can tell me what room my sister is in?" I asked. "Her name is Gianna Muccio."

Her smile faded. "I'm sorry. We don't give out room numbers for our customers."

"Oh, come on," Josie groused. "It's not like she's a stranger."

The woman looked at Josie and frowned then pointed her finger at me. "If she's your sister, then why don't you already have her room number? Can't you call her and ask for it?"

This was just what we needed right now—Sherlock Holmes posing as a desk clerk. "She didn't answer her phone when I called. Please, this is really important. She could be in some type of danger."

She gave me a doubtful look. "I'm sorry. Rules are rules."

"For God's sake." Josie slammed her hand on the counter. "Just give her the room number, lady. We're not mass murderers."

"Is there a problem?" A distinguished-looking gentleman with graying hair at the temples moved to the woman's right and observed us with interest.

The woman waved a finger at me. "She wants the room number for her sister. I explained we can't give those out."

He looked at us like we were clueless. "Sorry, ladies. No can do."

"This is crazy!" Josie exploded.

People were starting to stare. Afraid that we were about to be kicked out, I gave them both my most gracious smile and grabbed Josie by the arm, leading her away from the counter and the sets of eyes that followed us with curiosity. "I'm sure she's in the casino. We'll look for her there. Thanks anyway."

Josie was still mumbling under her breath as we walked to the other side of the hotel. Screens with colorful images came into plain view, and a variety of beeping noises could be heard from the machines.

"Look," I said. "It's not going to do Gianna any good if we get ourselves kicked out of here."

"I know." Josie's tone was irritated. "But I still think it's a stupid policy." She scanned the room. "Should we try here or the non-smoking section?"

"Definitely non-smoking," I said. Like myself, Gianna hated cigarette smoke, but not enough to deter her from visiting the casino entirely. Our mother, to her credit, didn't smoke that often and never in the house. Still, Gianna felt it was her duty to preach to Mom about her bad habit every chance she got.

There were several non-smoking areas. Since it was the shank of the evening, the place was crowded, and even in the labeled sections that stated cigarettes weren't allowed, smoke permeated the air so thick that it seeped into my clothes. Mike would surely smell it on me when I got home. Not that it mattered because I planned to tell him where I'd been. I hadn't wanted to relay it in a text earlier for fear he would worry.

No more secrets between us—at least not from me. *Ugh. There you go again, Sal.*

The noise was mind-blowing. People at one of the craps tables were screaming over a recent win. A live band was set up in a corner of the room, and I had to cover my ears for protection from the heavy metal music. I searched the room in confusion. Then, all of a sudden, it dawned on me why Gianna would come here. It wasn't just for the machines. She wanted to blend in with the crowd, in case someone happened to be looking for her. This thought didn't sit well with me.

"You did what?" A sharp voice sounded behind me.

I whirled around, puzzled why someone was yelling at me, but an angry female voice answered quickly. "So what? I know it's going to hit soon."

It was the same couple that had been in line at check-in. They were standing in front of a ten-dollar poker machine. Too rich for my blood. They looked like they were about to choke the life out of each other.

"You hit five hundred, and then you dumped it all back in already?" the man said in an incredulous tone.

"It's going to hit big, I just know it, Sam."

Sam didn't seem convinced. He started to drag the blonde woman away from the machine while she, in turn, started screaming and hitting him with her purse. Security rushed over to escort them both out.

"You're an addict!" Sam yelled. "I'm getting a divorce before you mortgage the house out from under us."

"Too late!" she screamed back at him.

Josie nudged me. "Told you so."

I shook my head in disbelief at the spectacle and then turned in the opposite direction. Back in a dimly lit corner of the room, a petite young woman with beautiful chestnut-colored hair sat at one of the penny machines, idly pressing the button. Her expression was bored. She wore large dark glasses, and her hair was pulled back into a ponytail, but I'd recognize my beautiful sister anywhere.

I nudged Josie and pointed. We both walked over and stood beside the machine until she looked up at us. Her manner instantly changed from indifference to relief, and she brought a hand to her mouth. "Oh my God."

When she stood up, I hugged her tightly to me, a small sob escaping from my lips. "I've been so worried about you."

On closer inspection, Gianna looked like she hadn't slept in weeks. She leaned over and hugged Josie.

"Are you okay, hon?" Josie asked.

Gianna's voice trembled as she nodded. "Yes. I'm so glad to see you guys."

I glanced around us. "Why don't we go up to your room so we can talk in private for a while?"

She nodded and led the way out into the hallway where we all piled into the elevator. She pressed the button for the fifth floor and then stared at me, her eyes mournful. "How did you find me?"

"You left a free night stay card in your desk. Call it intuition on my part."

Her chocolate-colored eyes started to fill. "I'm so glad you did. I've been missing you like crazy."

The elevator door opened, and we all walked down the hallway together. I put an arm around my sister's slim shoulders. "Why didn't you return my texts? I've been so worried about you. We all have."

"I'm sorry," Gianna said sadly. "My phone died shortly after I texted you, and I forgot to bring my charger with me. I've been meaning to go get a new one. I—I kind of left in a hurry."

Josie glanced at me worriedly. I told myself that I wouldn't panic, but the quivering in Gianna's voice caused my concern to skyrocket. I stared at her hands, which were shaking. This was not normal behavior for my sister. *What was going on?*

We sat down on the edge of her bed, and I reached for her hand. "I have some bad news about your client, Bernardo."

Gianna nodded and looked at the floor. "I know. I saw his picture on the news." She sighed. "I was afraid that might happen."

Panic enveloped my body. I grabbed both of Gianna's hands and peered into her eyes. "The police want to question you. I didn't tell them where you were because I wanted to talk with you first and find out what exactly happened. I know you didn't have anything to do with his death, honey."

Gianna started to sob like a child. I reached out and wrapped my arms around my sister, hugging her to me as I used to do when we were kids and she'd fallen off her bike.

"Do you know how he died?" I asked.

"Yes," she said through her tears.

Josie bit into her lower lip. "Sweetheart, just tell us what happened. We're here to help you."

Gianna wept softly in my arms. "You can't help me," she whispered, "because I'm the one who killed him."

CHAPTER TWELVE

My blood ran cold. Okay, I must have heard her wrong. "What are you talking about? You're not a murderer." *Please, God, let this be some kind of mistake.*

Gianna wiped at her eyes with the back of her hand. "I thought he was okay afterwards. Honest. But I *must* have killed him. It's the only explanation I can come up with." She started to cry again. "Sal, I don't know what to do. I guess I should go home and turn myself in."

I clutched her tightly by the shoulders and forced her to look at me. "Tell me exactly what happened."

Josie sat down on the other side of Gianna. "That slime made a pass at you, didn't he?"

Gianna's expression was full of misery. "Bernardo said he wanted to talk about the trial. He was convinced they'd retry him. So I told him we could go back to the bakery and speak there."

"Why didn't you just tell him you wouldn't represent him again?" Josie asked.

"That's not the way it works," Gianna replied. "As a public defender I don't have any choice of who I represent. I'm not allowed to turn clients down, and it's very likely he would have been assigned to me again anyway."

She blew out a breath and continued. "I told Bernardo that until we heard back about another trial, it would be best if we stayed away from each other. He seemed to understand."

I stroked her hand. "Go on."

"Then he asked me if I had any aspirin. Said he had a bad migraine. So we went upstairs to my apartment." Gianna stared at the floor. "I went to get him a glass of water, and when I turned around—Bernardo grabbed me. He told me he was in love with me and that he was leaving his wife. I was in complete shock. I never even saw this coming. So I asked him to please remove his hands, but instead he kissed me and wouldn't let me breathe. I tried to free myself."

Her hands were shaking so bad that I steadied them with my own. "I figured it was something like that. What happened then?"

"There was a frying pan sitting on the counter," Gianna said. "I managed to grab it and smacked him in the head with it. Then he released me."

"That wouldn't have killed him." At least I hoped not. "How many times did you hit him?"

"Only once. But if that didn't kill Bernardo, then what the heck happened to him?" Gianna asked. "I've been over this a million times in my head."

"Tell us what happened after you hit him," Josie said.

She sighed. "I was so angry. I told him to get the hell out of my house and never come back."

Josie and I both raised our eyebrows. My sister hardly ever swore.

"Wow," Josie said. "You *were* mad."

Gianna nodded. "Furious. That guy could have ruined my career. I practically pushed him out the door and down the stairs."

"This doesn't make any sense," I said. "His body was found in the back room of the bakery."

Gianna's mouth fell open in amazement. "What? They didn't say on the news where he was found, only that he had died. I guess I had hoped it was all a bad dream. I thought maybe he'd gotten behind the wheel and tried to drive away and then suffered an aneurism or something because I had hit him." She examined my face closely, as if looking for a sign that I believed her.

There was no doubt in my mind that she was telling the truth, but finding Gianna had not cleared things up as I'd hoped. Instead, I found myself even more confused. "Okay. Let's go over this one more time. You pushed him out the door of the apartment. He went down the stairs. Did you see him leave?"

"Yes. He said I'd be sorry and that he wasn't going to

split the—"

"Wait a second," Josie interrupted. "You *saw* him leave the bakery?"

Gianna nodded. "He slammed the glass door so hard I was afraid it might break. Then I ran back upstairs to my apartment. I felt like I was suffocating and needed to leave, fast. So I threw some things into a suitcase and took off. I've been here for two days trying to decide what to do next." Her face was full of misery. "At first I didn't even know where I would end up. I just drove, needing to put some distance between me and everything in my life." She studied me. "But I can't run from my problems forever. Has that ever happened to you?"

"Yes." While Colin and I were married and living in Florida, I'd come home early from work one night and found him in bed with another woman. My high school nemesis, in fact. I'd calmly shut the bedroom door, retreated to my car, and proceeded to drive the entire night. "I once drove to Georgia in the middle of the night, remember?"

Gianna threw her arms around me. "I shouldn't complain, not when you've been through so much."

"Forget about me. Did you lock the bakery door when you left?"

My sister looked at me in surprise. "Why, of course I did."

"I'm not mad, Gi. But please try to concentrate for a moment. You were upset. You were angry. The man tried to take advantage of you. How else could he have gotten back in? You're certain you locked it?"

She started to shake again, and I found myself wishing I hadn't asked the question. Still I had to know. Something was not adding up here.

A tear rolled down Gianna's cheek. "When I came down the stairs, I left through the back room because my car was parked out in the alley. He wasn't in there. I swear it."

"I believe you." Although this also made no sense.

She shut her eyes, trying to remember. "I *thought* I locked the front door at the time, but I was so upset. You're right—I can't be positive, Sal. All I heard on the news was that he had died. They probably didn't reveal a lot of details because it was suspicious. So somehow he snuck back into the building. Or maybe he broke in and then collapsed."

I wondered if Brian could tell if Bernardo had somehow broken into the bakery. With all the damage that had occurred, I didn't know if there was a way to find out. "He didn't die from the fire. There was blunt trauma to the right side of his face. Someone hit him with an object, several times."

She stared at me, puzzled. "Like I said, I only hit him once. What fire are you talking about?"

When I told her about the bakery, Gianna started to cry again. "Oh my God. This is all my fault."

I couldn't stand seeing my sister fall apart like this. Gently, I cupped her face between my hands. "Listen to me. You did nothing wrong. You were only defending yourself, and I don't believe you killed him. So you're in the clear."

She blew her nose into a tissue. "Maybe according to you guys, yes. But how do I prove it to the police?"

"We'll talk to Brian." Josie grinned at me. "Your sister has an *in* with him."

I chose to ignore her statement. "He knows you didn't kill him, Gi."

"But we can't prove that I didn't," Gianna protested. "I should go right back and fill the police in, but there's more, Sal."

Oh, jeez. "Tell me."

Gianna paused for a moment and put a hand to her chest, as if trying to steady herself. "After Bernardo asked me to go away with him, he confessed that he needed to get out of town right away. He said something about having enough money to tide us over for the rest of our lives."

Icicles formed between my shoulder blades. Bernardo must have been talking about Luigi's money, or shall we say Luigi's illegal funds from his racketeering business. I racked my brain, trying to figure out what to do next.

"Sal?"

Gianna's pale face watched me, and I grabbed her hand. "Bernardo's stepfather, Luigi, came to see me. He wanted to know where you were. He knew about the money. It sounds like Bernardo stole it from him."

Gianna's face was now the color of powdered sugar. "Oh

my God. Bernardo told me stories about his stepfather. He said the man used to beat him as a kid. When his wife—Bernardo's mother—died, he always complained that she'd stuck him with a loser for a stepchild. I confess I didn't like Bernardo, but I was sorry for him when he told me that story."

"That may have been all it was, just a story," Josie muttered.

What should we do now? I wanted Gianna to come home, but maybe she was safer here for the time being. If Luigi thought she had something to do with the theft, or maybe even that she'd killed Bernardo for the money—well, it was too awful to imagine what he might do to her.

Gianna wound a strand of hair around her finger. "It's my job to uphold the law. And now I can't even make a decision by myself. What a crappy lawyer I am. Maybe it's not too late for me to try a different profession. Spike likes me. Hey, what if I became a dog groomer or something like that?"

"Okay, stop it," I demanded. "This is what we're going to do. You will lie low here for a couple more days. I'm going to do a little snooping on my own and see what I can find out about Bernardo and what may have happened to him that night. Somehow someone else got into the bakery, hit him—maybe with my rolling pin—and killed him. His family is all looking for you. I'm not taking any chances with your safety."

"Sal." Gianna's expression was pained. "I'm not going to let *you* put yourself in danger for me. You're getting married in a couple of weeks."

"Piece of cookie," I grinned. "Gee, don't I sound like Grandma now?"

She didn't laugh. "I don't want you involved in this. Mike would hate me if something happened to you. Heck, I'd hate myself."

"The court would see that you had protection if you came home, right?" Josie asked.

Gianna shrugged. "They might send a patrol car by a couple of times a day but probably wouldn't do more than that. It doesn't matter, I need to go back. I'll move in with Mom and Dad for now." She rolled her eyes at the ceiling. "Lord, help me."

I shook my head. "No way. I don't trust this Luigi

character. He'd find a way to get to you." Plus, if Gianna went back, maybe my entire family would be in danger. "It's better this way for now. Promise me you'll sit tight for a day or two while I try to find out some more details."

"This is my problem, Sal. I said I don't want you involved."

"I'm already involved. Bernardo died in my bakery. Another day or two won't make much difference." I reached into my purse and gave her my iPhone cable, which I had used earlier at Mom and Dad's to charge my phone. "Take this. I'll buy another. But don't text me or anyone."

I didn't want the police to find her yet. Then again, maybe I should tell Brian, and he could come back with me to get her. But where would she stay?" What if Luigi and his goons were watching my parents' house? "Josie and I will make a trip back to see you, if not tomorrow then on Wednesday. Hopefully we'll know something more by then."

Gianna pressed her lips together stubbornly. "I hate not taking responsibility for my own actions. I never should have become a lawyer. This is more difficult than I ever imagined."

Baffled, I looked over her head at Josie, who raised her eyebrows in return. "Don't say that. You were born to be a lawyer." I thought of the countless times when Josie, Gianna, and I had played court as children. Gianna had always been the attorney, Josie either the judge or the juror, and me the criminal Gianna was defending. I hardly ever went to jail back then, though.

"Growing up, you and Grandma were the only ones who didn't laugh when I said I wanted to be an attorney. Mom and Dad thought it was so cute. A passing phase." A look of agitation crept into my sister's face. "All I want is for people to take me seriously."

"Hey. It was one bad case. Things will get better," I assured her.

Gianna shook her head. "No one takes me seriously in the courtroom." She hesitated and twisted the tissue between her hands as if groping for the right words. "I never told you guys this before, but the first day I showed up for court, the bailiff thought I was in the wrong building. I'll never forget his words.

'Sweetie, the modeling agency is down the street.'"

I winced. "Ouch."

"Yeah, ouch is right." Gianna's nostrils flared. "And then there was the time I was questioning a witness in Bernardo's case, and one of the spectators yelled something about how nice my butt—insert different word here—looked in the suit I was wearing. He was thrown out of court, of course, but I was beyond humiliated."

My heart ached for Gianna. It was both a blessing and a curse to be as beautiful as she was. "You can't let that stop you, honey. You've worked so hard your entire life for this."

She leaned her head against my shoulder. "I wish I was strong like you."

Her statement both shocked and pleased me. If Gianna had seen my meltdown at the fire the other night, she might feel differently now. "I'm not as strong as you think."

"Bull," she spoke quietly. "You're one tough cookie."

We all laughed, and then she lifted her head to look at me, her tone serious again. "How would you even find out who might have killed him? Or where the money is now?"

"Brian might know something," I said. "I can always reach out to him. Josie and I should try to get back into the bakery tomorrow if we have time. Maybe the cops missed something. There might be a clue to the killer's identity somewhere. Or maybe Bernardo left something behind that could incriminate the person."

Josie snorted. "Yeah, like a couple of million bucks. Mike will be pissed if you go in there again without a police escort, you know. He's not convinced the place is safe."

"Well, maybe Brian will take us." I really didn't want to call and ask him. He might think it was an attempt to spend more time with him, and I didn't need that aggravation right now.

I tucked a few loose strands of hair back behind Gianna's ear. My voice shook. "I don't know if we're going to be able to use the building again, so you may have to find a new apartment. At the very least, you'll need some other type of accommodations for a while."

"Don't worry about that," she assured me. "I feel so bad about the bakery. It probably never would have happened if I hadn't taken him there. What will you do until you have another location set up? Can you run something from yours and Mike's house? Maybe some kind of to-go business?"

I shook my head. "The kitchen is way too small, and there's not enough counter space." Then I told Gianna about relocating the bakery to our parents' house. She stared at me as though I had two heads.

"You are kidding, right? Why on earth would you choose to run a business from there? I love Mom and Dad, but they're not exactly normal, Sal."

"Gee, whatever gave you that idea?" Josie asked in mock disbelief.

"It's just temporary," I assured my sister.

Gianna snorted. "Yeah. Temporary insanity."

CHAPTER THIRTEEN

———

"So, what's the plan, Stacey?" Josie asked when we were on our way home.

I glanced at the clock in the van. It was nearly midnight, and we had an early day ahead of us tomorrow. "Stacey who?"

"Cagney and Stacey, remember? God, I love your grandmother."

I smiled in the darkness. "If we have a lull in business tomorrow at some point, maybe we can break away and get over to the bakery. Do a little investigating of our own. If Sarah doesn't mind covering, that is. If it's too busy, we'll figure out another time."

"Might as well use Sarah to our advantage while we can," Josie agreed. "I can't believe she's ditching you when you need her the most."

I pulled my phone out of my purse to check for messages. "I don't blame her. She has a child to think of, and it's got to be really tough for her making ends meet every month." I'd given her a raise awhile back, but the poor thing wore the same clothes nearly every day and the same pair of shoes all the time.

"Sarah really needs some new clothes," Josie said, as if reading my mind. "How do you think she'd feel if I gave her some old ones of mine? I think we're about the same size."

I hesitated. It seemed like a touchy subject. "I don't know. She's kind of proud. Maybe it would offend her."

"Well, can I at least offer her a pair of shoes?" Josie asked. "The pair she has is so worn out that the dang heel broke off on one, and not to mention how ugly those Oxfords are. Who wears chunky heels like that these days? They look like something Mrs. Gavelli would own."

"We don't all have your size five foot," I said tartly. "If it makes you feel better, offer her some. But please try not to embarrass her in the process."

Josie pointed a finger at herself. "Me, embarrass people? That would never happen."

"Right," I mocked then straightened up in the seat. "Maybe we could give her a new pair of shoes and an outfit as a going away present. We'll say it's for her job at the supermarket. She might accept it then." Lord knows I didn't have much money to spare these days, but Sarah had been an excellent employee, and I wanted to do something nice for her.

Mike had sent a text about a half an hour ago. *Just got home. Where are you?* I was debating about what to say. I'd hoped to beat him back to the house, but no such luck. "I'm telling Mike we found Gianna."

Josie stopped for a red light and made a face. "Fine. As long as he doesn't tell Rob where we went. If I were you, I wouldn't bring up about going to the bakery tomorrow either, unless Mike can manage to go with us. Do you think he could break away from his job? What's he working on, by the way?"

"I think it's unlikely he could meet us. He's got a roof to finish, and he just started another job. He's working fifteen-hour days so he can get caught up before our honeymoon."

Josie put her blinker on to turn left onto my street. "Did you guys decide where you're going yet?"

I shook my head. "We can't afford much of anything right now. Maybe we'll go to Cape Cod for a few days. I'd love to go to Hawaii someday, though." It wasn't about to happen, but I could dream, right?

"Bad choice," Josie said. "A complete waste of money."

"Why? It's gorgeous there. And I'd love to tour the islands."

She kept her eyes fixed on the road, but a sly smile formed at the corners of her mouth. "Honey, let's be realistic here. You two lovebirds would never leave your room all week, if you catch my drift."

My mouth fell open in surprise. "You *are* bad."

"No. Just honest."

Josie pulled into my driveway. Through the open living

room window I could hear Spike bark once in greeting. Mike had left the porch light on for me, and I could see a lamp on in the living room as well.

Josie grinned and cocked her head in the direction of the house. "No fooling around with the sexpot in there tonight. We've got a long and strange day ahead of us tomorrow."

I laughed. "Well, that's one way of putting it."

"See you in the morning, kiddo."

I shut the van door and dug my house key out of my purse. I was surprised that Mike wasn't at the front door to greet me, but Spike was.

"Hi, big guy." I leaned down to pet him then shut and locked the door behind me. Mike was stretched out on the couch, snoring softly. The television was tuned to a ballgame that was currently in extra innings. I shut it off and looked down with admiration at the man I loved. He was quite the vision, dressed in jeans and nothing else, feet bare, and his arms crossed over his chest. Desire spread through me as I watched his well-sculpted chest rise and fall slightly. Poor baby was all worn out. Well, I'd find a way to wake him up in a hurry.

Smiling to myself, I took a quick shower to get rid of the smoke smell from the casino and donned one of the new pieces of lingerie I'd bought for our honeymoon. It was pale blue, trimmed with lace, and very sheer, leaving little to the imagination. I fussed a bit with my hair then went back into the living room.

I leaned over Mike and rubbed his arm then kissed him softly on the lips. "Hey, Sleeping Beauty. Wake up."

Mike's eyes flickered open. He looked exhausted but smiled as his eyes met mine. "Hi, baby. When did you get in?"

I ran a finger down his smooth chest seductively. "About twenty minutes ago."

He yawned and raised himself into a sitting position. "Everything okay with Gianna?"

The answer was no, but I didn't want to tell him about my plans to snoop around further. He wouldn't like it. "It will be. She's coming home soon, I hope. Why were you working so late? I thought the roof was almost done?"

"Not quite. I ran into some problems, and the guy who

was helping me got a more permanent position, so I'm on my own. Plus, I started another job today, and I'm on a tight deadline to get it finished." His dark blue gaze glinted with mischief as he focused on me—or more specifically, my nightie. "Oh, wow. Is that new?"

"Mm-hmm." I did a 360-degree turn for him while he whistled appreciatively. I was pleased that my mission to seduce him was being accomplished. Not that it ever took much anyway. "I was saving it for our honeymoon, but thought I'd give you a preview tonight."

He drew me onto his lap, wrapped his arms around my waist, and kissed me deeply. "I like the sound of that. Hope it's an all-night preview."

I laughed and got to my feet, reaching for his hand. "Come on. Let's go to bed."

Mike rubbed his eyes again. "Okay. You go ahead, and get comfortable, baby. I need to take Spike for a quick walk, and then I'm all yours."

I leaned over Mike and kissed him, gripping his thick, dark hair between my fingers. "Don't be long."

I started to walk down the hallway and felt his eyes still on me. I turned around to see him watching me with a devilish smile. "What?"

His eyes shone, and he winked. "Nothing. I'm just enjoying the show."

I grinned and went into the bedroom, lit a candle on my nightstand, turned out the light, and then got under the covers to wait for Mike. I would have set the alarm clock, but he was up at dawn these days and would wake me before he left the house. I had told Josie I'd meet her at my parents' at seven o'clock sharp. Sarah was scheduled to come in at eight. She had to drop Julie off at camp first, and that didn't open up until seven thirty. All I needed was to get a little ahead moneywise so that I could put the money back in Mike's account and then hopefully start saving toward another location for the bakery.

Five minutes passed then Spike ran into the room and jumped onto the bed. Bewildered, I petted the dog and wondered why I hadn't heard the front door open. What the heck? "Mike?"

There was no answer. I stepped out of bed and padded

down the hallway in my bare feet. Mike was still sitting upright on the couch, fast asleep again.

I sighed with disappointment and reached for the afghan on the back of the couch to cover him. He'd wake up eventually and come to bed. I knew he was worn out but had really been looking forward to some alone time with him. Well, we'd make up for it on our honeymoon. I smiled to myself. Josie's earlier comment had been right on the money. Cape Cod would probably work out just fine.

As I walked back into the bedroom and blew out the candle, my mind started wandering again. Was there something else going on with him? What about this new job? Could he be working for some voluptuous blonde and afraid to tell me? *There you go again, Sal.* There was no reason for me not to trust him. I was inventing problems. If it hadn't been for Colin's cheating, I doubted I'd even be having these thoughts.

I got into bed and pulled the covers up to my nose, thinking of the fortune cookie message again. Mrs. Gavelli or no Mrs. Gavelli, those pieces of dough had to go. Weariness won over, and I closed my eyes.

"Princess."

"Hmm."

Someone shook my arm. "Hey." I opened my eyes to see Mike bending over me, dressed in jeans and a dark blue Adidas T-shirt. His hair was still damp from the shower, and he smelled wonderful—of that spicy aftershave I loved.

He sat down next to me on the edge of the bed and leaned down to kiss me tenderly on the lips. "It's six o'clock, baby. Time to get moving."

"Oh," I groaned. "It feels like I just went to bed." I raised myself into a sitting position and yawned noisily.

Mike grinned and pushed the covers off me. "Damn. I'm sorry about last night. I can't believe I missed out on this." He fingered the lace on my nightie.

I placed my arms around his neck "It's all right. We have plenty more nights ahead of us. A lifetime of them, actually."

"I'm counting on that." He crushed his mouth against mine, causing a flurry of passion and longing to erupt from deep within me.

When we finally broke apart, I uttered a low moan. "Nothing's coming between us tonight—I don't care how tired you are."

He laughed, but I could have sworn I saw a flicker of guilt reflected in his eyes. No, I must have imagined it.

"As soon as I get home, I'm all yours," Mike promised. "But I'm going to be pretty late again."

Ugh. I knew he was trying to clear his schedule, but selfishly, I wanted him here with me. However, we did need the money, especially since the fiasco with my bakery. "What's the other job?"

Mike hesitated for a moment then planted a kiss on my neck. "I'm putting in new flooring at Webster's Restaurant. They want it finished by the end of the week, so that's going to mean some more late nights until then."

"This honeymoon can't come soon enough." I stroked the stubble on his chin and forced him to look at me. "Hey, is there any chance you can break away today?"

He wove his fingers through my hair. "I'll be lucky if I find time to eat lunch. Why? What's going on?"

He was going to be upset, so I skimmed over the truth a bit. "Josie and I want to run by the bakery and grab some things."

Mike stared at me, unconvinced. "I thought you got everything out of there already."

"Not quite." If I told him it was to snoop, he'd really be upset. "We won't be long."

His jaw set in a determined lock. "I don't want you in the building, Sal. I'd rather you wait until Dave can get out there to inspect the place. He's supposed to go over tomorrow or the next day when he gets back in town. I'll double-check with him."

A lightbulb clicked on in my head. "Maybe I could meet him when he goes over?"

He toyed with my hair and gave me a shrewd look. "I guess that would be all right. Get what you have to, and then leave immediately. Understand?"

"Yes, sir."

Mike's smile returned, and he kissed me again. "Good luck today, sweetheart. I'll text you later."

Mike got off the bed and walked toward the bedroom

door with Spike trailing after him. He turned around, and I stared at his rugged, handsome face. His mouth curved into a seductive smile. "One more thing."

"Yes, my love?"

The pupils in his midnight blue eyes grew dark and increased in size as he pinned me with his gaze. Another rush of heat swept over me. "Make sure you wear that nightie again tonight."

With that, he was gone.

I jumped out of bed and rushed to take a quick shower, all the while marveling about how lucky I was. How foolish I'd been last night to think that maybe something else was going on with him.

I arrived at my parents' just minutes after seven o'clock. Josie's minivan was already there. When I went into the kitchen, she had the mixer going and was making *genettis*. The Italian glazed cookies sprinkled with nonpareils were one of my father's favorites. No doubt he'd be in there before long, pestering her. I hadn't seen his car outside and wondered if he'd made a trip to Denny's on the sly for a Grand Slam breakfast, complete with extra cholesterol.

Grandma Rosa was sitting in the dining room, coffee in hand, reading the morning paper. It was weird to see her relaxing because even at the age of seventy-five, that was not her style. However, I knew she wanted to stay out of Josie's way. I leaned down to hug her.

She patted my cheek. "Good morning, *cara mia*. Are you ready for a busy day?"

I poured myself a cup of coffee from the carafe in front of her. "I hope we get customers, Grandma."

"They will come. It is too bad we could not tie your father up in the basement, though. That man and his *pazzo* hobby may frighten people away. If I did not live here, I would be frightened too." Grandma Rosa studied my face carefully. "Your sister. You have found her?"

I went on to tell her what had transpired last night and that Josie and I had plans to return to the bakery to look around. She nodded in approval.

"Dear heart, I know how much you love your sister," she

said. "But this is not good for you either. There is to be a happy wedding in a few weeks. You should not be putting yourself or Josie in any danger right now."

"Did I hear my name?" Josie joined us, wearing a spotless white apron, her long auburn hair pinned into a tidy bun on the top of her head. In the bakery we'd had pink ball caps to wear, but I'd forgotten to bring them over. If they were even still useable after the fire, which I doubted.

I poured my best friend a cup of coffee, and she sat down. "Sorry. We haven't even opened yet, and I'm already slacking when I should be out there helping you. I was telling Grandma about going back to the bakery. Mike said this morning it should be fine as long as the engineer is there. I hope he can meet us today."

Grandma Rosa pressed her lips together, unconvinced. "You two need to be careful."

Josie kissed her on the cheek. "We will, Rosa. You can count on it. Gianna needs to stay where she is for now. You saw those Napoli pigs last night. They're convinced Gianna's part of Bernardo's scheme. They won't listen to reason. We've got to find out who's responsible for Bernardo's death and burning down the bakery."

My phone pinged, and I stared down at a text from Sarah. *Julie's sick. Need to find someone to watch her today. Can't send her to camp like this. Will be late. So sorry.*

I blew out a sigh and showed the message to Josie and my grandmother.

Josie shook her head. "Every week. Man, she has more issues with one kid than I have with four."

Grandma Rosa took a sip of her coffee. "That one, she has many problems. It is not good."

"Well, I hope this new job works out for her." I put the phone back in my pocket. "But she won't be able to bring Julie there, I wouldn't think. And what are we supposed to do for help in the meantime? I guess we should place an ad in the paper. She's leaving at the end of the week."

"Nice of her to give you two weeks' notice," Josie quipped.

Grandma Rosa got to her feet. "I will help today if you

need me. I am going to visit Nicoletta for a while, but call if you need anything."

"What would we ever do without you?" I asked. My grandmother was always there whenever Gianna or I needed her.

She chuckled. "You would be lost."

Josie pushed her chair in. "By the way, Father Grenaldi just called, and he wants one hundred cookies today. Jelly-filled, shortbread, spice, and oatmeal crème pie cookies. Twenty-five of each for the Altar Rosary Society meeting being held at the church tonight. He wants to pick them up at noon. Since I already have the dough on hand for everything except the spice ones, it's not going to be a problem."

I sniffed at the air, loving it. "It smells like my bakery again." Despite my dread over the location, the thought cheered me to no end. We could do this, and hopefully it would only be for a few weeks. Maybe after the honeymoon we'd be able to start off fresh someplace else. I kept trying to convince myself everything would be fine. With my parents, you never knew what they'd throw at you next. Their house was like a crazy carnival ride most days.

For the next two hours, Josie and I baked and filled the display case. My father arrived, sporting a gigantic grease spot on the front of his shirt, and my previous suspicions were confirmed. He grabbed a couple of cookies out of the case and went outside to water Grandma Rosa's garden. Josie growled as he walked away but said nothing. I had to give her credit—she was trying.

Sarah texted again, saying she would arrive within the hour. She kept apologizing, and I sympathized with her. How awful it must be to have no support system in your life.

I filled the jelly cookies and prepared them for baking while Josie rang up an order for a customer. Suddenly, I heard a noise from the vicinity of the living room and grimaced. My mother was out and Grandma Rosa in the kitchen, so I knew it had to be a customer who had lost their way. I hurried out there, anxious to avoid questions about the coffin.

A woman, dressed in a black designer suit and white silk blouse, was standing on the staircase, her arm extended on the wooden rail. She was tall and slender, hair the same shade of ebony as mine, but while mine curled, hers was long and sleek. Her eyes, dark and inquisitive, observed me thoughtfully.

"The bakery is out this way." I pointed in the direction of the kitchen.

"Sorry. I must have gotten mixed up. I'm looking for Sally Muccio," she said in a deep ethereal voice.

"Hi, I'm Sally. Can I help you with something?"

Her dark eyes glowered. "Let's start with your sister."

Something told me this wasn't a social call. "I'm sorry?"

The woman's snow queen smile created a cold chill to the very core of my being. "Suppose you cut to the chase, and tell me where your sister is hiding."

"Who the hell are you?" Josie was standing behind me.

The woman wrinkled her delicate nose at Josie. "Excuse me. This doesn't concern you, honey."

Josie stepped forward angrily, but I grabbed her by the arm. I forced myself to remain calm, but dread descended over me anyway. "Well, how about you tell us something, then? Who are you, and what do you want with Gianna?"

The woman gave me an apprising look. "I'm Victoria."

A warning the size of a church bell clanged inside my head as the next question fell out of my mouth. "Victoria who?"

"Victoria Napoli. I'm Bernardo's grieving widow."

CHAPTER FOURTEEN

———

Josie's eyes went wide with alarm, and I had no doubt that they mirrored my own. *Keep calm, Sal.* Great. More members of the delightful Napoli family. This was just what we needed.

"Where is the little hussy?" Victoria demanded. "I'm guessing that she's living here now that her place went up in flames."

Grandma Rosa stepped into the room, a stern look upon her face. "Do not speak about my granddaughter this way. When you come into this house, you show respect."

Victoria looked my grandmother up and down, and I half expected a nasty retort, but instead, her face went crimson. "I'm sorry." She covered her eyes with her hand. "I just don't know what to do anymore."

Grandma Rosa raised a coffee cup. "Would you like some?" she asked Victoria. "Or some cheesecake perhaps? Come into the dining room."

Victoria gave Grandma Rosa a genuine, warm smile. It was impossible to be angry when you were around my grandmother. Plus, I knew firsthand the wonders her cheesecake could work. "Some coffee would be great, thank you."

We walked through the living room together, and I saw Victoria's head do a double take when she spotted the coffin, but she said nothing.

"Would you like to sit down?" I stammered, not knowing what else to say.

She nodded. Grandma Rosa handed her a cup and then set out cream and sugar. Victoria glanced at my left hand, studying my one-carat, marquis diamond engagement ring.

"Nice gem. How long have you been married?"

I twisted the ring on my finger, unable to keep the smile off my face as I thought of Mike. "The wedding's next month."

She snorted. "Do yourself a favor, honey. Head for the hills. All men are jerks."

Well, we know your husband was. "Why do you want to see Gianna? What did she ever do, except try to help your husband?"

Victoria glanced around the room. "Is she here?"

"No," I replied.

"I don't believe you," she said tightly.

I must have looked annoyed because Grandma Rosa reached over and laid her hand on top of mine in an attempt to silence me. "My granddaughter is not here. And she had nothing to do with your husband's death."

Victoria toyed with her spoon. "She was the last person to see Bernardo alive. I know he was carrying on with her, so I'm guessing she knows where the money is. *My* money, to be exact."

I clenched my teeth in annoyance. Everyone was staking their claim to this sum of money that was rumored to be in the million-dollar range. I was sorry the man was dead, but why did he have to die in *my* bakery? Gianna's life was now in danger because of it.

"I thought that was Luigi's money," Josie commented. "At least that's what he told us when he stopped by for a chat."

Victoria stared at us over the rim of her coffee cup. "My father-in-law came to see you? It figures."

"Look," I said. "I don't know what's going on with your family, but let me reassure you that Gianna was *not* carrying on with your husband. Her job was to represent him in court. That's all." *And she didn't even want to do that.*

Her expression was amused. "Boy, are you naïve. Bernardo always got what he wanted as far as women were concerned. He was planning to run away with her. He even admitted it to me when I confronted him earlier that same day."

Grandma Rosa studied Victoria for a moment. "Perhaps that is what he told you, yes. But Gianna did not even like your husband."

"Grandma," I hissed in warning.

She shook her head at me. "No, Sally, Mrs. Napoli should know the truth. Gianna thought your husband was slum."

Victoria stared at my grandmother, confused. "We have a beautiful home, in a nice part of town. You must have our house mixed up with someone else's."

"She meant to say scum," I explained.

"Oh," Victoria nodded. "Well, that part's true enough." She wrung her hands together in obvious distress. "Look. He was a piece of crap, I'll admit. He screwed around on me many times. I can overlook that, though. I just want my money. Hell, I earned it from having to put up with him."

"How long were you married?" Josie asked.

"About two years." She sniffed at the air. "Smells like something's burning."

"My chocolate chips!" Josie screeched and made a beeline for the kitchen. I heard her slam the oven door and start cursing. Burned to a crisp, no doubt. The entire time we ran the bakery, Josie had never burned one cookie. Working here though was an entirely different matter.

Grandma Rosa spoke up. "Why would you stay with such a man when he was unfaithful to you?"

My thoughts exactly. True, my ex had cheated on me too, but as soon as I'd discovered his indiscretions, I'd walked out the door and never looked back.

I figured Victoria would be offended by the question, but if so, she didn't act like it. Instead, she laughed. "You're such a cute old lady. You remind me of my grandmother, rest her soul. Yeah, I've asked myself that question many times. Bernardo was handsome but a total bum. He had no interest in working for a living and loved being involved in the so-called family business. It made him feel powerful. He enjoyed seeing the look of fear in people's eyes. Sure, I could have left if I wanted to, but I chose to stay."

"Why?" Josie was standing in the doorway, arms folded across her chest.

Victoria sipped her coffee. "Because I knew about the money he was lifting from Luigi and wanted my share. Plus, the sex was great."

Ew. A mental picture I could do without.

"Mamma mia." Grandma Rosa shook her head.

"Do you have any children?" I hoped the answer was no, for the children's sake, at least.

Victoria shook her head. "No brats for me. No time, no interest in wiping snotty noses." She eyed me curiously. "I bet you want at least a dozen. You look the type."

"Thank you." I considered her remark a compliment.

She stretched her legs out underneath the table, obviously growing more comfortable with us. "Listen. All I want is what's rightfully mine. Bernardo asked me for a divorce right before he died. I told him I'd go along with it if he split the dough with me, and he agreed. I should have known he'd pull this crap. Typical."

I stared at her in amazement. "Well, somehow I don't think he planned on dying."

"Yeah, but someone else did, and now they have my money. Who knows—maybe Luigi ordered him killed. Sergio or Rufus might have had something to do with it too."

"What's a Rufus?" Josie asked.

"He's Sergio's goon of a pal. Built like an army tank. He goes everywhere with Sergio. Those two will do whatever Luigi says. Sergio would never dare risk his father's disapproval."

Grandma Rosa spoke up. "So Bernardo was the black horse of the family."

"Sheep, Rosa," Josie offered.

Victoria barked with laughter and smiled at my grandmother. "You are so adorable. Yeah, that's about right. First, he tried to win Luigi's approval then finally realized it was impossible. So he started embezzling from the company. But he got a little careless, and then, once you add in tax evasion, the stupid jerk was on the verge of getting himself locked up." She smiled. "And just when Bernardo thought he was scot-free, he goes and gets himself killed. Funny how that happens, huh?"

Josie and I exchanged a glance. Was Victoria responsible for her husband's death? She certainly had a motive. Then again, she was only one of a long list of people who were happy to dance on Bernardo's grave.

Victoria rose. "I have to go. The wake is tonight, and people will be stopping by my house. Look. I'm not trying to cause trouble for your sister. I just want what's rightfully mine."

I thought my family was abnormal sometimes, but they paled in comparison to the Napolis.

"Tell your sister I'll be waiting to hear from her. If he told her where he put the money, she'd be wise to cooperate. I'm the least of Gianna's worries. If Luigi finds her, he won't exactly ask questions first, if you get my drift."

Oh, I got her drift all right. She gave us all a curt little nod and crossed the hallway into the living room. I heard a small squeak, and Josie and I both rushed in. I had a pretty good idea of what had caused her startled outcry.

Dad was sitting at the computer desk, talking in earnest to someone. Mrs. Quincy from across the street was stretched out inside the coffin, her hands folded over her stomach.

Oh no. My business was being run in the middle of a loony bin.

"Domenic, what did you do to her?" Josie demanded.

Mrs. Quincy's eyes flickered open. She waved at me and Josie then turned her head back in my father's direction, making no attempt to sit up. "This is mighty comfortable, Domenic. Will it last for an eternity, though?"

"Why don't I go get you some coffee, and we'll talk about it?" My father lumbered to his feet. "You stay right where you are."

As I stared at the bewildered look on Victoria's face, I found myself wondering once again how to keep customers away from the living room. Should we put up another sign to redirect traffic? I doubted anything would work, but hey, we could always try.

Victoria visibly shuddered when my father waved to her and walked into the kitchen. She turned to stare at Mrs. Quincy lying in the coffin with her eyes closed then finally found her voice. "This place is nuts." She slammed the door behind her.

Josie smacked the palm of her hand against her forehead and started toward the kitchen. "Perhaps we should think about filing for bankruptcy. The bakery is doomed as long as your father is around, Sal."

"I'm here," Sarah called and rushed in through the living room door. She looked frazzled and was wearing a white blouse with a huge stain down the front of it. When Sarah noticed me and my grandmother staring at it, she blushed. "I'm sorry. I spilled coffee on myself during the drive. This day has been a nightmare so far."

Grandma Rosa motioned toward the stairs. "Gianna's clothes are upstairs. You should go to her room and see if you can find another blouse to wear. The apron will not cover that stain."

Sarah frowned. "I-I don't want to impose."

"Oh, it's fine," I said. "Gianna wouldn't care. Go ahead on up."

Sarah started upstairs, and Grandma Rosa returned to the kitchen. I was about to follow her when my cell phone rang. The number was unfamiliar, so I figured it must be business related. "Good morning. Sally's Samples."

"Hey," a deep male voice said. "Is this Sally?"

"Speaking. How can I help you?"

"I was wondering if your bakery made deliveries."

The man was doing a wonderful imitation of an obscene phone caller, his voice just above a whisper and accompanied by a great deal of heavy breathing. I was tempted to disconnect but couldn't afford to turn away potential business. "Well, it depends on your location. I don't have a driver available."

Maybe my father would be willing to help us out. Then again, he might end up scaring off a potential customer if he mentioned this new business venture of his. If Dad stayed home though, he was certain to run off more of our customers. Kind of a lose-lose situation for me.

"I'd like six dozen chocolate chip cookies. Could I have them delivered at one o'clock this afternoon by the hot-looking babe with the flaming hair and temper to match?"

An ice-cold chill ran through me. I was certain I knew who this voice belonged to now. "Um, what's the name and address?"

"Ninety-five Simmons Way. It's a furniture warehouse. Still need the name?" I could tell by his tone that he was taunting me.

Oh, I knew the building all right. It was only about five minutes away from my bakery, but everyone in town knew the business—or should we dare say *operation*—that was run from its location. My suspicions were confirmed. "Give me a moment while I grab a pen and write the address down. Don't go away."

"Look, I know the lady is busy, but it would be nice if she delivered the treats in person," he chuckled. "It's—ah—kind of in her best interest to make the trip. Correction. It would be in your sister's best interest. *Capisce*?"

"I—uh—understand completely. Please hold on so that I can check Josie's schedule. It won't take a minute."

So that was it. They'd found Gianna, or at the very least knew where she was. My hands shook while I covered the receiver. I ran into the kitchen and nudged Josie, who had the mixer going. She was making buttercream frosting for a batch of sugar cookies. She turned it off, wiped her hands on her apron, and looked at me, puzzled. "What's wrong?"

Afraid that the man still might be able to hear me, I whispered in her ear. "I think Sergio's on the phone."

Josie's blue eyes grew large and round. "What the hell does he want?"

I pointed a finger at her chest. "*You.*"

CHAPTER FIFTEEN

————

The day had gotten off to a slow start, but by noon we had sold over three hundred dollars in products. Not bad for our first morning. Grandma Rosa even rang up some sales for us. We kept bumping into each other in the kitchen, but that couldn't be helped. There were also several times that I had to reroute people heading in the direction of the living room and my father's intriguing business.

I was in the middle of making a batch of fudgy delight cookies—vanilla cookies with a droplet of fudge in the center—when a piercing scream filled my ears. Josie was over at the display case, bagging an order for a customer, while Grandma Rosa was talking with one of our neighbors by the cash register. Sarah was on the phone, taking an order.

Fearing the worst, I ran into the living room just as an elderly woman hurried by me, a bag of cookies in hand.

"Mrs. Arnold," Josie asked, "what happened?"

The elderly woman looked like she had just seen a ghost, or more than likely, a fat, balding Italian man sitting beside a coffin. "You people are twisted. I'm never coming here again." She bolted out the screen door, crying.

The other customers in the kitchen exchanged a confused look, but I was confident I knew what had happened.

Josie collected money from her customer and pointed at the screen door. "Be sure to use this exit. We, um, have to make repairs to the other sections of the house today."

"What kind of repairs?" The man she was waiting on asked with interest.

She slammed the register shut. "There are some things around here that just *have* to go."

That was an understatement. My father and his so-called

business venture were beyond repair.

Josie and I entered the living room. My father was seated at his computer desk, engrossed in an article he was reading on his laptop. I glanced at the title of it and winced. "Secret Confessions of a Funeral Director."

"Dad, what did you do to Mrs. Arnold? She said she's never coming back to the bakery again."

He gave me a disbelieving look. "Ah, she was overreacting. I just invited her to take this baby for a little test drive." He patted the lid of the coffin. "Is it my fault it slammed shut while she was inside?"

Josie groaned aloud and threw up her hands. "Domenic, you're killing us."

He laughed. "Hey, you made a funny, Josie."

Ugh. I tried in vain to reason with him. "Dad, I know this is your house. But could you please indulge us for a few days and move that thing out of here? It's really bad for our business."

My father thrust his hands forward. "How can it be bad? You eat in one room, and then you come in here to talk about restful accommodations. Makes perfect sense to me."

If there was one thing I knew, nothing about my father made sense. It never had.

We heard the kitchen screen door open and a man's voice in greeting. Grandma Rosa called to us. "Sally, Josie. Father is here."

She meant Father Grenaldi. We crossed the hallway, went through the dining room, and back into the kitchen. Grandma Rosa chatted with Father as Josie and I got his order ready. The cookies were already made. We only had to box them up.

Father Grenaldi raised his bushy white eyebrows as he handed me money. "I haven't seen you in church the last couple of weeks, and the wedding is coming up soon."

"I'm sorry, Father. We'll try to make it this week." I handed him his change. Sometimes I still wondered why Mike and I hadn't run off and eloped. My mother's side of the family was devout Catholic, and she insisted we needed to get married in the church to "cancel out my first disastrous marriage." Yes, those were her exact words. It didn't matter to her that Colin was already dead. Maria Muccio's mind, like my father's, was a mystery I had never managed to solve.

Mike wasn't Catholic but agreed to go along with a church wedding for my sake. We were supposed to be attending mass every week, but as Sunday was our only day off, it was difficult to make it sometimes. Not to mention how much we enjoyed lazy Sunday mornings in bed.

"Sal," my mother called. I heard the click-clack of her high heels on the floor and turned, just as Josie gasped out loud. My mother was dressed in a bright orange bikini that barely covered the necessities. She turned around, giving us the whole effect. I shut my eyes in embarrassment and wished I could disappear. My mother was wearing a thong. Even though I was more than twenty years younger, I never would have dreamed of wearing such a getup. Then again, I wouldn't look nearly as good as she did, either.

"What do you think? I'm going to wear this in the swimsuit competition. They asked specifically for us to wear thongs. I got to choose the color, though. Do you think it's too revealing?"

Grandma Rosa clucked her tongue against the roof of her mouth in disapproval. "My dear daughter, there is nothing that it does *not* reveal. You might as well be naked."

My mother caught sight of Father Grenaldi standing there and gave him a little finger wave. For once, she looked embarrassed. "Oh, hi, Father. Sorry. I didn't see you. Excuse my skin." She giggled.

"Excuse her lack of judgement," Grandma Rosa added.

Father Grenaldi stood there, frozen in place, his eyes bugging out of his head. He looked at my mother like he'd just seen the pearly white gates himself. His face turned whiter than his hair, and the boxes of cookies slipped from his arms.

"Father?" Grandma Rosa waved a hand in front of his face.

Father Grenaldi gave a small cry before he pitched forward, and his head crashed onto the vinyl floor.

* * *

"We've got to get out of there." Josie grumbled as she settled herself behind the minivan's wheel. "Your parents are driving the business into the ground."

I couldn't help thinking that my father might be able to use that as a slogan for his potential business. *What the heck is wrong with me?*

After we'd managed to revive Father Grenaldi and make sure that he was all right, we'd left him sitting in the dining room with Grandma Rosa having coffee, a dazed expression on his face. Grandma Rosa had banned my mother from the kitchen, so she and my father had gone upstairs to "watch television." Like we were all too stupid to figure out what they were really doing.

Since things had settled down a bit, Josie and I had left to make a special delivery, or at least that was what we'd told my grandmother and Sarah. Grandma Rosa had glanced at us sharply but said nothing. I had a sneaky suspicion we weren't fooling her.

I pulled my seat belt around me. "What can I do? There's currently no rental space in town that would work for us."

"Maybe we'll have to run the bakery out of a basement somewhere." Josie took a left at the end of the street. "I'd work just about anywhere right now to get away from your loony parents. Anyhow, what exactly did Sergio say on the phone?"

"He wanted to know if we made deliveries," I said. "And he asked that you be the one to bring the cookies. 'The hot-looking babe with the flaming hair and temper' were his exact words. He said it was in Gianna's best interest that we come. I don't like it. What if they found her?"

"If he asked for me, he won't be happy to see you tagging along," Josie pointed out.

I stared at her in disbelief. "Yeah, like I'd really let you go alone. Right."

She shrugged. "I can handle him. Don't worry."

"These aren't your average customers. The whole family is dangerous, Jos. Luigi wants his money back, and nothing or no one is going to get in his way."

"The warehouse is right across the street from the diner. We'll stay outside. He can't do anything to us in broad daylight."

The whole thing made me uneasy. What did they want from us? Did they know something about Bernardo that could hurt Gianna further? What if they followed us last night? Holy cow, I'd never even thought of that. "I should have asked Brian to come with us."

Josie pulled the van up in front of the building. "Oh sure. That definitely would make them happy if we brought a cop along." She placed the van in park and unbuttoned the bottom three buttons on her pink blouse and tied the ends together, revealing her flat stomach.

I watched her, mystified. "What the heck are you doing?"

Josie held a compact in front of herself and applied bright red lipstick to her mouth then fussed with her hair. "Trying to look the bimbo part. Might as well give Sergio what he wants."

"I *know* what he wants. You're playing with fire." *Great.* I winced at my unintended use of the word.

She winked. "A little sweet talk and I'll have Sergio eating out of my hand. I know his type. The guy is a two-faced liar. It wouldn't surprise me if he killed Bernardo and is trying to pin it on Gianna." She opened the door. "I'll get the truth out of him. Consider this a form of recreation."

Unconvinced, I got out of the vehicle. I didn't like this game at all. Sergio was dangerous, and the stakes were high. Plus, what if he had that pal of his with him? What was his name again—Ruckus?

We removed the two boxes of cookies from the back of the van. As Josie slammed the door and we turned around, Sergio appeared with another man at his side. I yelped, and we both jumped about ten feet in the air.

Sergio smiled. "Take it easy, ladies. No reason to be afraid of us."

No, not at all. Just a wolf in sheep's clothing—or rather a thousand-dollar Gucci three-piece suit.

"Um, it's sixty dollars for the cookies," I stammered. "We don't take personal checks."

Sergio reached into his wallet and handed me a hundred-dollar bill. "Keep the change, sweetheart." He turned to Josie, and his dark eyes widened with delight. "Looking good today, red."

Josie giggled appreciatively. She played the game better than most, but I knew deep down that she was nervous. She'd even removed her wedding ring while we'd been in the van. If Rob found out about this stunt, there would be hell to pay. "Thanks," she said.

Sergio tried to put an arm around her, but I chose that moment to thrust the boxes of cookies into his hands. "We really appreciate your business."

He glared at me but said nothing as he turned and handed the cookies to the giant standing next to him. Sergio's friend was at least six-and-a-half feet tall and weighed well over three hundred pounds. The arms that clutched at the boxes were the size of tree trunks. Cold, gray eyes of steel observed me with interest and also chilled me to the bone. His head was shaven, but he sported a slim brown ponytail that hung down his ape-sized back.

"Who's your friend?" I already had an inkling of who the man was. This was my attempt to stall Sergio from putting the moves on Josie.

Sergio nodded to the brute. "This is my buddy, Rufus." He poked his friend in the side and then squinted through the sunlight at me. "Rufus wants a girlfriend."

Rufus grunted and nodded at me. "She'll do."

Yikes. I opened my mouth, but no audible sound came out. I stared helplessly at Josie who gave me an encouraging nod as she went into full bimbo mode. "Ain't he cute, Sal?"

Adorable. "Um, we have to get back to our bakery. Maybe you could let us know what kind of information you have for us?"

Sergio placed an arm around Josie's shoulders, and I watched as she tensed slightly. She cut her eyes to me and then smiled at Sergio with fake adoration.

"I think we got off on the wrong foot the other day," she said coyly. "I didn't realize at first how cute you were even though Gianna told us so. Right, Sal?"

Well played. "Is my sister inside the warehouse?" What if they had her tied up in there? My stomach quaked with terror at the thought.

Sergio shook his head. "Haven't seen her since the trial. Look, I know your sister ain't responsible for Bernardo's death. My dad only cares about getting his money back."

I gave him what I hoped was an incredulous look. "This is why you wanted to see us? To tell us something we already knew? I thought Gianna was here."

Okay, so perhaps sarcasm had seeped into my speech just a tad too much. Sergio removed his arm from Josie's shoulders and narrowed his eyes at me. "Don't disrespect me, sweetie."

I shivered in the hot sun as I stared into his enormous, dark eyes. Alarm bells were clanging in my head. "Sorry, but everyone knows my sister is a good person. There's no way Gianna took the money, and she definitely didn't hurt Bernardo."

"I wouldn't care if she had," Sergio answered. "I just want the dough back. To hell with his dead body." He wrapped his arm around Josie again, and she giggled on cue.

This was starting to make me nauseous. "We really should be going."

"I'm gonna make you ladies a deal," Sergio said. He drew Josie closer to him. Nervous, I glanced around. There wasn't another person in sight. Even the diner seemed strangely desolate for this time of the day. "If this little fox goes out with me, I'll talk to my dad and convince him to back off your sister."

Rufus placed a hand on my shoulder, and I jumped. Okay, I would have tried to jump if his hand had not been weighing my entire body down.

Sergio nodded toward his buddy. "And you've got to go out with Rufus."

Rufus smiled down at me. I looked up at him, *way* up. My five-foot-three-inch stature barely reached his stomach. He opened his mouth, and the stench of his breath almost knocked me over. "I like you."

Oh my God. What had we gotten ourselves into?

"Um, that's not good enough," I blurted out to Sergio. "*Everyone* needs to leave Gianna alone. Tell your sister-in-law to back off too."

Sergio's eyes widened. "Victoria came to see you?"

I nodded. "This morning."

Josie tried to wiggle out of his grasp. "Sorry. I'm a bit claustrophobic, big guy."

"Hmm." Sergio eyed us suspiciously. "I wouldn't be surprised if that chick has the money and killed Bernardo for it. He wanted out of the marriage, you know."

"That's what Victoria told us. So you have no idea where the cash is now?" I asked.

"That wench has probably already ripped their house apart looking for the dough, but I'm guessing he didn't put it there. If it's in a bank account somewhere, she'll get first dibs." Sergio scratched his chin thoughtfully. "Looks like someone might have to take care of her too."

Rufus removed his hand from me long enough to crack his knuckles. Fear traveled down to the pit of my stomach as I watched him with equal parts of fascination and horror.

"How did Bernardo even get the money?" Josie asked.

Sergio snorted. "He's been ripping off my dad's clients for years. It was his job to collect. Then he started skimming off the top, telling people the rates had gone up. By the time we got wind of his scheme, he'd already been arrested. Pop thinks your sister staged the whole thing with that juror just to help get Bernardo off."

Furious, I stepped forward. "That's a lie. Gianna would never sink that low."

Sergio's face turned crimson, and he narrowed his eyes at me. "Are you insulting my family?"

With an uneasy look at me, Josie pulled him back in her arms. "My," she cooed, touching his arms. "You're so strong. I need someone like you to take care of me."

Good God. This lunacy had to end.

Josie's bimbo act bit appeared to be working. Sergio gazed into Josie's eyes and didn't bother to give me a second glance. "I can't believe a broad like you hasn't been snapped up already. Most of the chicks around here are married with a litter of kids."

"Ew," Josie frowned. "I'm never having kids. They'd cramp my style." She giggled again while I struggled to keep from rolling my eyes at her. "I'm afraid Sal can't go out with your handsome friend here, though. She's engaged to someone else."

I knew that Josie was trying to protect me from the brute, but perhaps that wasn't the way to go.

Rufus grunted in agitation, obviously not appreciating Josie's response. His enormous hand tightened around my arm again, encircling it in a grip that was both uncomfortable and made movement impossible.

"Too bad," Sergio shook his head. "Rufus don't like to share."

Uh-oh. I was no match for this goon. I tried to calm my nerves and focus on why we were really here. "Did Bernardo have any enemies?" *Outside his family, that is.*

Sergio and Rufus both laughed at this. It was nice to know that I'd provided some entertainment for them.

"Sweetheart, when you're in a family of power like ours, there's plenty of enemies," Sergio said. "People always want what you got. Sometimes they didn't like us putting the squeeze on them for money they owed." He gestured at Rufus. "Sometimes Rufus has to get ugly."

I had news for Sergio—Rufus was already there.

The goon smiled at me and then bobbed his head up and down. "Gotta do what I gotta do."

I attempted a laugh, but it came out sounding more like a frightened puppy's whine. "Well guys, it's been fun, but we need to get going. Let's arrange that double date sometime soon, okay?"

Sergio's eyes glittered in the sun. "Hey, I think we should have it now. No time like the present, right? He grabbed Josie's arm and pulled her toward the front door of the building. "Come on. Let me give you the guided tour, dollface."

Panic gripped me, almost as tight as Rufus's arm. These two characters were lower than pond scum. I wriggled around, trying to get the ogre to loosen his hold, which he only tightened in response to my struggling.

"You're cute," Rufus said. His voice sounded like Patrick Star's from SpongeBob SquarePants, and I guessed his mentality was spot-on as well.

How the heck are we going to get out of this mess?

"Excuse me." A deep authoritative voice growled from behind us. "Get your hands off her right now, or you're going to lose them."

I gulped, almost afraid to turn around. But I already knew who the voice belonged to.

Mike was standing there, arms folded across his broad chest, with that furious, jealous scowl on his face that I hadn't seen since our high school days.

This was not going to end well.

CHAPTER SIXTEEN

"All right." Mike's voice was calm, but his eyes continued to flash angry, blue sparks. "Suppose you two tell me what the hell is going on here?"

When I'd introduced Mike as my fiancé, Sergio and Rufus had decided to retreat back into the warehouse—in a bit of a haste too. Something told me we hadn't seen the last of them, though.

As usual, when upset, I started to babble. "I didn't want Josie to go alone. You know I didn't want that goon around me, but they said it was in Gianna's best interest for us to come here. We had to find out what they knew."

Mike closed his eyes for a moment. I suspected he was counting to ten—or maybe ten thousand. "You've been snooping again."

"We didn't have a choice. They said—"

He clutched me tightly by the shoulders. The anger was gone from his eyes and had been replaced with concern. "Listen to me." He nodded toward Josie. "Both of you. Stay away from that family. They are nothing but bad news. Let the cops handle this mess."

"Gianna's life could be in danger," I sputtered. "They think she has the money. Bernardo stole it from his stepfather's so-called business."

He sighed and looked toward the sky, as if praying for help from God and the heavens above to talk some sense into me. "Did you hear what I said? The Napolis are criminals. They're a hazard to your health. And now that loser is interested in Josie?" He stared at her outfit in disbelief. "What the hell would Rob say if he knew about this?"

Josie's eyes went wide with horror, and she quickly

adjusted her shirt. Rob and Mike had become good friends since Mike and I had started dating again. In fact, he was going to be Mike's best man at our wedding.

"You can't tell him," Josie pleaded. "He'd go nuts."

"I don't blame him," Mike said. "How do you think I felt when I saw that freak touching Sal?" He traced a finger down the side of my face. "I don't want anything to happen to you. Promise me you'll stay away from those goons—both of you."

"You're not making this easy for me," I choked out. "She's my little sister. I have to protect her."

"And I will protect you both," Mike said. "Get her to come home. She can't hide out forever. I know you, Sal. You're afraid everyone will be in danger if she comes back to your parents' house. Gianna can stay with us."

I thought I might burst into tears. "Really?"

He wove his fingers through my hair. "Of course, really. She's my family too, or will be in about three weeks. I know how much you love her. Why didn't you just ask me?"

Suddenly, I felt foolish. To be honest, I thought maybe Mike wouldn't have wanted to share our space with anyone. "I—I didn't know how you'd feel about it."

He gave me that sexy, lopsided smile of his. "As long as she's not coming on our honeymoon with us, it's fine."

"I don't think that will be a problem. Say, what are you doing over here anyway?"

Mike's smile faded. "I ran over to grab a sandwich from the diner. I'm glad I did since my timing turned out to be perfect." He pursed his lips together. "You're like the Pied Piper of Colwestern. Except instead of kids, there's always thugs following you around. Or the occasional murdering psychopath."

It was hard to argue with that statement. "We'll stay away from them. I promise."

"Good." He leaned down to kiss me. "At least there was one bright spot to my crazy day. Getting to see you."

I inhaled the scent of him. The front of his shirt was stained with tar, but the aroma of this morning's aftershave lingered on him, and as I looked into those gorgeous eyes and his handsome face, the need to be alone with him was overwhelming. I sensed he felt it too, but we both had other obligations to fulfill.

"This is a long way to come for a sandwich. Webster's Restaurant is at least twenty minutes away. Why didn't you eat there?"

The color rose in his tanned face. "Oh, I was over here talking to a potential customer about another job. Not sure I'm going to take it, though." He tweaked my nose. "How's business at the shop today?"

"It's going well," I said. "When my parents aren't around, that is."

"Hang in there. It won't be forever." He cradled my face in his hands and kissed me again. "See you tonight, princess."

"Try to get home early." I hoped I didn't sound desperate, but I really wanted to spend some time with him.

"I'll try." He nodded to Josie. "Be good. And stay out of trouble."

She smiled. "Thanks, Mike."

I watched him make his way into the diner before we got into Josie's van. She let out a huge sigh of relief. "I'm so glad he showed up when he did. I was getting a little nervous, Sal."

"You and me both."

"I'm not as good at the bimbo act as I used to be," Josie admitted. "After four kids, it tends to wear off. Now what do we do?"

I adjusted the visor against the sunlight. "We'd better get back to the house. After we close up tonight, we'll go back out and get Gianna. Can you come with me?"

Josie started the engine. "Rob's working the night shift, so that's fine. Hey, do you mind if we stop at Glenn's Jewelers while we're out here? I've been trying to get over and pick up my gold bracelet for the last week. I had them fix the clasp on it for me."

"Sure, go ahead."

Josie took a left at the end of the street, turned onto the next one, and found a parking space right in front of the jeweler. As I waited for her, I glanced around. The street, like mine, was zoned both residential and commercial. There were a few storefronts in addition to the jeweler on the left side and a couple of two-story apartment buildings on the right.

I noticed Mike's truck parked a few spots up from us. I had wondered where his truck was when we spotted him by the diner and was curious as to what type of a job he was considering. I knew we needed the money, but he was cramming too much in before our honeymoon. He wasn't getting any sleep, poor guy. And I, in turn, wasn't getting any romance.

I noticed a petite woman about my age come out of the house where Mike's truck was parked in front of. She was slim but curvy in all the right spots, with long, blonde hair piled high on her head in a messy knot. She wore a red bikini top with a pair of tight, white jean shorts that enhanced her tanned, slender legs. As I watched, she sauntered over to the mailbox and removed her mail. She continued to stand there, opening envelopes and reading their contents. I knew I'd seen her before, but I couldn't remember where.

Josie returned to the van. "Cripes. I know Glenn does good work, but forty dollars for a broken clasp? Seems a little high to me."

I pointed at the woman, who was now climbing the steps back to her house. "She looks familiar. Do you know her?"

Josie drove by the house, glancing sideways at the woman as she entered the building. "That's Marla Channing. Remember the woman who came into the bakery early one morning before we opened and said she was on her way home after a long night of work and needed something sweet?"

The words jarred my memory. "The one wearing the sequined cowboy boots and the gold miniskirt." A wardrobe my mother would probably kill for. "What does she do?"

"She calls it an entertainment venue, but it's actually a strip club over in Colgate."

My mouth went dry as sawdust. "So why is my fiancé parked in front of her house?"

"You don't have to worry," Josie said. "If Mike's there, I'm sure it's strictly professional. He has no interest in her anymore. Plus, he's the one who broke it off."

My mouth fell open. "He *dated* her? When?"

Josie paused to consider. "A few months before you came back home. Maybe a year and a half ago? Rob and I saw them at Ralph's one night. They were sitting at the bar together, and she was all over him. He ended it after a couple of dates. It was never anything serious—well, not for him at least. I heard she took it pretty badly."

It was no secret that Mike had always had more than his fair share of admirers, which included Backseat Brenda in high school. He'd once told me he'd never been able to get seriously involved with anyone else because he still loved me. Of course, that had done wonders for my ego. Still, the seed of doubt was busy planting itself in my head again. Had she lured him here, pretending to need a leaky faucet fixed? "Would she be hiring him for work? Do you think that's why he told me he wasn't sure if he was going to take the job?"

Josie pulled into my parents' driveway and shut the engine off. "Could be. Maybe he was afraid how you'd react if you knew. And for the record, I don't think you have a reason to worry. There's a reason she's an ex. From what I know, Marla's one of those needy, clingy types who suffocates any man she comes in contact with."

"Great. So he may be working for a stalker, then."

She laughed. "Oh, you're acting ridiculous. Besides, he's crazy about you. Please tell me you don't think he's cheating on you."

I exhaled a long, deep breath and counted to three. "I don't know what the heck is wrong with me." Then I told her about the fortune cookie message.

She wagged a finger in my face. "You see? I told you we should get rid of those things. They're playing with your head. Now, listen carefully. They. Don't. Mean. Anything."

"How can you say that?" I argued. "Think of all the times the messages have come true."

We opened the screen door and entered the kitchen. Grandma Rosa was waiting on a customer, and Sarah was rolling up fortunes inside the cookies. Great. Perfect timing.

Josie reached for a piece of waxed paper and grabbed two cookies off the tray. She held one out to me. "I am going to prove to you once and for all that these things are a bunch of crap."

"What's going on?" Sarah asked.

"Fortune cookies are controlling Sal's life," Josie

grinned.

Heat flooded my face in embarrassment. "That's not true. But you do have to admit the coincidence is a bit strange at times."

"It's like reading a horoscope," Josie said. "They're written in such a manner that makes you *think* it could happen. Your mind does the rest." Josie didn't write the fortunes for the cookies. We bought them from a novelty shop because it was easier. Still, even the one I'd received at the restaurant had been peculiar, not to mention accurate.

My best friend handed me a cookie and then cracked hers open. She snorted and waved the paper at me. "It says *Watch your step*."

I grinned. "Is that the fortune cookie talking or you?"

"Maybe it means I should learn to keep my big trap shut." She threw the piece of paper on the floor with a mock look of disgust. "And that's my Mrs. Gavelli imitation."

We all laughed, even Grandma Rosa.

Josie gestured to the cookie I was holding. "Go ahead— open it."

Grandma Rosa, Sarah, and Josie were all watching me. Reluctantly, I broke the cookie apart and read the message to myself then cut my eyes to Josie. "They don't mean anything, eh?"

Josie's mouth opened in surprise. "What's it say?"

I read aloud. "*If you have something good in your life, don't let it go.*" I shivered inwardly. "Okay, point well taken." I'd once doubted Mike ten years ago, and it had changed my life forever. I wasn't about to let that happen again.

Josie was silent for a second. "Well, I have to admit it's good advice for you. But I still don't think there's anything to those stupid strips of paper." She gestured to Sarah. "You open one."

Sarah stared at her like a frightened kitten. "Uh, no thanks."

Josie tied an apron on. "Do you think there's any truth to them, Sarah?"

Sarah's delicate complexion turned crimson. "No. They're silly. I think a person should rely on themselves to make their own fortune."

I exchanged glances with Josie. Sarah was always so timid. This might be a sign that she was ready to take charge of her life. Maybe it related to the new job, or perhaps she was dating a new man.

"I'm impressed," Josie grinned. "That sounded very philosophical."

Sarah's blush deepened. "I've just decided that I need to control my own destiny from now on. It's clear that I can't depend on anyone else. Everything is up to me."

Josie reached for another cookie and handed it to my grandmother, who was watching us in silent amusement. "Come on, Rosa. Your turn."

My grandmother wrinkled her nose at Josie. "You know that I do not bother with those *pazza* things." She directed a warning look at me. "Remember what I told you about them the other day."

"This is just an experiment," Josie argued, "to prove to Sal that they're useless. Come on. Indulge me."

My grandmother gave Josie an annoyed look then grunted and took the cookie. She broke it apart and read the message. "*A pleasant surprise is coming your way.*"

"See? She got a good one." Josie grinned at me.

"Oh, for cripes sake," I muttered. "Are you done embarrassing me for the day?"

Josie laughed and turned to throw the cookie into the garbage. Her foot turned slightly and collided with the garbage pail, causing her to lose her balance. She fell to the floor and yelped, reaching out to take the pail along with her.

Grandma Rosa and I were both at her side in a second. "Are you okay?"

She got to her feet slowly, putting weight on the arm that I held out to her. "I think so. I might have twisted my ankle but nothing serious."

I folded my arms across my chest. "*Watch your step.* What an interesting message."

"Oh, shut up." Josie winced in pain. "I'm still not convinced. You're so obsessed with those cookies that now you've got them working against me too."

I threw my hands up in the air. "Yes, I've been plotting the whole thing all along. It's my fault. I confess."

We heard the living room door slam, and I sighed. "Great. I don't want the customers coming in through there. I'd better go steer them this way before Dad offers them a nap in the coffin."

"Not to worry," Grandma Rosa said. "Your mama and papa have gone out. She had her bathing suit competition for that *pazza* contest of hers." She shook her head. "My daughter, at her age, parading around in almost nothing for the world to see. Where did I go wrong?"

"Heck," Josie said. "If I've got a body like hers at that age, you can bet I'll be showing it off too."

I stuck my tongue out at her playfully. "Rob wouldn't let you."

She snorted. "Well, that's true enough. He doesn't like me sharing my assets with the entire world."

I laughed and crossed through the dining room, already wracking my brain for some excuse to tell this customer as to why there was a coffin in the room. My father did enjoy making life difficult for us.

I stopped dead in my tracks when I came face-to-face with the so-called customer. There was no doubt in my mind that this was the pleasant surprise Grandma Rosa's cookie had warned of.

My sister.

CHAPTER SEVENTEEN

———

I rushed forward and threw my arms around Gianna. "Are you okay?"

She nodded and buried her face in my hair. "I'm sorry, Sal. I know you wanted me to stay at the casino, but I couldn't do it. I have to tell the police what I know. I couldn't live with myself otherwise."

I drew back and examined her face. A hint of color had returned to her cheeks, and the dark circles underneath her eyes were less prominent. "You don't have anything to be sorry about. I was wrong to ask you to stay there. That's not who you are. In fact, Josie and I were coming for you tonight."

Gianna pursed her lips together and nodded. "I thought about what you said. I've worked too darn hard to let anyone take this away from me. Everything's going to be fine. I've already called my supervisor and told him what happened. I said I'd talk to the police as well."

"With me, right there by your side."

She grinned. "You totally rock. Hey, you don't happen to have any of those Dutch chocolate cookies on hand, do you? I need chocolate so badly right now."

"I think that can be arranged." I looped my arm through hers, and we walked into the kitchen together. Josie was packing dough to store in the freezer, and Sarah was washing dishes. Josie shrieked when she saw us and started over, limping.

She threw her arms around Gianna. "I'm so glad you're back, kiddo."

Gianna hugged her and then glanced down at Josie's foot. "Did you hurt yourself?"

"Yeah," I chuckled. "She didn't watch her step."

Josie narrowed her eyes at me but said nothing.

"Come," Grandma Rosa said to Gianna. "Let us go into the dining room and talk there." Gianna wrapped an arm around my grandmother's waist while I grabbed some cookies from the display case and placed them on a paper plate. I left Sarah in the kitchen to wait on any customers that might happen along.

I filled Gianna in on our meeting with Victoria and our fun datefest with Rufus and Sergio. Her face turned pale. "I told you I didn't want you involved in this mess, Sal. It's my problem."

"Not so," I argued. "Someone wanted Bernardo dead, and my bakery suffered in the process. I already have a vested interest, so to speak. Hey, did Bernardo ever happen to tell you about any other enemies he might have had?"

"Outside of his family, that is," Josie murmured as she set a cup of coffee down in front of my sister.

Gianna shook her head. "Honestly, it didn't seem like he had fans anywhere. When you extort money from innocent people for your own benefit, there's a good chance no one's going to like you very much. He did talk about his stepfather a few times. He said they'd never had a good relationship. And he mentioned there were problems with his wife. That may have been to judge my interest in him, which I should have caught at the time. I figured they might divorce."

I folded my arms on the table. "Did he come on to you during the trial? There must have been many circumstances when you found yourself alone with him."

Gianna reached for a cookie. "He didn't try to get physical until that night in my apartment, but there were a couple of weird moments. Once, he asked me if I had a boyfriend. Another time he mentioned that I looked beautiful, but I had no idea he was entertaining notions about running away with me. I mean, why would I think he was interested?"

"No reason," I said smoothly. "Bernardo was a lot of things, but he certainly wasn't blind."

Gianna blushed and spoke in her ever modest way. "Oh, Sal. You're just being ridiculous."

"We found out that Bernardo has children from a previous relationship," Josie said. "Did he mention that to you?"

Gianna finished chewing the cookie and reached for

another. "He never said a word. I'm not surprised though. Probably your classic deadbeat dad." Her hand flew to her mouth. "Oh jeez. I can't believe I just said that."

It made me sad to think of children growing up without a parent. My thoughts shifted to Mike and his awful upbringing—a father who had deserted him at the age of five, and a stepfather who'd smacked him around whenever the mood struck. I'd witnessed a couple of those incidents myself before he too had split on Mike and his mother. Sure, my parents were a couple of oddballs, but at least my childhood had been a happy one. Despite their eccentric ways, I'd never doubted their love for me or Gianna. And of course, Grandma Rosa was in a class all by herself.

Gianna turned to Grandma. "You don't think Mom and Dad would mind if I move back in to my old bedroom for a while, do you? Unless Dad's already using it as an embalming room or something like that."

I laughed and placed a hand on her arm. "You're going to spend the night at my house."

She raised her eyebrows. "No way. I don't want to intrude. I'm sure Mike would be thrilled about having a third wheel around."

"It was Mike's idea," I said. "We'd both feel better if we could keep an eye on you. That Luigi character and his slimy son are dangerous. Mom and Dad mean well and would try to keep you safe, but then again, they *are* Mom and Dad."

Grandma Rosa grunted. "What am I, chopped kidney? I would help keep my granddaughter safe too."

Gianna glanced at her, amused. "You mean liver, Grandma."

"Whatever." Grandma Rosa thrust her finger in my direction. "Don't I keep you safe from Nicoletta?"

She had a point there. "No one will get to her with Mike around. Besides, we have an alarm system." I rose from the table. "I'm going to see if Sarah needs any help. Be right back."

Sarah was alone in the kitchen, sweeping the floor. She turned her head when she heard me approach.

"Sally, I was just coming to get you. I have to leave. Julie's babysitter has another commitment this afternoon, and I can't find anyone else."

"Of course, Sarah. Please text me later, and let me know how she's doing. I hope it's nothing serious."

Sarah shook her head. "No, it's just a slight fever. Julie will be fine." She grabbed her purse from inside one of the kitchen cabinets and then looked up at me again, the color rising in her cheeks. "I'm sorry to have to tell you this, but tomorrow's got to be my last day."

Shoot. This was a major disappointment since I still needed her. "I thought you were going to stay through Saturday?"

Sarah lowered her eyes to the floor. "I know I said I would and had planned to, but it's not possible. I'm so sorry. With Julie being sick, plus the new job, I need a couple of days to regroup before I start work on Monday. I'd also like to do something special with Julie. I feel like I've been neglecting her lately."

I was overcome with pity for the woman. "Of course, Julie has to come first. It's just—well, I can't tell you how much I've appreciated having you here. We're sorry to see you leave. Plus, I have to confess that I'm really going to miss that beautiful little girl of yours."

She smiled. "Julie adores you. You're going to make a wonderful mother someday."

My cheeks warmed at the compliment. That was my greatest hope. "Thank you. Don't worry—I'll have your check ready for you tomorrow."

"Thanks, Sally. I'll see you in the morning." Sarah started for the door then turned back around, her gaze direct with mine. "It's hard to deal with change sometimes, isn't it?"

"It is. But it will all be worth it in the end," I promised.

As I watched her leave, I thought of my own divorce and the decision I'd made to return back home from Florida. Had that really been less than a year ago? It felt like another lifetime.

I poured myself a cup of coffee and reached into the refrigerator for some half-and-half. The container slipped from my grasp and fell to the floor. I ran over to the counter and grabbed some paper towels then got down on all fours, cleaning up the mess. There was a light tap on the screen door. "Come on in."

The screen door opened, but I didn't bother to look up. "Be with you in a second." There was silence from the person standing behind me, and I started to feel a bit self-conscious. I adjusted my blouse and fastened the button that had come undone and looked up. I looked up to see Brian watching me with those brilliant green eyes and a hint of a smile at the corners of his mouth.

Ugh. Great. Now he would think I was putting on a show for him. Before I could get to my feet, he extended a hand, and having no choice, I took it. "Thanks."

"That's the best thing I've seen all day." He grinned.

My face burned from embarrassment. "What are you doing here?"

He folded his arms across his broad chest. "I saw Gianna's car outside. I'd like to talk to her for a minute."

It was difficult not to groan. "Come on, Brian. She just got back. She's planning to go down to the police station tomorrow and tell them everything that happened with Bernardo."

"Ordinarily that would be fine," Brian said. "But I have some questions for her regarding a new development we've run across. It could be associated with the fire and really can't wait."

I didn't like the sound of this, or the grim expression he wore. "She's napping."

He gave me a disbelieving look. "Really?"

"Uh-huh." My sister needed a break from all of this. "But I'll tell her you stopped by."

"Oh, hi, Brian." Gianna walked into the kitchen and placed her cup in the sink.

"Hello, Gianna." He turned back to me with a smug grin. "My, she woke up fast. Didn't she?"

I threw up my hands. "Fine. Come into the dining room. Want some coffee?"

"No thanks." He followed me through the doorway, and even though I couldn't see him, I swear I could feel his eyes raking over me.

Josie's eyes sparkled as she observed him. "Well, look who's here. The man with the fast gun and even faster hands."

Everyone was silent, and I desperately wanted to disappear. I swore to myself I'd get even with my friend later.

Brian's light complexion turned a deep crimson. "Well, I guess I deserved that one." He gestured to the chair next to Grandma Rosa. "Okay if I sit down?"

Grandma Rosa nodded. "It is a free state."

Brian stared at her, baffled, but didn't comment. He removed his hat and hung it on the back of the chair then reached into his shirt pocket and withdrew a plastic bag with something shiny inside. He placed it in front of Gianna. "Have you seen this before?"

She drew her eyebrows together and examined the bag. Inside was a silver chain with the name *Gianna* intertwined through the center. "Yes. It's mine. Mom and Dad gave it to me for my sixteenth birthday. Where'd you get this?"

Brian seemed uncomfortable. "It was in Sally's shed outside the bakery. Next to an empty gas can."

The four of us stared at Brian, dumbfounded. Sure, gasoline had started the fire. Why had I not realized before that it had been *my* gasoline—from the can inside *my* shed—which Rob had filled earlier that same day?

"Why would it have been out in the shed?" Gianna wanted to know. "I haven't even worn that necklace in years. This makes no sense."

Brian raised a hand. "I know you didn't start the fire, Gianna, but you have to admit it seems a bit strange." He turned to me. "Clint called me earlier to say he sent the report to your insurance company. From what was implied, it isn't looking very good for you right now as far as reimbursement goes."

I thought I'd mentally prepared myself for this fact, but a wave of depression still descended over me. "Yeah, I had a feeling this might happen."

"I noticed that the lock on your shed was broken," Brian continued.

"Yes." Maybe if I'd remembered to ask Mike to fix it sooner, none of this would have ever happened. "So anyone could have gone in there and taken the gas to start the fire."

Brian turned to Gianna. "Suppose you start by telling me what happened that night?"

Gianna twisted her hands in her lap. "Bernardo came to find me at Sal's party. He wanted to talk about the trial and the possibility of his being retried. When we got to the bakery, he asked me if I had any aspirin. He followed me up the stairs and—" She colored slightly and bent her head. "He made a pass at me."

Brian's face was stern. "What then? Did you hit him?"

I winced, remembering his comments the other day about the marks on the right side of Bernardo's face. "She didn't kill him. Gianna was only—"

His expression was annoyed as he turned to me. "Please don't interrupt, Sally. I'm only interested in what Gianna has to say."

I bit into my lower lip to hold back a retort. *Well, excuse me.*

"My," Josie grinned. "And here I thought you were interested in *anything* Sal had to offer."

Good grief. She never knew when to quit.

A muscle ticked in Brian's jaw, but he didn't comment. "Go on, Gianna."

"I hit him with a frying pan," she confessed, "but only once. He seemed a little dazed but otherwise fine. Then I threw him out of my apartment and practically down the stairs."

"You saw him leave the building?" Brian asked.

Gianna nodded. "Yes, but I must not have locked the door. I mean, how else could he have gotten back in?"

Brian pursed his lips. "There's more. An unlocked briefcase was found in the trunk of Bernardo's vehicle. We went over it carefully, but the only prints we could identify were his."

Josie rested her chin on her hand. "Was there money inside?"

"Here's the confusing part." Brian leaned forward on the table. "There was one lone dollar bill in it."

We all stared at him in amazement.

"You found one dollar in a briefcase?" Gianna repeated.

He pursed his lips as he watched her. "Any thoughts?"

I snapped my fingers. "I wonder if—"

Brian glared at me. "I'm sorry, but is your name Gianna?"

I sat there, fuming in silence. I guessed Brian was doing this to embarrass me since he'd obviously been humiliated by Josie's statement. Fine. I would bide my time.

Gianna tapped her index finger on the table as she considered the question. "Bernardo told me he had enough money to tide us over for the rest of our lives, and he wanted me to run away with him at that moment."

"So whoever killed him obviously has the money now," Josie mumbled. "Plus, they tried to frame Gianna by planting her necklace in the shed."

"This is ludicrous," Gianna said. "Bernardo's entire family is out to get me."

I raised a hand and waited until I caught Brian's eye. "May I?"

He nodded, a smirk on his lips.

"I wonder if someone was trying to make a point," I said, "by leaving a one-dollar bill. They must have had some type of history with him. His wife, Victoria, came to see me. She thought he'd planned to leave town with Gianna too, but maybe she was saying that to throw people off her trail."

"Holy cow," Gianna breathed. "I just thought of something. That night, when Bernardo told me he was divorcing Victoria, he mentioned she'd be lucky if she got one dollar from him."

Josie's eyes opened wide with surprise. "I bet she's the one. It would fit."

"What did Luigi say about all this?" I asked Brian. "Have you talked to him?"

"Not directly, but my partner did. He claims it's his money, but he has no legal grounds to prove this, and if he's foolish enough to try, he could be looking at a long line of charges against himself. So let's just say he isn't very happy right now." Brian looked at my sister. "The senior Napoli basically accused you of the crime."

Gianna's nostrils flared. "Maybe I should go talk to him myself."

"No," Grandma Rosa shook her head. "That would not be wise."

"You're not going anywhere near him." I had another

thought. "Could Luigi have taken his own money? What if he killed Bernardo in order to file a claim on the missing money, but he had the cash all along…is that possible?"

Brian's jaw tightened. "We've thought of that, but why would he drag Gianna into it?"

Her lower lip trembled. "If it hadn't been for that juror asking me out, Bernardo probably would have gone to prison, and I think that's what Luigi wanted."

Brian rose. "I've got to get back to the station. I'd appreciate it if all of you would stay away from the Napoli family, okay?" He turned to Gianna. "There's no need for you to go down to the station tomorrow. I'll relay everything you said, but my boss will probably want to talk to you at some point."

"That's fine. Thanks, Brian," she said gratefully.

He nodded at Josie and Grandma Rosa then his gaze met mine. "Would you walk me out? I'd like to talk to you for a moment."

I pushed my chair back and glared at Josie, praying she wouldn't say anything. She kept her eyes fixed stoically on the carpet.

When we reached the screen door, he held it open to let me exit first. I walked with him to his squad car, neither of us saying anything. Finally, he turned to face me.

"I just wanted to tell you again how sorry I am about the other night. It was totally uncalled for and unprofessional of me."

God, this was uncomfortable. "It's okay, Brian. Really." He was standing so close that I was able to inhale the woodsy scent of his cologne. While he looked handsome as always, I felt nothing but friendship for him. Another man was in full possession of my heart.

He grinned. "I actually lied in there. I'm not going back to the station. I have a date tonight."

My ears perked up. "Wow. Who's the lucky girl? Do I know her?"

"Her name is Ally Tetrault. She's a nurse at Colwestern Hospital."

I opened my mouth in surprise. "Ally was in high school with me. I haven't seen her since I moved back home. Please tell her I said hello."

Brian groaned in obvious frustration then smiled. "Of course she had to be a classmate of yours. Pretty hard to find someone around here who doesn't know you."

"Ally's terrific," I said. "I hope it goes well."

Brian got into his car and started the engine. I leaned against his open window, and he reached over to take my hand in his for a moment, saying nothing. For the teeny tiniest moment, I felt a little bit jealous of Ally, and then it disappeared forever. I released my hand from Brian's and gave him a thumbs-up. "She's a lucky girl."

He smiled, his green eyes cascading more warmth than the bright June sun. "Take care of yourself, Sally."

With that, the squad car pulled out of my parents' driveway and disappeared down the street.

CHAPTER EIGHTEEN

———

After closing down the bakery operation for the night and then eating dinner with Grandma Rosa, Gianna and I had returned to my house. It was almost nine o'clock by then, and I was exhausted from the events of the day. My parents had not returned from the contest, but my mother had sent me and Gianna a text of her in the orange thong bathing suit. She said she'd placed second in the swimsuit competition. The finals were not being held until Thursday morning, but she would be busy most of tomorrow posing for pictures with the other contestants. I prayed my father would accompany her. Every day that he and that coffin spent in the living room, my business died a little more. No pun intended.

Gianna decided to turn in early and settled into the guest room to watch some television. I had sent Mike a text earlier, asking what time he might be home. I'd brought him back some peppers stuffed with meat and rice—one of his favorites—that my grandmother had prepared for supper. I hadn't received a response yet and felt myself getting antsy. I texted him again and this time received an immediate reply.

Sorry, baby. Trying to finish up a few things. Keep that nightie ready.

I took Spike for a walk, which he seemed to appreciate. Fortunately, Mike had installed a doggie door for him in the kitchen that led to a small fenced yard out back since we both worked long hours and couldn't run home often during the day. I let him run around the yard for a bit and realized I'd forgotten to bring the mail in. I walked down the driveway to the box and grabbed several envelopes. One was addressed to Mrs. Sally Donovan (To Be.) I smiled to myself. How I loved seeing my married name in print. I opened the envelope without further thought, assuming it was probably from a venue hoping to gain business from the wedding.

Inside was a typed note that smelled heavily of a man's fragrance. Aqua Velva, maybe? It read:

If you don't want to get burned like your shop, stop asking questions.

My heart hammered against the wall of my chest. Terrified, I ran into the backyard, scooped up Spike, and shut us into the house, slamming and locking the door behind us. I activated the alarm, planning to shut it off before Mike got home. I texted him again, but there was no response.

What had I done? I hadn't purposely tried to make trouble this time. Victoria had come to me with questions about Gianna. Sergio and Rufus had sent for Josie and me. Luigi had come to my parents' house—I hadn't gone to him. The only thing I'd done was try to find my sister and keep her safe, yet somehow, I had managed to tick off a killer again. This was getting to be an all too common occurrence. Who the heck was behind this?

Of course, I didn't know all of the enemies Bernardo had made, but it seemed likely that I might have already encountered the murderer. Victoria, perhaps? The man had cheated on her numerous times, but she went along with it. What woman in her right mind would be fine with that?

Crap. I didn't want to, but I placed a call to Brian, letting him know about the note. His phone rang three times and then went to voicemail. Oh, that's right. He was out on his date. I left a quick message telling him about the note. Within five minutes, Mike called.

"Where are you?" My voice trembled.

He caught the anxiety in my voice. "Baby, what's wrong?"

I told him about the note. "Can you come home now?"

There was a slight hesitation before he spoke. "All right, I'm on my way. Don't turn the alarm off until I'm in the driveway."

I disconnected and stole a peek into Gianna's room, but she was already sound asleep. As much as I wanted the company, I didn't have the heart to wake her. She needed the rest. I returned to my room and pulled the covers up around me. Spike jumped up on the bed, and I cuddled him against my chest. I didn't like being afraid. And why had Mike hesitated on the phone?

It seemed like forever, but ten minutes later Mike's headlights shone in the driveway. As I went to shut off the alarm, I busied myself with rapid mathematic calculations in my head. Webster's Restaurant was at least twenty minutes away. How had he gotten here so fast?

I waited by the door for him, trying to decide how I'd ask where he'd really been. He opened the door and then immediately shut and locked it behind him, set the alarm, and then drew me into his arms. "You okay?"

I buried my face in his chest. "Yes, now that you're here."

He kissed the top of my head and wrapped his arm around my shoulders as we walked into the kitchen. He peered into the refrigerator at the Pyrex dish I'd brought for him. "Oh, wow. Your grandmother made stuffed peppers?"

"Give me the dish, and I'll heat it up for you."

Mike grabbed a bottled water out of the fridge and then spotted the note I'd left on the countertop. I watched his jaw harden as he read it. "This is from one of those Napoli characters. I'd bet on it." He carefully placed it inside a plastic sandwich bag then handed it to me. His eyes darkened as he reached for me again. "It took every bit of restraint for me to not punch that goon in the face when I saw his hands on you today."

"Lucky for us you showed up when you did." I changed the subject. "How are the floors coming at the restaurant?"

I felt him tense slightly against me "Everything will be done in a few days." The microwave dinged, and I grabbed his container. Mike sat down at the table and began to eat. He closed his eyes for a moment. "I'm starving. I swear—your grandmother is the world's best cook."

"You got here pretty fast from the restaurant." I couldn't help myself.

"Hmm." He examined the rest of the mail but didn't answer me. "I guess you'd better call Jenkins and tell him about the note. Or go down to the police station tomorrow."

I crossed my arms in front of me. "I left him a message." I should have stopped right there, but of course I had to press the issue. "How'd you get here so quickly?"

He glanced up at me and smiled. "I was already on my way home when you called."

"Oh." I leaned over and kissed him on the forehead. "Well, I'm going to bed. Night."

"Hey." Mike put the fork down and placed his hands on my waist. "Is there something else bothering you?"

"Not at all," I lied and ran my hands through his thick hair. "It's just been a long day."

He placed a finger on my lips. "I've got to return a couple of calls, and then I'll be in. Don't fall asleep on me, baby."

"I won't." I forced a smile to my lips, but the truth was I felt a bit insecure at the moment. It was obvious from Mike's manner that he was intentionally keeping something from me. Was he working at Marla's house? We loved each other, so why couldn't he trust me with the truth?

I got into bed and turned the television on for company as I waited for him. I clicked the channels until I came to an old rerun of *I Love Lucy*. Comforted, I snuggled back against the pillows and yawned. When Mike came to bed we'd talk, straighten everything out, and have some quality alone time. I was sure of it.

I vaguely remembered Mike kissing me, and I murmured something in response about getting up soon. The next thing I knew, sunlight was streaming in through the window, and I stared at the alarm clock. Six thirty. I jumped out of bed and raced down the hall, but he was already long gone. Damn. This time I'd been the one to fall asleep. What a pair we were. The doubts kept pouring into my head. Why didn't he wake me up last night? Didn't he want to be intimate with me anymore?

There you go again, Sal. Your insecurities are really getting tiresome.

Mike had made coffee, and I poured myself some, taking the mug into the bathroom with me. Gianna had left a note saying she needed to be at the courthouse early and she would text me later. I showered and dressed quickly, poured more coffee into a travel mug, and drove over to my parents' house.

When it was time to open, we had several people waiting at the kitchen door. We were so busy we had to allow people in two at a time. My mother breezed through, dressed in a one-piece, bright blue, tube top concoction that barely covered her rear. She bussed me on the cheek. "How do I look, honey?"

"Amazing." It happened to be the truth.

She opened her clutch purse, the same obnoxious shade of blue as the dress, and handed me two twenty-dollar bills. "I'm in such a good mood today. Give everyone outside a cookie on me." She glanced into the case. "Looks like you have enough fudgy delights for the crowd. Why don't you guys hand them out and then tell your customers to stop over for the final judging of the beauty contest tomorrow morning. Anyone can come. It's open to the public."

Josie was frosting her own version of black and white cookies. She looked up and rolled her eyes at me.

"Mom, are you trying to buy votes?"

"Of course not! Although," she admitted, "it doesn't hurt to have a cheerleading section. I'm guaranteed to place at least third because of the bathing suit competition. My, it would be wonderful to win."

"You're *gonna* win, baby," my father spoke in a self-assured tone as he patted her on the backside. "No doubt about that."

I winced in discomfort. Customers in the kitchen and at the back door were staring at them. As much as I loved my parents, did they always have to embarrass me so?

"I'll give everyone a cookie. I promise. Um, why don't you guys go out through the living room?"

"Domenic." Mrs. O'Brien spoke up as Josie bagged her order. "I want to take a look at that coffin before you leave. My mother's not long for this world, and I've got to get a leg up on the preparations."

"Sweet Lord," Josie whispered under her breath.

My father beamed with pride. "Of course. We have time. Maria, let's show her the finer points of the casket. Bring your cookies with you," he said to Mrs. O'Brien.

"Hey, I want to see it too," the next customer in line said. "I've been hearing about this casket all over town. It's like—

legendary."

"What about your order?" Josie asked.

He waved his hand dismissively. "Ah, I can get cookies anytime. But lying in a coffin—alive—is priceless."

Josie's jaw almost hit the floor. "This is unreal. We'll have to come up with a new motto. 'Sally's Samples. Come for the cookies, but stay for the coffin.' Unfreakinbelievable."

I sighed and let a few more customers trickle in the door. We were almost caught up when Mrs. Gavelli barged into the kitchen without waiting her turn. She did not look happy.

"You." She pointed a finger at my chest. "I hear all about what you do."

Great. Another person was ticked off at me. Maybe she'd leave me a note in the mailbox too. "What are you talking about?"

"You no wanna make fortune cookies anymore," she huffed. "Well, is too bad. You make them or else I tell everyone how you take Johnny in the garage all those years ago."

I leaned against the kitchen wall, defeated. "Mrs. G, he took *me* into the garage."

"Yah, that's what they all say," she spat out. "Now you give me fortune cookie. And I'd better get good one."

"You tell her, Gram." Johnny's face appeared at the screen door. He caught sight of Josie and winked. "If you give me a cookie, I'll follow you into the garage too."

"Cripes," Josie muttered. "You belong on a leash."

Mrs. Gavelli broke the cookie apart, and her leathery looking complexion turned whiter than confectioner's sugar as she read her message. She glanced at me in a disapproving manner. "That not nice."

Perplexed, I glanced over her shoulder and read aloud. "*You are a sick individual.*"

Josie removed a tray of oatmeal chocolate chip cookies from the oven and laughed so hard that she almost dropped them. "I couldn't have said it any better myself."

Mrs. Gavelli gave her the look of death, threw the cookie on the ground, and stomped out the door, banging it shut behind her.

Johnny exchanged a grim look with my grandmother.

"I'd better go see that she's okay."

My grandmother shook her head. "I will go to her." She then gestured at me and Josie. "You tell them."

"Tell us what?" I asked, confused.

Grandma Rosa patted my cheek. "Johnny needs to have a talk with you. I will go make Nicoletta some tea." She opened the screen door and then closed it quietly behind her.

We were customer-free at the moment. Sarah looked ill at ease among us and said she had a phone call to make. She disappeared out back, leaving Josie and me alone with Johnny.

"Okay," I said. "Spill it. What's going on?"

The laughter in Johnny's eyes died as he returned my gaze. "Gram has cancer."

"No." Josie clamped a hand over her mouth in horror.

I went to Johnny and threw my arms around his neck. "I'm so sorry."

Johnny hugged me back. When he released me, I noticed his mouth quivering. "That's why the fortune upset her so much. She really thinks there's some truth to those things, crazy as it sounds."

"Gee." Josie cocked her head at me. "I know someone else like that too."

I sighed and focused on Johnny again. "What type does she have? How bad is it?"

"Bone," Johnny said. "It's the reason I came home. She needed someone to take her to chemo and stuff. Your grandmother has been wonderful, but let's face it—she's no spring chicken herself. And after everything Gram's done for me in my lifetime, I thought a little payback was in order. There was an opening at our old high school for a history teacher, so I applied for it and got the job."

"That's wonderful," I said. "But you still didn't answer my question. How bad is it?"

"She has a good chance," Johnny said. "They caught it early. The oncologist said attitude makes a big difference too. She's determined to live long enough to dance at my wedding, so she says."

Josie leaned on the counter, fascinated. "I didn't know you were dating anyone."

He grinned saucily at her. "As a matter of fact, I have a lunch date today. With a certain brilliant lawyer we all know and love."

"Shut up," Josie said.

"Holy cow," I smiled at him. "You and Gianna?"

The color rose high in Johnny's cheeks. "I saw her car pull into the driveway yesterday. Before she could even make it inside, I ran over to talk, proposed lunch, and she accepted."

It didn't surprise me that they had a lunch date, but I was a little shocked my sister hadn't told me. We always confided in each other. "Why, that little sneak. She's never kept secrets from me before."

"She was probably afraid we'd tease her about it," Josie said. "Which, of course, I intend to do."

Johnny winked at me. "Or maybe she's afraid you'll be jealous."

I swatted his arm with a dish towel. "Oh, knock it off."

He laughed and then grew serious again. "I'm not sure where this is headed, if anywhere. I know she's been through a lot—the recent breakup with Frank and now this whole mess with that shady client of hers. But I have to confess I've had my eye on her for a long time. And a good thing is always worth waiting for." Johnny's gaze met mine as he reached for the door. "Guess Mike knows something about that too."

Heat warmed my cheeks, and I lowered my eyes. "Thanks."

Johnny clenched his fists at his sides. "I hate seeing her go through this. You guys are like family to me. I'd do anything for Gram, and that includes the Muccio clan as well."

Ever the kidder, it was obvious by the tone of his voice that Johnny wasn't fooling around this time. The serious look in his dark eyes sent a slight shiver down my spine, but I managed a smile. "Get out of here. Go show my sister a good time."

Johnny's devilish grin returned, and he let himself out the door.

"Well, I'll be damned," Josie said. "He certainly does worship the ground Gianna walks on. Pretty nice to have a guy that'll do anything for you. And they haven't even officially started dating yet."

How far *would* Johnny go to protect my sister? *Okay, stop it, Sal.* "She deserves the best."

"Just like her big sis."

I said nothing, thinking about the missed opportunity for romance again last night. Although, this time, I had no one to blame but myself for falling asleep on Mike.

Sarah reappeared and removed some sugar cookies from the oven. She set them on the counter on a trivet and started measuring out tablespoons for another tray. Everything took twice as long in this environment.

"What time are we meeting the structural engineer?" Josie asked.

"Not until five," I said. "He couldn't make it any earlier. Maybe we'll find that Bernardo's killer left a clue behind to their identity while we're there."

"Don't get your hopes up. Then again, we have known killers to be careless in the past," Josie agreed.

I turned to Sarah. "Are you okay closing up without us?"

She looked up at me. "Oh no. I have to pick Julie up by four today. I didn't think you'd mind if I left then, what with it being my last day and all."

"Okay." Jeez, it seemed like Sarah couldn't wait to be rid of me and my bakery. "I understand." I looked down and saw she was still wearing the shoe with the heel missing. I wasn't sure how she managed to walk in the thing. I would have felt off-kilter all day. "We'll just plan to close up a little earlier tonight."

"I'm sorry, Sally," she mumbled. "You've been so good to me, and I feel like I keep letting you down."

"Don't worry about it, Sarah." Maybe it was a good thing she was leaving. The constant apologizing and excuses were starting to wear on me a bit. I would miss Julie, though. Since I hadn't had a chance to pick up a good-bye gift for Sarah, I wrote out a check and added a hundred dollars to the usual amount then handed it to her.

She glanced at it, clearly thunderstruck. "Sally, you made a mistake."

I waved it aside. "Buy something for Julie with it."

Sarah's lower lip trembled. "Thank you." She placed the check in her jeans pocket. "I wish there were more people like you in this world."

The musical notes on my cell phone sounded. I gave Sarah a pat on the shoulder before I answered. "Sally's Samples. Can I help you?"

"Hi, Sally. Marah Webster here," an elderly woman's voice greeted me. "I saw the advertisement you placed in the paper. How's the new location working out?"

I laughed. "It's taking a while to get used to the surroundings, so to speak, but we're managing. What can I do for you?"

"It's my granddaughter's birthday today," she said. "She loves those *genettis* that you make. Can I get two dozen of those and two dozen sugar cookies? I'll have my daughter pick them up in an hour if that's okay. I can't get away from the restaurant right now."

I jotted the order down on paper. "You're in luck. Josie just made a batch of the *genettis* this morning. We'll have it ready for you. The restaurant's swamped, huh?"

"Oh goodness, yes. This is our busiest time of the year. We get so many people on their way to the falls who stop by here for lunch or dinner first. It's such a nice compliment, you know."

"It must be a pain with the floors not being finished. But you're in good hands at least," I teased.

"I'm sorry?"

"The floors that Mike's putting in for you," I said.

She was silent for a moment. "Sweetie, I haven't seen Mike in weeks. Did he say he was working here?"

An ice-cold chill swept over me and nudged my shoulders apart, settling between them. "Um, no. I must have confused you with somebody else."

"Oh, okay then. I've got to run, dear. The lunch crowd is absolutely crazy. Tell your grandmother I said hello."

She disconnected, leaving me with the phone frozen to my ear. Josie and Sarah were both discussing the texture of the fudge frosting and paid no attention to me. I walked into the living room, past the coffin standing open—and empty for a change—and out the door. I sat down on the front steps and stared out at the soft billows of clouds gathering in the sky. It was another beautiful June day. I took several deep breaths in an effort to calm the anxiety growing within me.

Mike had been lying to me. I was certain of that. The question that kept zooming through my head at a furious pace was…why?

CHAPTER NINETEEN

"Okay," Josie said as we settled into her van on the way to the bakery. "You've barely said a word all afternoon. What's eating you?"

I turned my head toward the window as she backed the vehicle out of my parents' driveway, thereby managing to avoid her direct and all-knowing gaze. "Nothing. I'm fine."

She placed a hand on my arm. "Sal, you talk to me about everything. Let's hear it."

I shook my head stubbornly, blinking back tears.

"Hey." Her voice was gentle. "This isn't about Mike, is it? You're still not thinking about Marla, are you?"

Resigned, I turned around in the seat to face her. "I really don't know what to think. He told me he was working late every night to install flooring at Webster's Restaurant. I talked to Mrs. Webster today, and she didn't know anything about it."

Josie blew out a breath and was quiet for a moment. "I'm sure he has a good reason."

"A good reason for being dishonest? It had better be *darned* good. I'm not going to start our marriage off with a pack of lies between us."

She stopped for a light and narrowed her eyes at me. "Don't go there, Sal. He loves you. Maybe he's got a job that he's ashamed of. What if he's installing toilets or working in a sewer somewhere?"

I cocked an eyebrow at her in disbelief. "That's crazy. Why would I care about something like that? I'm proud of him no matter what he does."

"Then give him the benefit of the doubt," Josie said. "You haven't seen much of him lately, so maybe he's been putting off telling you. Or what if the job fell through, and Mrs.

Webster thought he should be the one to tell you. Maybe Mike's embarrassed."

I knew she was trying to help, but the churning in my gut told me there was more to it than that. "I don't care what time he gets home tonight—we're going to have a serious talk. I've been lied to before, and I'm not about to go through it again."

"Don't even attempt to compare Mike to that louse you were married to." Josie pulled up in the alley that ran behind the bakery.

My mind shifted back to the condition of my shop. If it wasn't for the discolored wood and the acrid smell still in the air, everything would have appeared to be normal from the outside. Mike had installed a new door on the back of the building. He'd said I had to have something in place to prevent looters from getting in, whether the building was salvageable or not. My heart told me he felt the place was beyond repair but didn't want to tell me yet, another reason why he wanted his friend to check the place out.

If there was some way we could continue to run the bakery here, I wanted Mike to start working on it right after our honeymoon, or when he finished whatever the heck he was doing now. *Ugh. There you go again, Sal.* I didn't want to think about the lie again.

The glass door in the storefront had some cracks and was probably still useable, but Mike had advised us to use the back door. He said Dave would meet us there.

Josie looked at her watch. "We're a few minutes early."

"Let's take a look inside," I said. "We were in a hurry the other day, so I want to see if there's anything else salvageable."

She snorted. "Right. I know what you're thinking, Nancy Drew. You're not going to find anything. The police already looked the place over."

"I don't care. Brian finding Gianna's necklace was not a good thing. Someone is trying to implicate my sister in this mess. Whoever killed Bernardo and stole the money is one and the same person. It's weird, but I feel like I should already know who did this. Come on."

I inserted the new key Mike had given me into the door, and with apprehension, we entered the back room. The door closed noiselessly behind us. I looked around our former kitchen and prep area with dismay. The place smelled of mildew, and the floor was blackened. I sighed and took a broom, starting to sweep up the debris.

Josie wiped at her eyes. "Sal, why bother? Do you really think this place is going to be useable again? I'm guessing not."

I bit into my lower lip, determined not to cry. "It would make me feel better at least."

She shook her head in resignation and walked out into the storefront. I reached the broom underneath the appliances and soon had a huge pile of dust and debris sitting in my dustpan. The plastic trash receptacle had disintegrated from the fire, so I went out to the alley and emptied the dustpan into the trash bin. I caught sight of a car leaving the alley, but it was too far away to see what kind it was or who was driving. I hoped Dave hadn't decided to ditch us for some reason.

I turned around to go back inside but completely missed the step and tripped. The dustpan went flying from my hands and landed under the sink. As I stooped down to retrieve it, I noticed a small, thick piece of what appeared to be burnt wood against the wall and picked it up. I stared at it, confused. For some reason I thought I should know what it was. Ah heck, what difference did it make? The place was a disaster. Disgusted, I threw the wood on to what was left of our prep table. I hoped Dave would show up soon. It hurt to see the repercussions of the fire firsthand, and I wanted to get this over with as soon as possible.

I glanced up at the hooks on the walls. The aprons that had been hanging there were now charred bits of burned cloth, beyond recognition. The ball caps were also ruined. With a sigh, I started to clean off the shelf above them. As I extended my arm to the back, my fingers connected with a piece of metal. I pulled it off the shelf and found myself staring at a gold charm bracelet.

Shoot. This belonged to Julie. She had insisted on helping wash the dishes last time she was here—much to Josie's dismay—and I had suggested she take the bracelet off and place it up on the shelf for safekeeping. We'd all forgotten about it afterwards.

I grabbed my cell phone out of my jeans pocket and

dialed Sarah's cell phone, fingering the little charms as I waited. They consisted of a *Happy Birthday* sign, a cat, the letter *J*, and a soccer ball. The fact that the metal had not endured damage from the fire cheered me up some. I thought with a pang of the sweet little face from the last time she was here, when she'd chattered on about how much she wanted a kitten until Josie exclaimed she was giving her a headache.

"Hi." A little voice giggled and interrupted my thoughts.

I smiled to myself. "Hi Julie. It's Sally. Is your mommy—?"

"Sally!" she squealed. "Mommy's out."

Confused, I glanced at the phone. "What do you mean she's out? She left you all alone?"

"Well, sometimes she does," the little girl admitted. "But she's just outside right now. I'm a big girl, so I can take care of myself."

I was perplexed. Julie was only eight years old. I knew Sarah didn't have an easy life, but I couldn't imagine leaving my own child alone at such a young age. "Oh. Well, I found your bracelet. Maybe Mommy can stop over to get it tonight and bring you too."

"I'm not going to get to see you anymore." Her voice sounded wistful.

My heart dissolved into a giant puddle as I pictured the child with her blonde pigtails and enormous blue eyes set in a perfect oval face. How lucky Sarah was. "Your mommy won't be working here, but we can still see each other."

"No. We're moving away."

I must have heard her wrong. "Sweetie, your mommy's taking another job, but it's not that far away. I'll still see you."

"No," the child cried. "We're leaving tomorrow."

Curiosity got the best of me. "Where are you going?"

Julie giggled. "Mommy said it's a secret. She just bought me the Cinderella gown from the Disney store, so I bet I'm gonna go see her and all the other princesses."

That had to set Sarah back quite a few bucks. Maybe she'd used the extra money I'd given her "Oh, I bet you look so pretty in it."

"I do," she agreed. "Can I have some more fortune

cookies before we go?"

"Of course. You can have all the cookies you want, as long as it's okay with your mommy. If she can't come, I'll bring them over tomorrow. You also left—"

"No. Bring them tonight," she insisted. "We're leaving tomorrow. I want to see you and Josie again. Her cookies are even better than my mommy's, but don't tell her I said that."

Her little voice was squeezing my heart so tight I found it difficult to breathe. "I promise. But I thought Mommy was going to work in the grocery store."

"Mommy doesn't have to go to work ever again. Okay, I'll tell you. I think she's going to take me on the Disney cruise."

Wishful thinking on the child's part, but I played along. "Wow. That's so awesome. Did she tell you that's where you're going?"

"Well," Julie said in a singsong voice, "she said our ship has come in. So I think that means we're going. Can you come too?"

My eyes grew moist. "I wish I could, sweetheart, but I have to make more cookies for the customers."

"Okay," she said reluctantly. "I'll tell Mommy you called. Will you say goodbye to Josie for me? She's going to miss me a lot, isn't she?"

"Totally." Okay, so it was a bit of a stretch, but there was no reason to hurt the little girl's feelings. I longed for a child so much that I literally ached from the want at times. Josie, on the other hand, often compared herself to the old woman who lived in a shoe. She was a good mother and loved her boys in a fierce and protective way but was brutally honest when she said she had no time or inclination to entertain anyone else's children. Hopefully someday mine would be an exception to her rule.

"Bye, Sally. I love you."

A tear rolled down my cheek. "I love you too, Julie."

As I put the phone back into my pocket, an uneasy feeling of dread settled over me. Why had Sarah lied about the job? What would make her leave town all of a sudden? Something here wasn't adding up.

After a couple of minutes, I glanced at my watch. Five fifteen. I was getting annoyed with this guy. I knew he was doing

Mike a favor, but hey, my time was valuable too. My phone pinged at that moment with a text from Mike.

Dave said you called him to cancel. Why?

What the heck was going on? I texted back. *I never called him. Why would I cancel?*

His message came back a minute later. *Don't know. Thought maybe the kitchen got really busy, and you couldn't get away.*

No. Josie and I are at the bakery waiting for him.

I waited another couple of minutes, and then my phone pinged again. *If you're inside that building, I want you out. Now. Don't think it's safe. Just texted Dave, and he said he'll get over later but couldn't give me a time. I'll meet him if you can't.*

I was tempted to say something about how could he meet the engineer when he had so many other jobs going on but stopped myself just in time. I wouldn't go there now. *Okay we'll leave now. What time will you be home?*

The answer came quick. *Probably not till midnight. Want to get these floors done for the Websters by this weekend.*

The hand that held my phone started to shake. Another lie. *How many more, Mike?* My throat grew tight with tears as my fingers flew across the screen. *Please come home early. We need to talk.*

What's wrong?

I hesitated before answering. I loved this man so much and knew he loved me too, so what was I doing? Why were doubts getting the best of me again? Catching Colin in a compromising position flashed through my mind, and I thought of Grandma Rosa's words. *See before you jump.* I honestly didn't think Mike was cheating on me, but why wouldn't he tell me what he was doing? I knew I needed to think this through some more before reacting—or overreacting.

I typed out a brief message. *Nothing. I just miss you.*

It won't be for much longer. Miss and love you too.

I swiped at my eyes and put the phone back in my pocket, glancing around the room again. I could hear Josie on the phone by the front door. She must have been talking to Rob. I tried to envision what might have happened Saturday night when Bernardo was here.

Gianna thought she had locked the door. If so, how had Bernardo gotten in? Even with the fire, Brian said there didn't appear to have been a forced entry beforehand. Bernardo could not have been hiding because Gianna was parked in the alley and would have seen him in the back room before she left. Either he had a key, or she hadn't locked the door.

I thought about Brian's comment that the perpetrator had been left-handed. True, Gianna was left-handed. But who else? I tried to remember the day when Luigi had dropped by my parents'. I thought he and his son, Sergio, were both right-handed but couldn't be positive. Victoria? Not sure. And Rufus? No question about it. I remembered how the ape had laid his enormous right hand on me in a possessive manner.

My eyes came to rest on the black piece of wood on the table. I picked it up and flipped it over in my hands. There was a red spot on one side, and my chest constricted at the sight. Blood? Could this have been a possible murder weapon? Was Bernardo hit with it? I walked into the storefront with the wood cupped in my hands.

Josie said goodbye to whoever she was talking to and turned around to face me. "What are you looking at?"

I held the object out to her. "Do you know what this is?"

She leaned in closer and took the piece in her hands, examining it. "Looks like some kind of heel to me. It might be the one that Sarah lost."

A light bulb clicked on in my head, and the room started to spin around while my inner thoughts began to sicken me. No, it couldn't be. But the more I thought about it, the more I had to admit that it all made sense.

"Who do we know that's left-handed?" I asked.

She furrowed her brow. "You mean as in Bernardo's killer?"

I nodded. "Anyone who comes to mind. Just throw it out there. Of course, there's Gianna."

Josie frowned. "I think Sergio might have been, but I'm not positive."

"Who else can you think of?"

"Well, Sarah is, but what does that have to do with—?" Josie's face went pale beneath her freckles. "Shut up. How could you even suggest such a thing?"

Bile rose in the back of my throat. "I'm literally getting sick thinking about it," I confessed. "But it does fit, and another thought occurred to me. What if Julie is Bernardo's child?"

Josie covered her mouth in horror. "Sal, you don't have any proof. Just because we found Sarah's heel doesn't make her a killer. She worked here, for God's sake. Of course we'd find some of her stuff around."

I placed a hand over my chest to steady my intense heart rate. "Hear me out, okay? First off, Sarah's left-handed. We found her heel with what I think is blood on it. She never made it to my party the other night, remember? She had time to commit the crime. I've been racking my brain over and over all week, wondering how Bernardo could have gotten back into the bakery."

"But Gianna told you she wasn't sure if she'd locked the door," Josie protested.

"No, but Sarah is the only one of us besides Gianna and Mike who has a key to the building."

Josie rubbed her arms as if for warmth. "I don't believe it, Sal. Hell, I don't *want* to believe it. Please come up with another conclusion. We've worked side by side with the woman for months, and now you want me to think she's a cold-hearted killer who set the bakery on fire? No freaking way."

I drew my phone out of my jeans pocket. "Come on. Let's get out of here. I'll call Gianna from your van."

"What for?"

"I want to see if she can check out Julie's birth certificate. Then we'll have our answer."

"There's no need," a voice sounded softly from behind us.

Josie and I both whirled around. Sarah was standing there, eyes wild, her face devoid of color. She regarded us in silence as she held a large sharp butcher knife in her hand.

"What are you doing?" Josie asked shakily.

Sarah stepped forward and motioned us away from the front door. "There's no need to call Gianna. I'll tell you everything you want to know."

CHAPTER TWENTY

My legs went numb. This had to be a bad dream. Here I was being confronted by a killer yet again. From knives to guns to being duct-taped and left to die, I'd pretty much seen it all by now. Was there a sign on my back that read *Please try to kill me*?

"Sarah." Somehow I managed to keep my voice steady. "Put down the knife."

Her eyes, which had reminded me of a frightened doe's when I'd first met her, were now cold and angry as they gazed into mine. She gestured toward the back room. "Both of you in there. Don't try anything funny, either."

We both backed up into the kitchen area, exchanging a quick glance between us and then at the knife. Once we were pressed up against the table, Sarah reached for Josie's arm and yanked it behind her back, pressing the knife to her throat.

"Sarah, stop it!" I started forward, but Josie's fearful eyes kept me rooted in place.

"I'm sorry." Sarah's voice was monotone. "You've been good to me, Sally. God knows you're one of the few people in this life who has. I'm sorry you had to be involved."

"Sarah, the structural engineer's going to be here any minute," I lied. "You're not going to get away with this."

She smiled. "Who do you think called him to cancel?"

I was perplexed. "How did you even know who he was?"

"You left his name and number on the counter earlier," Sarah replied. "The flip side of the note had a recipe Josie had written out for me, so I wound up taking the paper home and a good thing I did. After Julie said she'd talked to you, I knew I'd have to come out here, and Dave would have been in the way. Lucky for me he was running late when I called and pretended to be you, so it worked out well." She waved the knife up and down. "Piece of cake—oops, I mean cookie. Ha-ha, get it?"

I swallowed hard, still trying to come to terms with everything. How were we going to get out of this without someone getting hurt? Josie, always so full of energy and sarcasm, had practically gone limp in Sarah's arms as the knife was pressed against her throat. Was there a chance anyone would come here? No. My parents were off at the beauty pageant event doing God knows what. Gianna might be with Johnny or still at work. Mike thought I was on my way home. There would be no reason for anyone to come by. We were on our own.

"Sarah." I tried to appeal to her motherly instinct. "You don't want to hurt Josie. She's got four little kids. You're a mother too, so you know what it's like. Don't do this."

She blinked back tears but tightened her grip around Josie's throat, pointing the knife at her with the other. "I don't want to, but there's no other choice for me. It all just spiraled out of control."

"Bernardo was Julie's father, wasn't he?" I asked gently.

She let out a long, ragged breath and nodded, her gaze even with mine. "He was so handsome and suave. I met him at a bar one night. I was new in town and out with a couple of girlfriends. He approached me, and then we talked for hours. We really hit it off, you know. After the bar closed down, we went back to my place for a nightcap. And then, things happened."

Sarah's face flushed a bright red as she continued. "When I found out about the baby, he said he'd help, but it was all a lie. He never paid me one red cent. God, I was such a fool. I even took the baby over to his house one day, and he refused to let us in. Wouldn't even look at our beautiful little girl. He said it was all my fault for not using birth control, so why should he help? I decided she was better off without him back then." Tears streamed out of her eyes, and I watched as one landed on the blade of the knife, where it glistened.

Josie whimpered like a child, and that seemed to jar Sarah out of her flashback. She paused for breath then continued.

"At first, I was going to fight him for child support but never had a test done. Stupid, I know. So after a few months, Julie and I left town to live with an aunt of mine. When she relocated last year, I decided to come back to Colwestern. Julie's been asking questions about her father lately, and I thought maybe he'd want to see her. I called Bernardo a few months ago, thinking maybe his feelings had changed, but no. I even threatened to tell his new wife, and he laughed and said go ahead, that she wouldn't care less. He said he had no interest in seeing me or Julie ever again and to leave him the hell alone."

I glanced anxiously at Josie's face. Her blue eyes were filled with terror, pleading for me to help her. If I made a sudden move, Sarah could slice Josie's throat in one quick motion. I had to keep her talking for a while and hope that an opportunity to disarm her might arise.

"How did you know he was here that night?" I asked.

"I didn't at first," Sarah admitted. "When I got home, I realized I'd left my cell phone behind. I stuck Julie with one of my neighbors and ran back out. I pulled up in the alley and saw Gianna's car leaving. Once I got inside, someone was banging on the front door. I think Bernardo thought I was Gianna, until the door opened."

"So you let him in," I prompted.

Sarah smiled. "Yeah. You should have seen the expression on Bernardo's face. But that didn't stop him from mocking me. He said he was leaving town and that he had plenty of money with him. Wasn't it too bad I'd never see any of it? Not even a single dollar. 'Nothing for my so-called bastard,' is how he put it." She blinked back tears. "His own flesh and blood. Well, I got even with him."

That explained the one-dollar bill in the briefcase. After Sarah had killed Bernardo she must have taken his car keys and removed the money from his briefcase.

The room was silent except for Josie's labored breathing. I felt completely helpless. At that moment I heard a strange noise coming from above. It almost seemed like the building had moved. We needed to get out of here soon.

Sarah seemed oblivious to the noise as she continued to hold the knife against Josie's throat. "He walked toward the door, laughing, and I just kind of lost it. I took my shoe off and hit him in the head with it. He was stunned for a minute but then reached out and lunged for me. I ran into the back room to try to leave through the alley. He picked up the rolling pin and hit me in the shoulder. Then he grabbed me by the throat, like this." She squeezed Josie's neck until she made a gurgling sound.

"Stop it, Sarah!" I screamed. "You're hurting her."

She looked up at me angrily. "What about all the times I've been hurt? What about my daughter who's never had anyone to call Father? Don't we deserve some happiness?"

"Of course you do." *Although you don't go around killing people in the process, despite how rotten they might be.* "But you don't set people's buildings on fire or let other people take the rap for murder, like my sister."

She stared at me, open-mouthed. "I didn't know what else to do. I hit Bernardo again with the heel of my shoe, and he fell down. I hit him over and over. Too many times to count. The blood was running down the side of his face, and then I realized that he wasn't moving. I knew he was dead and was afraid somehow they'd figure out it was me. I had to try to cover the whole thing up. Then I remembered the gasoline in the shed." She shrugged her shoulders. "So, I had no choice but to set the place on fire. I was going to send you some money after I went away. Honest."

The callous manner in which she talked about Bernardo's death and the arson sickened me. I wondered, with a pang, if Julie had ever been the victim of her psychotic behavior, but this wasn't a good time to ask. I exchanged glances with Josie, whose eyes then darted back in the direction of the knife resting against her throat.

Sarah had become completely unglued, and I was afraid of ticking her off any further. I also did not want to be in this building any longer.

"Sarah, you were going to let Gianna take the blame for what you did." Another thought crossed my mind. "That day when I told you to go up to her room and get yourself some clothes—that's when you found the necklace, wasn't it?"

She narrowed her eyes at me angrily. "I did what was necessary to throw suspicion off me. Gianna would have gotten out of it somehow. She's a lawyer, for God's sake. Plus, she's beautiful and will make tons of money defending scumbags like Bernardo. I saw them together once, you know. Outside the courthouse. I knew he was in love with her—it was so obvious. Gianna's probably got guys throwing themselves at her feet. She deserves to suffer a bit, like I have."

What was this woman thinking? Gianna had always been sweet to Sarah, even lending her money one day for lunch when she'd forgotten her purse.

My reasoning skills went right out the window, and anger surged through me. If there was a Guinness world record for most psychos encountered in a year, I'd definitely win, hands down. I couldn't let this woman destroy us. Josie's life and mine were both at stake here.

"And even you," she said bitterly. "Your fiancé is gorgeous and adores you. I've watched the way he looks at you. It's like there's no one else in the world. Why can't I have that? You have no idea what it's like to raise a child on your own. You don't know what it's like to suffer."

"That's not fair," I said quietly, taking a step toward her. "My ex-husband cheated on me and put me through hell. He never wanted children, and I'd gladly give my arm for..." I broke off as I watched the knife waver in her hand. "Colin was murdered, and they arrested Mike for the crime. You know all this. Now I have to rebuild my entire business. My life isn't perfect—no one's is. But you can't give up, Sarah. Sometimes you just have to pick yourself up and continue to put one foot in front of the other, no matter how painful it is."

"But it's not right," Sarah wailed. "I've waited and waited, but my prince charming has never come. Every time I meet a guy who seems interested, they find out about Julie, and it's good-bye Sarah, nice knowing you."

"Their loss," I said.

"Well, I don't need a man anymore. I have all I want—a suitcase full of money and my little girl. Everything else is unimportant."

My heart swelled when I thought of that sweet child. She deserved so much better than this. "Did you leave Julie home by herself again?"

Sarah's face contorted with rage. "I do what I have to. As soon as Julie got off the phone, she couldn't wait to tell me that you were bringing her fortune cookies. She also mentioned that she'd told you we were going away and that I didn't have to go to work anymore. I was afraid you'd figure it out before we left tomorrow, so I had to come and find out for myself."

"You put the note in my mailbox last night, hoping that I'd think it was Luigi who'd killed Bernardo," I said.

Sarah's mouth twisted into an evil smile. "Correct. He was in the bakery last week buying *genettis* while you guys were out. I recognized him immediately, although he had no idea who I was. I caught the scent of that Aqua Velva a mile away. There's no way I could pass up an opportunity to try to frame him for the murder of his stepson."

"So you'd been planning this for a while?" I kept hoping for an opportunity to charge her. We were running out of time.

"Ever since Bernardo dumped me and my precious little girl, I've wanted revenge. I'm a patient person, so the wait didn't bother me."

Also crazy, but I wisely kept that part to myself.

Sarah's nostrils flared. "Who did he think he was to try to make us disappear? What, did we embarrass him? Well, he learned the hard way." She pulled Josie's head back roughly by the hair, forcing her to cry out in pain. "Once I get rid of you two, I'm out of here."

My heart stuttered in my chest as I watched Josie's eyes roll back in her head. Then I thought of Julie, and the rage boiled over. "Shame on you. I thought you were a good mother, Sarah. I'd give anything to have a little girl like Julie."

"Don't you dare judge me," Sarah said fiercely. "You don't know what I've been through."

Sure, this woman had been through a lot. But she'd also killed a man and shown no remorse for it. She was more upset about burning down my bakery than the murder. I'd worked by her side for the last five months and never once suspected she was capable of such a crime. When had I become such a crummy judge of character?

My heart continued to pound against the wall of my chest. Outside of my family, Josie, and Mike, was anyone trustworthy anymore? I wondered what was running through Sarah's mind. Then again, I probably didn't want to know.

Stay calm, Sal. Don't screw this up. Pointing out what

Sarah had done to Bernardo wasn't going to help, so I tried another angle. "I'm not angry about the bakery."

The knife moved away about an inch from Josie's throat but not enough so that I felt comfortable making a move. "You're not?"

"Of course not," I said. "This is all material stuff. All I want is for you to let Josie go. You don't want to hurt her, Sarah. Let me try to help you. Killing us won't do any good. Maybe Gianna can help too."

Sarah's lower lip trembled. "No one's ever wanted to help me."

I tried to soothe her. "Don't say that. I'll do what I can. But you need to let Josie go. And then I'll go back with you to your house to get Julie."

Josie looked at me in alarm but didn't dare speak, afraid the sound might trigger a reaction in Sarah.

Sarah laughed. "You're lying. You just don't want to die."

Well, that part was true enough. "Please let Josie go. You don't want her kids to be without a mother, do you?"

"What does it matter?" she shrilled, tears streaming down her face again. "If they find out what I did, they'll take my Julie away from me."

The knife wavered in her hand as the emotions took over, and then another noise from overhead was heard almost simultaneously, and the building moved. When Sarah glanced upward, I sprang forward to try to grab the knife, feeling the blade slice into my hand. Josie screamed and managed to insert her elbow backwards into Sarah's stomach. Sarah doubled over in pain, and the knife slipped from her grasp. Josie and I were both distracted for a split second too long by the blood flowing from my hand. I sprang forward to grab the knife off the floor, but Sarah reached it ahead of me. She backed up against the new door, holding it high above her head in triumph.

"Try anything again," she hissed, "and you're both dead."

Before she could continue, the back door was pushed open from the outside. It smacked Sarah right in the head. She let out an *oof* as the impact knocked her to her knees. The knife flew out of her hands and landed at Josie's feet, and she quickly grabbed it.

We both looked up to see Grandma Rosa standing there, a puzzled look on her face. She glanced down at Sarah sitting back on her haunches, sobbing. Josie was standing next to her, shaking the knife wildly as she stared at my hand in horror. "Sal, are you okay?"

An intense pain traveled through my right hand and up my arm. "It stings like crazy." The blood continued to drip on the floor as I spoke.

"After all that Sal has done for you," Josie rasped. "This is how you repay her, Sarah?"

Sarah covered her face with her hands. "I'm sorry. I never meant for it to turn out this way."

Josie gritted her teeth. "You're just sorry you got caught." She continued to grip the knife tightly in one hand and reached the other into her jeans pocket for her phone to dial 9-1-1.

Grandma Rosa took some tissues out of her purse and wrapped them around my hand while she examined it. "You should go to the hospital. It does not look very deep, but we still need to have it checked."

I winced from the pain but managed a smile for her. "Your timing was perfect. But what are you doing here?"

"Nicoletta had some of your fortune cookies," Grandma Rosa explained. "She had a chemo treatment yesterday and has not been feeling well. So when she asked me to open one, I could not refuse her." Her eyes regarded me solemnly. "I still do not believe in those silly things, but when I saw the message, I decided to come anyway."

She reached into her housecoat pocket and pulled out a slip of paper which read *Take a chance. Loved ones need you.*

"So you see, *cara mia*," she continued. "Sometimes these messages can prove to be useful."

She was a true wonder. "What would I ever do without you?"

Grandma Rosa shrugged. "You would be lost." She stared at Sarah still crying on the floor, and clucked her tongue. "I told you that one had problems. Even I did not see this mess coming, though."

"You saved our lives, Grandma," I said.

She looked pleased. "I am a good Cagney and Stacey, yes?"

I laughed and kissed her on the check. "The best." I didn't even bother to correct her this time. As far as I was concerned, my grandmother could be any detective team that she wanted.

CHAPTER TWENTY-ONE

———

Brian and his partner arrived within minutes of Josie's call. Sarah was led away, sobbing and yelling obscenities at them.

Jeez, you think you know a person.

Josie had some paper towels in the back of her van and wrapped them around my hand before she drove me to the hospital's emergency room, with Grandma Rosa following. Fortunately, the waiting room was empty, and I was able to be seen right away. I needed a few stitches and almost whined out loud when they told me. I hated needles and hospitals. If I wanted a family someday, though, I guessed I would have to learn to get used to them.

Grandma Rosa sat there and held my other hand, whispering comforting words to me until the doctor was finished. It reminded me of the time when I was seven and had been running out back, chasing Gianna, and had fallen, creating a huge gash in the side of my head. My parents weren't home at the time, so my grandmother had been the one to rush me to the hospital. I remembered how I'd cried when I had to have stitches, but afterward Grandma Rosa had put me to bed, let me watch cartoons until late at night, and brought me cheesecake. There didn't seem to be any problem that she couldn't solve.

Josie had called Mike for me and explained what had happened. When Grandma Rosa and I returned to the waiting room, he was sitting with Josie. Although he looked incredibly handsome as always, the look of exhaustion on his rugged face was undeniable. He had spatters of paint in his dark, curly hair, which was in a state of disarray. The front of his T-shirt was dirty, and there was paint on his jeans as well. He rushed forward when he saw me, his midnight blue eyes filled with love and concern.

He gathered me in his arms and hugged me tightly against his chest. "Are you all right?"

I held up my right hand. "Five stitches. It could have been a lot worse."

Mike drew my hand to his mouth and kissed it, bandage and all. "Thank God."

"You should have seen her, Mike," Josie grinned "Sal was awesome. She ran right at Sarah, not even thinking about herself. She just wanted to make sure Sarah didn't hurt me."

Mike's lips compressed together into a fine, thin line. He frowned and said nothing for a minute, and I knew he was struggling for composure. Finally, he spoke. "You could have been killed. Both of you. I told you to stay out of that building until Dave checked it out."

"I could hear noises coming from above while we were inside," Josie added. "It didn't sound good."

I winced. *Thanks for the help, Jos.*

Mike drew back and held me at arm's length, his eyes pinning me with their direct gaze. "Why didn't you listen to me?"

As I'd been getting my stitches, I'd debated about what to say to him, given the lies he'd been telling me. I thought maybe I'd act indifferent or cool, but when I saw the expression of concern in his eyes, everything fell away. "I'm sorry. We only planned to go in for a minute. Then Sarah arrived, and things got out of hand."

Mike sighed heavily and drew me against him. "I'm just thankful you're both all right."

The door to the waiting room opened, and Brian entered. He was in jeans and an American Eagle T-shirt, obviously off-duty. He nodded to Mike and Josie then looked at me and the bandage on my hand. "Are you okay, Sally?"

"Yes. Thanks for getting to the bakery so quickly when Josie called you."

"Not a problem." He gestured at the chairs. "Maybe we should all sit down for a minute."

After we were settled, everyone turned to Brian expectantly. His expression was grim. "Thank God you guys got out of that building when you did. It definitely could have been a lot worse."

Mike narrowed his eyes at him. "What happened?"

"Seems like part of the second floor fell onto the first," Brian said.

"But the fire wasn't even upstairs," Josie protested. "I don't understand. How could something like that happen?"

A muscle ticked in Mike's jaw, and he swore under his breath. "I knew it. It was probably a weight-bearing wall that collapsed." He ran a hand through his hair, clearly frustrated. When he spoke again, his voice was gruff. "You're like a cat with nine lives, Sal. But I've lost count of how many you might have left."

So had I, and the thought did not make me want to jump with joy either.

Brian's gaze met mine. "Sarah confessed to everything. She's been locked up and will be transferred to another jail in the morning."

Josie visibly shivered. "I can't believe we hired a murderer. I never would have thought she was capable of such a heinous crime. You can't trust anyone anymore."

Brian nodded. "You two seem to have a way of attracting these kind of people. Sort of like magnets for disaster."

"Gee, thanks for the compliment," I mumbled.

He went on. "It sounds like Bernardo egged Sarah on, and she snapped. From what she told us it seems like she'd been planning some type of revenge for years. It's just too bad she didn't stop and think about how her actions might affect other people."

My mouth went dry. "Has someone checked on Julie? Is she okay?"

Brian's face reddened with anger "Sarah told us about Julie, so I left my partner to take care of the report at the station and went out to the house with another officer. The little girl was sound asleep and all by herself. That woman won't be winning any Mother of the Year awards, that's for sure."

"But she was okay?" Mike asked.

Brian nodded. "I woke Julie up, and we took her to the station. She has a great-aunt in Syracuse who's on her way to get her."

Without thinking, my mouth opened, and the words tumbled out before I could stop them. "I could take Julie for the night, Brian. Until her aunt gets here. What's going to happen to her now?"

He scratched his head. "I believe the aunt's planning to take her long-term."

"Do we know anything about her?" I burst out. "Maybe she has issues too. You can't hand her over to that woman without knowing."

Everyone was silent, looking at me. My heart broke for that precious little girl, and I put my face in my hands.

"Hey." Mike placed an arm around my shoulders. "Sal, this woman is Julie's family—a blood relative. It's not up to you to decide."

I burst into tears. "It's so wrong that that sweet little girl has to suffer because of her mother's faults. I'll take her if no one else will."

Mike stared at me in amazement. "Do you realize what you're saying?"

"Julie's an innocent victim," I sobbed. "Both her parents failed her. She deserves a chance at a better life." I reached for his hand. "We could give her a good life."

He said nothing for a moment, just held my hand and stroked my fingers softly. Perhaps he was thinking about his own miserable childhood. Then those beautiful blue eyes smiled into mine. "If they'll let you have her, Sal, it's okay with me."

I glanced up at everyone. Grandma Rosa smiled at us, and Josie was wiping tears from her eyes.

Brian cleared his throat. "Sally, you didn't let me finish. The aunt was very concerned about Julie. She mentioned that Sarah had had a nervous breakdown when she was a teenager, so apparently the woman's had problems for years. The aunt *is* Julie's blood relative, so she has a right to her. I know this sounds cruel, but what you want is of no consequence here."

It was as if someone had punched me in the stomach. One minute I was on the verge of being a mother, and then just as quickly it had all been taken away. I lowered my head. "Oh. I understand."

Mike kissed my hair. "You're a beautiful person for

wanting to do this, Sal. I hate to say this, but maybe someday, when Julie knows the whole story, she'd resent you for having a part in it, and I know that would destroy you."

I blew out a sigh. Mike was right, of course. "I wish I could do something for her. Maybe if I go see her—"

My grandmother, who had been sitting quietly on the other side of me, spoke up. "*Cara mia*, I think it is wonderful that you want to help the little girl, but you need to step aside. Mike is right. It is better that you do not see her again."

The tears rolled down my cheeks again, and I said nothing. Grandma Rosa patted my back. "Be strong, my dear. Sometimes there are things that we cannot fix, no matter how hard we try."

I wiped my eyes and glanced over at Brian, who wore a somber expression. "If something happens with the aunt, will you let me know?"

"Of course I will." He got to his feet. "I'm glad that you're all right and sorry about the bakery. But I'm thankful you guys made it out of there in time."

The door of the waiting room opened again, and Ally Tetrault walked in. She was tall and slender, with short auburn hair the same shade as Josie's and striking gray eyes. She was wearing pink scrubs and carried a large purse slung over her shoulder, obviously leaving for the day. She grinned at me. "Hey, Sal. I heard you were here. Long time no see. How's the hand?"

I waved it at her. "Still attached to the rest of me."

She laughed and touched Brian on the shoulder. "I thought you were off duty?"

Brian kissed her on the cheek. "I am but wanted to let Sally know about the details of an investigation that involved her bakery. I'm finished here now, so I can follow you over to your place if you're ready to go."

Josie wiggled her brows at me and then glanced down at the floor, a smile forming at the corners of her mouth.

"At your service, Officer." Ally waved to the rest of us and smiled at Mike. "I saw Gianna last week, and she said you guys were getting married next month. Congrats. You've got yourself a good one there."

Mike ran a hand through my hair. "That's one thing I'm sure of."

Ally turned back to Brian. The look of affection that passed between the two was unmistakable. As I watched them, I realized Brian's infatuation with me was finally over, and I felt nothing but relief this time.

"I'm starving." Ally reached for his hand. "It was good seeing all of you. Keep in touch, Sal. Maybe we can double-date sometime."

Mike mumbled something under his breath that sounded like "Try never," and I poked him in the ribs.

"Sure thing. You guys take care," I smiled.

"We'll need you and Josie to come down to the station for some further questioning tomorrow," Brian said to me.

I nodded. "No problem."

Brian turned away and held the door open for Ally. I watched them through the window as they crossed the street, holding hands and talking. I had to admit they made a cute couple.

"Wow," Josie breathed. "He didn't even give you a backward glance, Sal."

"Good. About time," Mike muttered.

Josie rose to her feet and crossed over to hug me. "It's after eight, and Rob has to work tonight. Forgive me if I bail on you now?"

I glanced from Mike to Grandma Rosa. "I'm in good hands. You go ahead."

Josie hesitated. "So we definitely have to find a permanent location now. Maybe we'll have to look in another town. Rob and I found a building for rent about forty-five minutes away in Cherryville. I called, and they said it can be shown only during the day. Seems the owner works nights. I know the commute's not ideal, but it beats running the business from your parents' house."

"No argument there." I turned to my grandmother. "Do you think you could handle the kitchen for a couple of hours tomorrow so that Josie and I can go look at it?"

Grandma Rosa looked uncomfortable and glanced down at the floor. "We will see."

I stared at her, baffled. My grandmother never refused me anything, but I didn't press the issue. Maybe she was taking Mrs. Gavelli to chemo. I'd talk with her later.

I gave Josie a thumbs-up with my good hand. "We'll figure something out. See you in the morning."

She smiled, hugged Mike, and kissed my grandmother then left.

Grandma Rosa eased out of her chair. "I made tiramisu. You two should come back to the house and have some."

I was all about the comfort foods right now. "That sounds good." I reached for Mike's hand. "What do you say, babe?"

He hesitated and glanced from me to my grandmother. "As long as you're okay, would you mind if I went back to work for a couple of hours?"

I was stunned. What the heck was going on? *Stay calm, Sal. Don't do anything stupid.* "To finish the Webster's floors, right?"

Mike watched me, confused. "Right. I want to have that job completed by the weekend. I finished the roof this morning."

Grandma Rosa shook her head. "You are working too hard. Have you eaten?"

"I'll grab something later, Rosa, but thank you." They exchanged a knowing look, and now I was totally perplexed. Here he was, lying to me, and all my grandmother cared about was if he was hungry. Had everyone gone crazy?

Mike planted a soft kiss on my lips. "I might be pretty late, so don't wait up."

I clenched my good hand at my side but could no longer keep my mouth shut. "I'd appreciate it if you could come home soon. We need to talk, Mike."

He seemed surprised by my reaction. "What's wrong? Is it about the wedding?"

I glanced over at Grandma Rosa standing behind Mike. She placed a finger to her lips. Why didn't she want me to say anything when I knew Mike was lying? I swallowed hard and forced the initial words back down my throat. "There's some things we need to go over."

Mike grinned in apparent relief. "Well, I'm not as good

of a wedding planner as your mother, but I'll do the best I can, for your sake. I'll try to finish up early." He traced a finger softly over my lips. "Love you." He gave my grandmother a broad smile as he exited the room.

Damn, he wasn't making this easy. I sat back down in the chair and drew my bandaged hand to my face before I burst into tears.

"Do not cry, *cara mia*. Everything is fine."

"Grandma, why didn't you want me to say anything to him? He's lying to me, and I have to know why. I can't live like this."

She reached for my other hand. "Sally, my dear, come. I know what you need."

In no time at all, I was sitting at the dining room table with Grandma Rosa, stuffing my face with tiramisu. I was exhausted but refused when she asked if I wanted to lie down for a while.

"I'm going to confront him when he gets home," I said. "I won't have our marriage starting out like this. I've been down this road before. Can you drive me home?"

Grandma Rosa stirred her cup of tea absently as she sat across from me. "*Cara mia*, there is no doubt in my mind that your young man loves you very much. Please do not go about making trouble."

"Me?" I cried out. "What trouble? *I* haven't lied about anything."

"Trust in your young man," Grandma Rosa said. "He is *not* cheating on you."

Deep in my heart, I knew she was right. But given what I'd been through in the past, I was still somewhat vulnerable. "Grandma, I have a long history of men cheating on me."

Grandma Rosa snorted. "Bah. It is not *that* long. Your clown of an ex-husband. That is all. Of course it does not excuse what he did to you. My heart aches for all that you went through. But do not make it sound like every man you ever cared for was unfaithful. That is not so."

She sipped her tea and then continued. "You thought Mike cheated while you were dating in high school. You never gave him a chance to explain, and then you went and married that—buffoon. Rest his soul." She made the sign of the cross on her chest. "You were wrong about Mike then, and you are wrong now."

My cheeks grew warm under my fingertips. "Okay. So technically it was only *one* man." Still, I couldn't help myself. I hated feeling insecure and knew I shouldn't dwell on the past, but Colin had created some very deep wounds that were taking longer than I thought to heal. Maybe they never would entirely. Mike was nothing like Colin, so I shouldn't be having doubts, but I knew that something was amiss. "Okay, if he's not cheating, then why is he lying to me?"

Grandma Rosa shrugged. "Be patient, my dear. I am sure he will tell you soon."

I rubbed my eyes wearily. "I want to marry him more than anything else in the world. I never even thought it was possible to love someone so much. In some ways it scares me."

"Do not be scared," Grandma Rosa said. "Be grateful for such a precious love. I had that once too and will always be thankful for it."

She sipped her tea again, and I watched her, curious. "You mean with Grandpa, right? I wish I could remember him." He had died when I was three.

She shook her head. "No, *cara mia*. There was another boy who stole my heart long before your grandfather." Her large brown eyes that were always so full of wisdom and strength looked unbelievably sad as they fixed on mine.

My chest constricted with pain as I watched her. "Then you mean Uncle Luca?" Grandma had dated him before her younger sister, Luisa, had stolen him away. Eventually they'd married, and Grandma and Luisa's relationship had never been the same. Aunt Luisa had been murdered shortly before my return to Colwestern last year, thus beginning my career of encountering random psychopathic killers.

Once again, Grandma Rosa shook her head. "No, my dear. This was another boy. I have never spoken of him to anyone. Remember the other night when I said I have had my tests too?"

I nodded. "Please tell me about him."

"His name was Vernon," Grandma Rosa said. "We met

one summer when his family moved into the house next to mine. I had just finished high school." She closed her eyes for a moment, remembering. "Like your Mike, he was handsome. Dark hair, dark eyes. All of the girls were crazy about him, especially your Aunt Luisa." She made the sign of the cross on her chest. "Luisa never liked anyone, except for the boys who wanted to spend time with me." She gave a little proud toss of her head. "Luisa was a nutsy cookie too but not in a nice way like your mama."

I laughed. "What happened to Vernon?"

She put another piece of cake on my plate. "He asked me to go steady with him. We were very much in love. Your great-grandfather—my father—did not like him. He was twenty-three years old to my seventeen. My father threatened to keep me under lock and key if I saw him again. I did anything I could to be with him. I told lies I am not proud of. Looking back, I would not have changed a thing. Sometimes the heart knows when it is meant to be with another. That is the way it is with you and your young man. I remember when you were only sixteen and told me that you had fallen in love. Do you recall that day?"

"Yes," I whispered.

"Even though you were so young at the time, I did not laugh at you. You are like me, Sally. You knew right away that you were meant to be with him, as I was with Vernon."

"So what happened to him?" I asked again, almost fearful.

Grandma Rosa's smile was sad. "He went away to the Vietnam War and did not come back. His body was never found."

I reached out my good hand and placed it over hers. I hated to see her in so much pain. It was obvious that even after all these years, she still grieved for her one true love. "I don't know what to say, Grandma. I'm so very sorry."

She kissed me on the forehead. "Sometimes life deals us cruel blows, *cara mia*. But it shapes the person that we are. Always remember that. I am grateful for the time I shared with Vernon and will treasure it in my heart for as long as I shall live. He also wrote me the most beautiful love letters when he went away. Someday I will show them to you."

"He's the one who gave you the brooch."

She nodded. "Yes, but I want you to have that. I have the letters and my beautiful memories. Always remember the saying."

I tried to make light of the serious situation. "See before I jump?"

Grandma Rosa smiled. "It is better to have loved and lost than to never have loved at all."

My darling grandmother really was amazing. Most of the time she got simple everyday puns and phrases wrong but then could recite beautiful lines of poetry word for word. How blessed I was to have her in my life. A tear rolled down my cheek before I could stop it.

She handed me a tissue and rose. "Come. You look very tired. Rest awhile before you go home. It is quiet here. Your parents are staying at a hotel near the contest tonight. The judges will make their decision tomorrow morning. Thank goodness all this silliness will be over soon, and then things will get back to normal."

I raised my eyebrows as I settled back on the couch. "You know that things will *never* be normal around here, Grandma."

"You are right about that." Grandma Rosa started toward the kitchen. "I will make you some hot chocolate. Things will be fine, my sweet girl. Trust your grandmother."

CHAPTER TWENTY-TWO

—————

The warmth from the sunlight on my face awakened me. I opened one eye, confused for a moment as to where I was. Then I realized I was lying on the couch in my parents' living room. Grandma Rosa had covered me with the patchwork quilt she had made for me when I was a child.

There was a clattering of dishes and a murmur of voices coming from the kitchen. The clock on the wall said eight o'clock. I remembered talking to Grandma Rosa, her going to make me hot chocolate, and then I must have dozed off. Damn. I'd better text Mike as he was sure to be worried about me. Yawning, I glanced at the screen of my phone. I had several messages. There was one from Josie telling me she'd be a little late this morning and another from Brian last night letting me know that Julie had left town with her aunt. There were a couple from Mike, the first of which had arrived at 2:10 this morning.

Just got in. Fed Spike and walked him. Guess you must have stayed at your parents? Call me if you're still up. I want you here with me. Love you.

He'd sent another one about ten minutes later. *Only three more weeks till I get to watch my beautiful bride walk toward me.*

A rollercoaster of emotions swept through me. What kind of job would keep him working until two in the morning? This was getting insane. What would I say when I saw him? My heart told me one thing while my gut veered off in a different direction. Maybe Josie had been right. Was he doing something shady for money?

Before I could even attempt to make any more sense of this, I needed my morning coffee. I padded out to the kitchen in my bare feet. Grandma Rosa was stirring something on the stove while Josie was making a thick dough to be used for shortbread cookies. Gianna was also there, leaning against the counter, talking to Grandma Rosa. She had stayed at my parents the night before but arrived after I had fallen asleep. She was dressed in a black suit and holding a travel mug of coffee, so I assumed she was headed for the courthouse. All three turned and stared at me.

"Well, look who decided to come to work today," Josie teased.

I walked over to the coffee pot and poured myself a mug then addressed my grandmother. "You should have woken me. I wanted to talk to Mike last night. This can't wait any longer."

"I talked to Mike a little while ago," Grandma Rosa said. "He called here to see if you were awake. He is coming by at noon to take you to lunch."

Now I was really confused. He stays out working until two in the morning, but he has time to take me to lunch? "I can't. Josie and I are going to look at a building at one o'clock. There isn't enough time."

"You will go to lunch first," Grandma Rosa declared. "It is settled."

I placed my hands on my hips. God, I was not in the mood for this today. "I don't have time for lunch. He can come here and say what he has to."

Grandma Rosa spoke sharply. "No. Stop acting like Silly Sally again. You will see him at noon and have your talk then. That is all."

"Grandma—"

"Enough. Do not be so insolent. Hurry upstairs to take a shower. Careful of your bandage. Then come back down, and do what you can to help Josie."

I shook my head. "What if—"

Grandma Rosa glared at me. "What is it you young people say…? Stuff said."

Josie laughed out loud. "It's *'nuff said*, Rosa."

My grandmother nodded in approval. "I like that too."

I glanced at Gianna, who was checking her face in a compact. "Going to work or maybe meeting someone for breakfast?"

Her cheeks reddened, and she meekly placed the

compact back into her purse. "So I see the cat's out of the bag."

I leaned against the counter. "Why didn't you tell me about your date with Johnny? You always tell me *everything*."

She lowered her eyes to the floor. "I don't know why, Sal. I'm sorry. Right after I accepted, I started to have doubts. I said to myself, do I really want to get involved with someone else again so soon? Then I decided what the heck—it was only a lunch date. Why not just go? I didn't want to say anything until I knew if it would be a disaster or not."

"And?" Josie and I both said in unison.

She grinned. "It went well. We met again last night after I got out of work and went to the movies. We're taking it slow, though."

I raised an eyebrow at her. "Hmm. Two dates in one day doesn't sound slow to me."

Gianna blushed but said nothing.

"It is good," Grandma Rosa said. "I always suspected he was sweet on you. Johnny was a rotten little boy, yes, but he has become a fine young man. Nicoletta is very proud of him."

"We're all forgetting one very important detail here," Josie interrupted. "Gianna might have Mrs. Gavelli as a grandmother-in-law someday."

"Gianna Gavelli," I teased. "It *does* have a certain ring to it."

Gianna's face turned as white as flour. "Okay, let's not get ahead of ourselves here. One marriage in this family is enough for a while, don't you think?"

We all laughed, and then Gianna spoke in a serious tone. "I didn't get home until after one and didn't see your text until then. I can't believe what you and Josie had to go through with that woman. It totally blows me away."

"How do you think we feel?" Josie asked. "We had a killer working for us. Next time we hire someone, Sal, we're doing a thorough background check. We can't afford to take any more chances."

"You're right about that," I agreed.

Gianna touched my arm. "Thank you for everything you did. You don't know what a relief it is for me to be done with that mess. I'm sorry Bernardo had to die, but I'm happy not to be a suspect anymore. I was afraid it might ruin my career." She reached for her briefcase. "I have to meet with a new client this morning."

Josie popped the cookies into the oven. "Give us all the dirt."

Gianna stared at her in disbelief. "You know I can't do that. Strictly confidential."

"Brian texted me this morning. He said that they recovered the money from Sarah's house. What will happen to it now?" I asked.

Gianna shrugged. "Since the Godfather—I mean Luigi—can't legitimately show that the money is his, I'm assuming that the police will confiscate it. I'm sure that will go over well with the Napolis."

That was the understatement of the year. "Wow, I'd hate to be anywhere near Luigi today."

Grandma Rosa shook her head. "Such a disgrace to Italians everywhere."

We all suddenly had our attention diverted by a loud giggle coming from outside. My mother and father were running around the backyard. She was wearing a gigantic, gold, sparkly crown on her head and a red sash that said *Mrs. Fox* over a short, tight white dress with spaghetti straps and four-inch silver sandals. My father stood on the bench of the picnic table and started to beat his chest and yell loudly.

A customer started toward the kitchen entrance, spotted my parents antics, and then turned and ran back to his car parked across the street.

"Your parents are great for business." Josie remarked. "He's not having another stroke, is he?"

Gianna and I spoke simultaneously. "No. It's their Tarzan routine."

Grandma Rosa turned away in disgust from the picture of her daughter and son-in-law. "Speaking of embarrassments. Your mother has always acted like a teenager, and now she has your father doing it too. Where did I go wrong?"

Gianna closed her eyes. "I can't look anymore. I'm afraid Dad's going to fall off. Why can't we have normal parents for one day of my life?"

"Dang," Josie grinned. "Those two are always full of surprises."

My mother rushed into the kitchen, her face glowing with excitement. She waved an envelope at us and then threw her arms around me. "I won, sweetheart! I won! Do you know what this means?"

"That's great, Mom." I said.

Gianna's face flushed in annoyance. "You know, Mom, while you were parading around in your skivvies yesterday, your daughter was almost killed. Josie too."

A shadow crossed over my mother's animated face, and she placed an arm around my shoulders. "I know. I talked to Grandma earlier this morning. Are you sure you're okay? How's the hand?"

I stretched it out to her. "I'm fine, Mom."

My father joined us in the kitchen, a pleased look upon his face as he slung an arm across my mother's shoulders. "Go ahead and show her, baby."

My mother held out a manila envelope to me. Puzzled, I turned it over and opened the clasp. Inside were two round-trip tickets to Hawaii and a hotel reservation. The date of the reservation was the same day as my wedding.

I stared at her, confused. "You won a trip to Hawaii? That's great!"

She beamed. "It's for you and Mike. For your honeymoon. Consider it a wedding gift from me and your father."

He patted her behind. "This is all you, baby. I can't take credit for it."

The entire room was silent as I continued to stare at her, stunned. "You're giving me the grand prize? Mom, I can't take this."

She reached over and smoothed my hair back. "I know money is tight right now, plus you never had a real honeymoon with Colin. And I know *this* marriage will last. So begin it right with the man you love, in a romantic setting, and start making me some grandchildren."

My lower lip trembled as I reached over to hug her. "Thank you so much. I can't believe you did this for me."

Her cheeks flushed. "Well, I wanted to win the trip for you and Mike, but I confess I did have ulterior motives. I scored a modeling contract with *Sizzilicious Magazine*. You should be seeing your mother in there before the end of the year!"

Gianna and I exchanged horrified glances.

"Mother," Gianna squeaked. "That magazine does nude centerfolds. Please tell me that you're not going to be featured in one, or I may have to kill myself."

"Oh, honey, I would never do that," Mom assured her. "I'll be modeling underwear. All tasteful stuff too. Hardly any thongs."

My grandmother raised her eyes to the ceiling. "Lord help us all."

* * *

After Gianna left for work, I'd gone upstairs to take a shower and borrow some of her clothes. She was moving back in with my parents today. She said it was because the case was over and her life was no longer in danger, but I suspected it was to be near Johnny as well.

My mother and father had gone off to attend a press conference for the contest. Grandma Rosa was next door visiting with Mrs. Gavelli. Our makeshift bakery was slow this morning. After the earlier episode with my parents, I found myself wondering how many people they were managing to scare away. Maybe a few more episodes and no one would want to come here at all. As it was, the coffin was attracting more attention than my cookies were.

I busied myself with making doughs and tried not to think about my upcoming lunch date. I had texted Mike and said Josie and I had an appointment to go see a building at one, but he hadn't responded. Maybe he wouldn't even show up. Perhaps my grandmother had gotten it all wrong.

Josie was quiet as she made up a batch of strawberry frosting for her famous vanilla cookies, an order for an upcoming baby shower. Since we'd been best friends for over twenty years, she knew my mind better than I did most of the time.

"Sal, stop torturing yourself."

I glanced at the clock. It was 12:10. "See? He isn't coming. I should have known. We need to leave if we're going to make our appointment." I drew my phone out of my jeans pocket and was just getting ready to dash off a somewhat snarky text to him when Mike's face appeared at the screen door.

"Hey," Josie greeted him as he walked in. "We were just talking about you."

I narrowed my eyes at my best friend then turned to face my fiancé. He was dressed in a striped blue and white oxford dress shirt that brought out his eyes, navy blue dress slacks, and black loafers. It was strange to see him out of his work uniform of jeans and T-shirts, but I had to admit he did clean up nicely. It had been a few days since Mike and I had been together in any intimate way, and as I stared into his handsome face, my heart began to beat rapidly. I was still upset, though.

"Didn't you get my text?" I asked. "Josie and I have to go see a building at one."

He reached for my hand. "Yeah, I got it. But there's something that can't wait." He glanced at Josie. "Can I steal the boss away for a while?"

Josie grinned and waved us toward the door. "I can manage the place for a while. You lovebirds go enjoy yourself."

I folded my arms across my chest. "We need to talk, Mike."

He practically dragged me to the door. "We will. But there's something you have to see first." His eyes that never failed to hypnotize me with their beauty held mine. "Please, baby?"

"Fine." I followed him to his truck, and he opened the passenger side door for me. After he settled in next to me, he reached over for my hand, and I stiffened. He watched me quizzically. "What's wrong?"

The time had come. I blew out a long breath and stared out the window while we made our way down the street. "I know you haven't been working for the Websters."

"Oh." Mike looked straight ahead, his expression serious. "How did you find out?"

"Mrs. Webster called to place an order yesterday."

He said nothing, his eyes still focused on the road. Finally, I couldn't stand it anymore. "Please tell me why you lied to me."

He grabbed for something over his visor and handed it to me. "I will. But you need to put this on first."

"A blindfold? No way. You know I hate the dark."

A wistful smile spread across his face. "Please, Sal. Do this one thing for me, and then I'll explain everything."

"Fine." I said again and placed the blindfold on, brooding in both silence and darkness. Mike reached for my hand, and I felt his lips brush against it. I thought of Grandma Rosa's words and tried to tell myself that everything was going to be all right.

The truck stopped suddenly, and I heard Mike get out. My door opened, and Mike lifted me down to the ground. "Can I look yet?"

"Not yet." He took me by the hand, and from the heat underneath my sandals, I knew we were on a paved sidewalk.

"Be careful, baby. There are three steps in front of us."

"Where the heck are we?"

I heard a jingle of bells as we entered some type of building, and then the door shut behind us. "Okay, I'm not in the mood for any games right now."

He laughed. "Ready for the reveal?"

"Yes."

He removed the blindfold while I blinked and glanced around me in confusion. For a moment I thought I had been transported back to my old bakery, but that couldn't be right. There was a gleaming, empty display case with a brand-new oak counter that ran behind it. Three little white tables were nestled against the large glass window in the front of the room. The place still smelled of fresh paint, a cream color similar to the one in my old shop. I turned to Mike with questioning eyes. He sported a huge grin that reminded me of a little boy's as he watched me with obvious excitement.

"What do you think, princess?"

Was this some type of déjà vu? "Where are we? Did you turn back the clock somehow?"

Mike laughed. "We're at thirteen Carson Way.

Remember how you saw the listing earlier this week and were told it had been rented? Well, that's because *I* rented it. I spent all week painting, installing new flooring and the counter, fixing the ceiling, and getting a display case delivered. The place was a mess when I first saw it, so I was able to finagle a better price because of it."

He went on, talking fast now. "I figured I'd let you order the appliances yourself. If you didn't want the place, or the old building was still usable, I could fix that one up over time, and we could turn a profit on it. But I knew this building was perfect because the layout was so similar to your old building. There's even an apartment upstairs if Gianna wants to move back in. If not, we can rent it out."

Stunned, I continued to stare at him. My mouth went dry, and I found myself incapable of speech, which didn't happen often.

Mike's eyes were shining. "I had to tell a lot of white lies, and I'm sorry for that. I probably should have asked you first but really wanted it to be a surprise. To tell the truth, I was hoping you wouldn't ask for any more money out of the account because I used most of it for the repairs and to pay the first month's rent. But it looks like your insurance company will pay out on the claim now, so everything should work out. We can rent this with an option to buy, just like your old place."

I walked over to the tables. I fingered the crocheted tablecloths, two white and one beige. I knew whose handiwork these belonged to. "My grandmother knew about this and didn't tell me?"

"I had to let someone in on the secret," Mike explained. "Everything's not finished yet, but I talked to your grandmother earlier this morning before you woke up. She said you were aware I was lying and that it might be a good idea to tell you what was going on before you got even more upset."

"I can't believe it." I was in total awe as I glanced down at the blue and white checkered vinyl flooring. "It looks the same as the one in my old shop."

"Pretty close. It wasn't easy to find," Mike admitted. "But I wanted the place to be perfect. This is my wedding gift to you, baby. Do you like it?"

His words took my breath way. "It's amazing. No, *you're* amazing." The place was incredible and just as I would have designed it myself. I didn't think it possible, but my original shop was back, sans the same location. Almost every detail was the same as my former bakery, and I immediately felt at home. Thanks to this wonderful man—*my* man.

Mike placed his hands on my waist and gazed tenderly into my eyes. The tears were already sliding down my cheeks as I stared back at him. "Thank you. No one's ever done anything like this for me before."

A smile warmed those incredible blue eyes as he wiped the tears away from my lashes with his thumb. "Maybe no one's ever loved you this much before."

"I love you too," I managed to say before I dissolved completely into sobs. He held me in his arms and let me cry. "I always have. Even when I was married to Colin, I could never get you out of my head or heart. I wouldn't let myself admit it to anyone then, but you are the only one I've ever truly loved."

He was silent as he lifted my face between his strong, calloused hands. I saw such a range of emotions in those deep-set eyes. Passion, admiration, and devotion—all I would ever need, and then some. Without another word, he covered my mouth with his, and I lost myself in his presence, the kiss, and everything our love stood for.

When we broke apart, Mike's voice was gruff as he tenderly stroked my hair. "This probably sounds like a bad pun, but I'd walk through fire for you, Sal. You're what gives my life meaning."

I smiled at him through my tears. "I can't believe you did that."

His face was puzzled. "What'd I do now?"

I grinned and pressed my lips against his. "You stole my line."

RECIPES

———

OATMEAL CRÈME PIE COOKIES

Prep time: About 30 minutes

Cookie ingredients:
1 cup butter-flavored Crisco or margarine
¾ cup brown sugar
½ cup granulated sugar
1 tablespoon molasses
1½ teaspoons vanilla extract
2 eggs
1½ cups flour
½ teaspoon salt
1 teaspoon baking soda
½ teaspoon cinnamon
1½ cup quick oats

Preheat oven to 350° Fahrenheit. In a large bowl, beat margarine or Crisco, brown sugar, granulated sugar, molasses, and vanilla. Mix well, and then add eggs, one at a time, beating until light and fluffy. In a separate bowl, mix together flour, salt, baking soda, and cinnamon then add to creamed mixture. Add in the oats, and mix until blended. Drop by tablespoonful onto parchment-lined cookie sheet or non-greased stoneware. Make sure the cookies are at least 2 inches apart for them to spread out—cookies will flatten. Bake 8–10 minutes or until just starting to brown around the edges. Do not overcook. Transfer to cooling rack.

For the filling:
2 teaspoons very hot water
¼ teaspoon salt
7-ounce jar marshmallow fluff
¾ cup butter-flavored Crisco

⅔ cup powdered sugar
1½ teaspoons vanilla

    Combine hot water with salt, and then mix until the salt is dissolved. In a large bowl, beat marshmallow fluff with Crisco, powdered sugar, and vanilla. Beat on high until fluffy. Add the salt water, and mix until well combined. Spread filling onto one cookie, and press second cookie on top. Ready to eat immediately. Makes 3 dozen oatmeal cookies or 18 cream pies. Store in airtight containers.

MOCHA COOKIES

1¼ cups flour
½ cup sugar
Dash of vanilla
⅛ teaspoon salt
½ cup finely ground hazelnuts
2 tablespoons finely ground coffee
1 egg
½ cup butter, softened

Preheat oven to 390° Fahrenheit. Combine flour, sugar, vanilla, and salt. Spread out some parchment paper, or prepare a clean work surface, and form a mound with the dry ingredients on the prepared surface. Beat the egg well, make a dent in the mound of ingredients, and pour the egg into it. Cut the butter into pieces, and add it to the egg. Knead the dough until ingredients are mixed well then cover mixture and let chill for about 15 minutes. Form balls about one inch in diameter (or a little smaller) then flatten until they're 6–7mm thick. Bake for about 10 minutes. Cookies may be a little soft when you take them out. Cool on rack before adding glaze.

For the glaze:
⅔ cup confectioner's sugar
1 tablespoon finely ground coffee
1 tablespoon hot water
Dark chocolate mocha beans for decorating

Mix the first three ingredients together, and then spread over the cooled cookies. Top each with a dark chocolate mocha bean and serve. Makes about three dozen cookies. Store in airtight containers.

OATMEAL CHOCOLATE CHIP COOKIES

1 cup margarine
¾ cup brown sugar
½ cup white sugar
1 egg
1 teaspoon vanilla
1½ cups flour
1 teaspoon baking soda
3 cups oatmeal
2 cups semi-sweet chocolate chips

Preheat oven to 350° Fahrenheit. Cream butter and sugars together until fluffy. Beat in egg and vanilla. Stir in remaining dry ingredients until well mixed. Add chocolate chips. Drop by teaspoonful onto parchment-lined baking sheet. Bake about 10–12 minutes. Cookies are done if the tops spring back when lightly pressed with finger. Remove from oven, and place on rack to cool. Makes about 3 dozen cookies.

SALLY'S SHORTBREAD

Note: These can be made as simple shortbread bars or as slice-and-bake refrigerator cookies.

1 pound butter (4 sticks)
1 cup sugar, plus additional ¼ cup for sprinkling
4 cups flour

To make simple shortbread bars:
Place butter in a large microwavable bowl, and microwave on low power (20%) for 2–3 minutes until very soft and creamy but not melted. Add the cup of sugar to the softened butter, and stir with a spoon until fully blended. Add the flour to the butter and sugar mixture, and mix gently with your hands until it comes together into a heavy dough. Do not over mix. The dough will be very sticky. Place dough in an ungreased 13 x 9-inch pan, patting it down evenly and into the corners with your fingers until the surface is smooth and even. Prick dough all over, down to the bottom of the pan, with a fork. Sprinkle a few tablespoons of sugar evenly over the top. Place the pan in the refrigerator for at least 30 minutes. Preheat oven to 375° Fahrenheit. Bake shortbread for 5 minutes, and then without opening the oven, reduce heat to 300° and continue baking for another 50 minutes or so, until shortbread is a light golden color. Cut immediately into 32 bars and place on cooling rack for 15 minutes. Remove bars from pan, and continue to cool. Once completely cooled, place in tins or airtight containers. Makes approximately 32 bars.

To make slice-and-bake refrigerator cookies:
Place butter in a large microwavable bowl, and microwave on low power (20%) for 2–3 minutes until very soft and creamy but not melted. Add the cup of sugar to the softened butter, and stir with a spoon until fully blended. Add the flour to the butter and sugar mixture, and mix gently with your hands until it comes together into a heavy dough. Do not over mix. The

dough will be very sticky. After mixing the dough, separate it into 4 equal portions and place each onto a separate sheet of waxed paper. Shape and roll each portion of dough into an 8-inch log in the waxed paper, and fold the ends closed. Refrigerate for at least 30 minutes. Preheat oven to 375°. Unwrap from the waxed paper, and slice each log into 8 rounds. Lightly dip the top side of each cookie into the sugar, place several inches apart on two baking sheets, and prick each cookie through a couple of times with a fork. Bake the cookies for 2 minutes then, without opening the oven, reduce heat to 300° and continue baking for another 20 minutes or so, until shortbread is a light golden color. Place pan on cooling rack for 5 minutes. Remove cookies from pan, and continue to cool. Once completely cooled, put in tins or airtight containers.

ABOUT THE AUTHOR

USA Today bestselling author Catherine Bruns lives in Upstate New York with a male dominated household that consists of her very patient husband, three sons, and assorted cats and dogs. She has wanted to be a writer since the age of eight when she wrote her own version of Cinderella (fortunately Disney never sued). Catherine holds a B.A. in English and is a member of Mystery Writers of America and Sisters in Crime.

To learn more about Catherine Bruns, visit her online at www.catherinebruns.net

Enjoyed this book? Check out these other reads available in print now from Gemma Halliday Publishing:

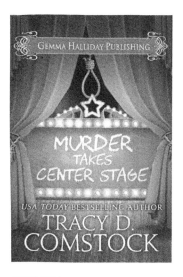

Made in the USA
Las Vegas, NV
14 August 2023